MAIL ORDER BRIDE

Montana Bargain

Echo Canyon Brides

Book 2

LINDA BRIDEY

Dedication

This book is dedicated to all of my faithful readers, without whom I would be nothing. I thank you for the support, reviews, love, and friendship you have shown me as we have gone through this journey together. I am truly blessed to have such a wonderful readership.

Contents

Chapter One

"Why didn't you tell me about this sooner?" Erin Avery's light brown eyes looked over the advertisement in the Clary, Missouri newspaper.

Her friend, Jessica Timberland, said, "I didn't think you'd be interested in becoming a mail-order bride since you don't have any interest in men at all."

They sat drinking coffee in the parlor of Jessica's farmhouse, which was located on the outskirts of the city. She had offhandedly mentioned an unusual ad in the personals that she had read a couple of weeks prior. Once she'd told Erin the main requirement was that the woman must be a doctor, Erin's ears had perked up and she'd demanded to see the ad.

Dr. Erin Avery had graduated almost a year ago from the Homeopathic Medical College of Missouri, but had yet to find a position because even though there were more women being granted medical degrees, the vast majority of medical institutions were still biased against them. She'd tried the various hospitals around the state and in neighboring states, but none of them had been willing to hire a woman.

She'd tried to start her own practice, but there were only a handful of people who were willing to become her patients. Due to her stagnant career, she was growing increasingly bitter and Jessica was worried about her jaded friend's mental state. However, Erin began channeling her anger and resentment into a fierce determination to succeed no matter what she had to do to make her dream of being a successful doctor come true.

Looking at the ad again, she read:

> Listen to Aunt Edna, ladies! I have quite the man for you, whom I personally know. He is a very handsome Chinese veterinarian who seeks a female doctor as a wife. She must meet the following qualifications: Be a practical woman of science who is able to handle stressful situations. She must desire children and be prepared to marry one week after meeting. In return, the lovely lady will receive help in setting up a medical practice and have the satisfaction of meeting the medical needs of a community that greatly needs such a service. The doctor in question is 31 years old, 5'10", 182 lbs., with an impressive physique, a kind heart, and a quick wit. He is honest, reliable, and definitely delectable. Please send letters of interest to Dr. Winslow Wu, General Delivery, Echo Canyon, Montana.

Jessica watched as a delighted smile spread over Erin's face as she reread the ad. "Don't tell me you like the idea?"

"Of course I like it. Someone who's actually looking for a female doctor? It's a dream come true, Jess. And I'm going. I'm going to write this man a letter that will make him sit up and take notice."

Jessica stared at her. "Erin, he's Chinese and you don't know anything about him. You can't just decide to marry someone before you've even exchanged letters with him. And he wants to get married within a week! That's very suspicious."

She knew how badly Erin wanted to be able to practice her

profession, but this was much too risky.

"If it means I get to practice medicine, I'll marry some eighty-year-old guy who's uglier than the backside of a mule. I don't care if he's Chinese, white, colored, checkered, or polka-dotted. It makes no difference to me," Erin said. "I'm everything he outlined in this ad. Plus, I think it's kind of cute that this woman is vouching for him."

"You don't know that it's really a woman who wrote the ad. This man could be insane or cruel or anything, Erin!"

"I'll be able to tell that from his letters," Erin said. "I appreciate your concern, but I'm a grown woman and I can take care of myself."

Jessica groaned. "I hate it when you get like this. It always means that no one is going to talk you out of something."

Erin nodded. "That's right. I didn't let Dad keep me out of medical school and I worked my way through on my own. I'll be damned if I'm going to let all those small-minded men keep me from putting my education to good use. The fact that this man wants a woman as a doctor makes me half in love with him already. It tells me that he's open-minded and not threatened by intelligent women. It's perfect."

"Love? I can't believe you actually said 'in love'," Jessica said, sitting her coffee cup on the coffee table.

Erin flapped her hand in a dismissive gesture. "It's just a figure of speech. I'm not looking for love. It's inconvenient and it'll just get in the way of my career."

Jessica pursed her lips and gave Erin a baleful look. "You're only saying that because of Garret."

"You're right. Look how that turned out. He seduced me— willingly, I must admit—and then let me know that it didn't mean anything to him. Once he got what he wanted, he was done with me. I don't need that kind of distraction in my life," Erin said.

"But you're talking about marrying a man you don't even know!" Jessica said. "If you don't want a relationship with a man, why get married?"

Erin remained calm in the face of Jessica's anxious protest. "So I can be a doctor."

"But he's going to expect to … you know … make babies," Jessica said.

Erin laughed at Jessica's embarrassed expression. "Yes, Jessica, I realize that he's going to want to be intimate. That's normally how babies are made."

Jessica's blush turned even darker. "So you're willing to have relations with a man only one week after meeting him? Because you know it's expected on the wedding night."

"Sure," Erin said. "If it means I get to be a doctor, so be it. Besides, it says he's handsome, so it won't be all bad."

Jessica put her hands over her face. "I don't understand you. I never have when it comes to this type of thing."

"Well, I'm sorry I'm not the swooning, sweet-natured, damsel-in-distress type of woman, Jessica. That might work for you, but not for me," Erin said. "Well, I have a letter to go write. See you tomorrow."

The early January wind swept down the main street in Echo Canyon, commonly referred to as "Echo" by its residents. It was a strange sight that greeted anyone who happened to be out on the street that evening. Dr. Winslow Wu, Win to his friends, walked along the hard-packed dirt street, followed closely by a very small burro. The cold weather made her frisky and she kept nipping at him as they strolled along.

He had no need for a lead rope because she followed him everywhere—whether he wanted her to or not. One of the few people who would use his veterinarian services had given her to him as payment for saving a foaling mare and her baby. At first, Win had refused to take Sugar, but he had rethought the offer, figuring that Sugar might come in handy for several reasons.

Win just hadn't known that the burro would become so attached to him. She was an escape artist and chewed through ropes, kicked out boards, and rammed gates in order to stay with Win. Finally, he'd given up and just let her come with him.

Stopping at one of the buildings along Main Street, Win looked up at the second-story windows and was pleased to see light in them. Going to a door that led to a set of stairs, Win took out a key and unlocked the door. No sooner had he pushed it open than Sugar shoved him to the side and began clambering up the steps, her hooves making a loud racket on the wooden boards.

Win smiled at the burro's impatient behavior. "Excuse me, madam."

He jogged effortlessly up the stairs after her. Sugar gained the top of the stairs and pawed at the closed door. Joining her there, Win waited for it to be answered.

"C'mon in! It's open!"

Sugar looked at Win. "What? You know how to do it. Open it."

Clamping her teeth around the knob, Sugar turned it and nudged the door open. She clip-clopped her way into the art studio of one of Win's friends, Billy Two Moons. Sugar let out a hee-haw of greeting to Billy.

The Indian youth put down his paintbrush and wiped his hands on a rag. "Hey, pretty girl," he said, hugging her and scratching her ears. "Are you causing trouble?"

Win said, "When isn't she? She almost got in the store today."

Billy kissed Sugar's forehead and said, "Well, maybe there was something she needed to buy."

"She doesn't need any more candy," Win said. "It's not good for her and it makes her more hyper than she already is."

Sugar rubbed her head against Billy's bare torso and kept it there. "Aw, you hurt her feelings, Win. Shame on you. Did your pa say something mean to you? Don't worry, Uncle Billy loves you even if he doesn't."

Win just gave Billy a steady look. "Don't encourage her."

The downstairs door opened again and they heard what sounded like the footsteps of several people coming up the stairs. Sugar's ears perked up and she turned towards the door. Her tail swished back and forth. This was her "guard burro" pose and she was ready to defend her territory if necessary.

Billy laughed at her as someone knocked on the door. "C'mon in!"

The door opened and Sheriff Evan Taft and his wife, Josie, entered the studio.

"Hey, guys," Billy said.

Josie barely had time to greet him before Sugar wanted Josie to pet her. "Hi, Billy. Hi, Sugar."

Sugar loved attention and made sure that everyone gave her some. Win laughed as she head-butted Evan, who always roughhoused with her. Evan grabbed her around the neck and tousled with her a little. As usual, she brayed and acted as though she would attack, but nothing ever came of it.

Josie threw a leg over Sugar's back and sat there in her coat. "Just call me Mary and Evan is Joseph."

Win gave her a dubious look and asked, "Why?"

She and Evan exchanged looks and Josie said, "Because this summer we will become parents."

Billy and Win got the joke and they were overjoyed for their friends. Billy hugged Josie, who had become a surrogate big sister to him over the past summer when she'd come to Echo as Evan's mail-order bride. The beautiful blonde with dazzling blue eyes and a willowy figure had charmed Evan right from the beginning.

"Wow!" Billy said. "That's fantastic. You're already starting to make deputies."

All of Evan's friends always teased him about him and Josie making their own law enforcement staff.

Win shook Evan's hand and said, "Congratulations. I'm really happy for you."

"Thanks, guys." Evan's green eyes shone with a happy light. "We couldn't be happier and Aunt Edna is over the moon."

Josie said, "She told me to make the baby grow fast so she can hold it soon. I told her that the oven is baking as fast as it can."

All of the men laughed and Josie slid off Sugar's back.

"How're the sales going?" Evan asked Billy.

The previous fall, Billy had bought the building to use as an art gallery and studio. The shop was on the first floor, along with the efficiency apartment where Billy lived. The entire second floor was his studio. It was very large with windows all along the whole length of it. Several friends had helped him enlarge the original windows so that even more light came in during the day.

Billy's other source of income had given him the funds to make the necessary repairs to the building, although it was still a work in progress. He, Win, and their friends, Lucky Quinn, Ross Ryder, and Travis Desmond, had all gone into the sheep herding business together. It had begun turning a small profit and his money had gone into getting his art career off the ground.

"Pretty good," Billy said. "People don't have a whole lot of money for extras like that, but hopefully that'll start changing soon. You have your bride and hopefully Win will find one soon."

Echo was a town on the verge of dying out. The gold and silver mines had dried up and many of the businesses had been forced to close. People had moved elsewhere to find work and so Echo was quickly heading towards extinction. There were men left behind who worked at various jobs, but single women were in short supply.

The previous March, Jerry Belker, who owned the wagon and wheelwright shop in Echo, had come up with the idea that if they could get more women to come to Echo the increased population would mean more business and boost the economy, thereby saving their town. Evan had reluctantly stepped forward to start putting the plan into action. So far it had worked.

Everyone had been surprised when Win had decided to go next since he didn't seem to be the marrying type.

"Speaking of that," Win said. "I got a letter today from a prospective bride."

Josie clapped her hands and slid a chair over to where Win sat. "Tell us everything."

He laughed at her eager expression. "Ok. Her name is Erin Avery and she's a doctor from Clary, Missouri. She's twenty-five and graduated last year from the Homeopathic Medical College of Missouri, which is a very good school. I've gotten a few letters, but I like hers the best. She's down to earth, intelligent, and very career-minded." When Josie opened her mouth, Win said, "Yes, she wants to have a family, too. And she sounds attractive."

Billy asked, "How attractive?"

Win frowned at him. "Well, she's 5'8" tall, brown hair, brown eyes, and says she has a womanly figure. Sounds attractive to me."

"She's only a couple of inches shorter than you," Billy said. "Does that bother you?"

Win was used to jokes about his height and it didn't bother him. He grinned. "Nope. That'll just make it easier to kiss her."

Billy laughed. "Yeah, that's true."

Josie said, "She's not even here and you're thinking about kissing her. I mean, you've only gotten the one letter. You might not be compatible at all."

"Only one way to find that out," Win said. "I'm going to tell her to come ahead whenever she's ready."

Evan's eyebrows rose high on his forehead. "Don't you want to exchange a few more letters at least?"

Win's black eyes glittered with amusement. "Look, I know my approach to this is different than you and Josie's, but I'm looking more at her qualifications as a doctor. Echo needs a doctor. I tried to talk Sean into staying but Earnest ruined that, damn him. He doesn't want to move Opal here with Earnest around."

Evan's upper lip curled in a snarl of hatred. Marvin Earnest was evil personified. Unfortunately, Evan had no proof of him breaking the law so there wasn't much he could do about the man—yet. Ever since Earnest had slept with his first fiancée, Louise, Evan had hated Marvin with a passion that knew no bounds. Marvin had done a lot of heinous things over the years, but there wasn't enough proof to arrest him.

Evan had been kidnapped on his and Josie's wedding day and he knew that Marvin was behind it somehow. He just needed to figure out how he'd pulled it off, but find out he would. At twenty-six, Evan was the youngest sheriff in Gallatin County history, and he was known far and wide for his determination and keen investigative skills. He could be creative in his law enforcement methods and didn't mind getting violent when it was called for.

"I know," Josie said. "I tried to convince him, too, but he wouldn't budge."

Sean and Opal Everett were friends of Josie's from Pullman, Washington where she was from. They'd come to town for Josie's wedding. During that time there had been an earthquake, a rare occurrence for their area, and Echo had been fortunate that Sean had been in town.

"So, I figure this is the best way to get us a doctor," Win said.

Josie said, "Well, it's very noble of you, Win, but what if you hate each other? You'd be sacrificing your happiness for Echo."

Win shrugged. "So be it. However, I'm hoping that we hit it off at some point once we know each other a little better."

"So why the stipulation of getting married in one week?" Evan asked.

"Once she's married, she won't be leaving," Win said. "And that'll take care of the no relations before marriage issue. I think that's a load of crap, anyway, but it'll get that out of the way."

It was well known that Win had no faith in any religion and didn't hold much respect for many social conventions of the time. He and Lucky, who was very devout in many spiritual aspects, argued about this subject all the time. Win didn't care what people thought about that and he made no apologies for his beliefs or lack thereof.

Billy went back to painting as he asked, "So she was fine with that?"

"Yep. It's a good sign that she's so practical. That'll make things easier. I couldn't believe that a few of the other letters came from supposed doctors; they sure didn't sound like it," Win said.

Josie said, "Just because a woman is a doctor doesn't mean she can't be looking for love, Win."

He smiled at her. "I know that, but their letters were just too sappy for me. I want a woman with a good head on her shoulders. That might not sound romantic to all of you, but it is to me. I find women who know their own minds to be very attractive. I don't mind a forward woman, either. Much better than some shy thing who can't even speak in the presence of a man. Nope, that's not my kind of woman."

Evan said, "It sure sounds like you know what you're after. I hope you get it."

"Me, too. Well, I guess I'll take my shadow there and go home and see what the other shepherd is up to. Have a good night all and congratulations again," Win said.

The others said goodnight to him and Sugar. He made her open the door and grinned as she clomped agilely down the stairs again.

Chapter Two

Jessica was terrified for Erin's wellbeing. She'd tried everything to convince Erin not to go to Echo Canyon, but with her typical stubbornness, Erin had stuck to her guns. They stood on the railroad platform, waiting for the train to arrive.

"Please don't go," Jessica said. It was a last-ditch attempt to change Erin's mind.

Erin gave Jessica an annoyed look. "Jess, I'm going and you might as well accept it. I'll come visit sometime and you can come there, too."

Jessica shook her head. "Nope. I'm happy right here. I'm not going to make that kind of trip alone and neither should you."

Knowing that her friend was only being protective, Erin gritted her teeth together to prevent a caustic remark from exiting her mouth. "Jess, I appreciate your concern, but please stop this. Either you give me a good sendoff or you can leave right now. The choice is yours."

Jessica's foot tapped agitatedly and she bit her bottom lip. "Ok. I won't say it anymore. I'm going to miss you so much."

Erin saw the tears in Jessica's blue eyes and sighed. "Please don't do that, either."

"I can't help it! My best friend is moving four states away and I'll probably never see you again. How am I supposed to feel? I won't even be there for your wedding."

That was Erin's only regret about leaving—not having Jessica as her maid of honor. However, Erin was willing to forgo that if it meant that she could make her dream come true.

"I know. I wish you could be there, too. I tried to get you to move with me, but you won't."

"No. I have the farm and Ma to take care of. I can't uproot her to go to the middle of nowhere," Jessica said.

Erin nodded as the train pulled into the station. "Ok, give me a hug and then go. It'll be too hard otherwise."

Jessica latched onto Erin for dear life, tears falling from her eyes. Erin grew a little weepy herself before putting up her defensive wall against the pain leaving Jessica and her home would cause her. Finally, Jessica let her go.

"I love you," Jessica said. "You write me the second you get there. Do you hear me?"

"I promise that I'll send a letter right away," Erin said. "I love you, too. Now, scoot so I can get on."

Jessica gave her another quick hug and then walked away, tears streaming down her face. Erin looked after her for a few moments and then turned around so she couldn't see Jessica anymore. Steeling herself, Erin gave the conductor her ticket and boarded the train.

Only Erin's sheer determination kept her going. The changes in railways were maddening and the wait times between trains were sometimes long. She was exhausted, but unable to sleep on the train much. She was grateful that the next stop would be an overnight one so that she could sleep in a proper bed.

Collecting her luggage, she made her way to a hotel and checked in. As soon as she reached her room, she dropped the luggage, locked her door, and lay down on the bed. She was asleep in minutes.

Feeling more refreshed in the morning, she boarded the last train, which would take her not quite all the way to Montana. There she would meet up with Win. She was excited to meet her future husband. She'd enjoyed their letters and she liked his dry wit.

> *Erin,*
>
> *I don't think you'll find it exciting here, but since you're so excited about setting up your practice, that'll be enough excitement, I'm sure. You'll be inundated with patients practically as soon as you get here, so be prepared. Everyone here is thrilled that you're coming, and so am I, of course.*
>
> *I think you'll find the office I chose to be adequate and I've already started getting some of the standard equipment and supplies you'll need. I'd rather leave the rest to you, since you're going to be the one using it the most. Lucky is very happy to hear that you can do dentistry work since he's had a toothache for a couple of weeks now. I looked at it, but I'm not really trained to diagnose human teeth, so that's better left to you, too. I offered to pull it for him, but he said, "I'll wait for the pretty lady doctor, thanks very much."*

Although they hadn't exchanged very many letters, Win's missives were long and gave Erin a good idea of what Echo and its citizens were like. She'd read them again a few times as she'd traveled and she couldn't wait to get there.

When the train slowed and stopped at the Cheyenne station, Erin quickly gathered her things and exited the train car. She waited for her luggage and then went into the depot to wait since the late February weather was so cold. Ever practical, Erin had opted for heavy trousers and blouses, which had kept her warmer than a dress and layers of petticoats, which she couldn't stand. This wasn't standard dress for a woman, but she didn't care.

She needed to go to the ladies' room, but she didn't want to take her two suitcases with her. However, she couldn't leave them in the lobby with so many people there. Someone was sure to take them. Even though it would be a nuisance, there was no other choice but to take them with her. Coming back into the lobby, she decided to go back outside to wait for Win.

To keep herself warm, she walked back and forth a little. As she neared the corner of the building, a man jumped out, grabbing at her reticule. She shouted and tried to pull away from him, but he grabbed her by the hair and hauled her around the side of the building. Most of the passengers had already been picked up and the few who hadn't been were too concerned with their own affairs to notice the incident.

Erin struggled with the man, but he was stronger than her. He'd kept hold of her hair and was using it to hang onto her. With all her strength, Erin pulled away from him, intent on keeping her bag. Not only was her money in it, but also some jewelry that was sentimental to her, and she'd be damned if this crook was going to get it from her.

She succeeded in getting away from him, but a very large section of hair was ripped from her scalp in the process. The pain was excruciating and she screamed for help again. Suddenly she heard the sound of fists connecting with flesh. As she leaned against the building for support, she saw another man fighting her assailant, although it didn't seem like much of a fight. The would-be robber lay inert on the ground. It had taken mere seconds for the other man to render him thus.

Afraid the second man also meant her harm, Erin began backing away, but then she saw her bag on the ground and stopped.

The man turned towards her and she instantly knew that it was Win. The Chinese man before her had piercing, dark eyes and chiseled features. Concern was etched into the lines of his face. She'd never seen a Chinese man who wore jeans or a cowboy hat.

"Win?" she ventured.

"Yeah. This is a heck of a way to meet, Erin. Are you hurt?" His eyes traveled over her as he picked up her bag.

Erin held the side of her head. "He ripped a bunch of my hair out and it hurts like hell. How bad is it?"

Win replied, "Let's get away from this guy."

Even though she was perfectly able to walk on her own power, she didn't mind when he took her elbow and guided her around to the front of the building. Win stopped her at his wagon and said, "Turn around."

Erin did and dropped her hand. When Win saw how much of her lustrous brown hair was gone, he swore. He wanted to go mete out some more punishment on the thief. Gently, he ran his fingertips over what was approximately a three-by-three inch area. A few droplets of blood stood out on her scalp. He took out his handkerchief and blotted them away.

"Well, it's going to be sore, but you'll live. I'd like to go make sure he doesn't, but I don't think you want to visit your future husband in jail," he said.

She turned around to face him again. She didn't have to tilt her head much to look up at him. She liked that she could look almost directly into his eyes, which she suddenly found mesmerizing. "No, I really don't."

Win frowned a little. "You're gonna need a haircut."

"What?" she asked. "It looks that bad?"

"I'm afraid so. Pulling it back won't cover the area since it's so big, and it'll grow at all different lengths, anyway. It starts behind your ear and goes right up the side of your head. You'd be better to just cut it off and start over," Win said.

Erin wasn't vain about much, but she felt that her hair was her best feature. It was thick, shiny, and very soft. The disturbing thought of having to cut it, combined with the shock of what had just occurred, was too much for her. She couldn't control the tears that welled up in her eyes. She tried to turn away before Win saw them, but he wouldn't let her.

Instead, he embraced her. "It's ok. You're safe," he said. "It's all right now."

Erin could feel the power in his arms as he held her. She had trained herself to endure all sorts of adversity without letting the strain show and she hated showing weakness. However, she'd never been physically attacked before, and she allowed him to comfort her for a few moments while she composed herself.

She backed away and said, "Thank you. Sorry for crying, but I've never had anyone rip my hair out before. I'm sure I look horrible."

Win admired her pluck and he knew that she wanted to keep it together. "I don't think so. Even looking like a half-shorn sheep, you're a fine-looking woman."

His witty compliment was just what she needed. "Thank you, Dr. Wu. I've never seen a Chinese man look so good in a cowboy hat before."

His smile captivated her. "And you won't see one anywhere else but right in front of you, either." He was happy both with her compliment and that he was able to make her laugh.

"Handsome and modest" she said, smiling.

"And don't forget intelligent," he said. "Dr. Avery, I think we need to go get your hair seen to. We'll find a barber."

"A barber? Don't you mean a salon?"

He hefted her suitcases into his wagon and said, "No. Most ladies' salons don't do such short haircuts, since men rarely go to them. Barbers do that sort of thing every day, though."

Mortified, Erin said, "I don't want to walk into a barber shop and have some man I don't know cut my hair."

"Ok. We'll just leave it like that then. You won't even be able to cover it with a hat since there was a little trauma done to a couple of places on your scalp. It'll irritate it too much."

"But I don't want it to show, either."

He said, "I have one other solution, but it depends on how much you trust me. I can cut it for you."

She thought he was making another joke, but when he didn't laugh with her, she realized he was serious. "You know how to cut hair?"

"Yep. My mother taught me. She was a woman of many talents," Win said. He'd been assessing her hair with a barber's eye.

Being practical, Erin figured since Win had just saved her from God only knew what fate, she could probably trust him to cut her hair. Better him than some stranger. "All right. You can cut it. It's better to have short hair than look like a half-shorn sheep."

"Good. I'll cut it for you when we check into the hotel," he said.

Erin nodded and climbed into the wagon. After making sure Erin was safely seated, Win went back around to the other side of the wagon.

Settling on the seat beside her, he asked, "Are you sure you're not hurt anywhere else?"

She gave him a sardonic look. "I'm a doctor. I'd know if I were hurt."

"Good. Let's get to that haircut then." Win picked up the reins and got the horses moving.

Chapter Three

Checking in at the hotel was a rather tense experience; the clerk acted rather cool with Win. He was used to such treatment, but even though she heard about it all the time, Erin hadn't seen it much. She expected him to get angry about it, but Win simply smiled at the clerk and did what needed done to get their rooms rented.

Following her up the stairs to the second floor, Win took the opportunity to look her over a little better. The trousers she wore gave him an excellent view of her shapely behind. Her back was straight and her long legs were much to his liking. He'd been right when he'd said that it would be easy kissing her—both because she wasn't much shorter than he was and also because she was a beautiful woman.

He became angry again when he thought about the jackass who'd assaulted Erin. He'd have liked to make the guy even sorrier, but he'd wanted to take care of Erin and get away before someone notified the sheriff about it. Because of his race, some wouldn't have been on his side despite the fact that he'd been defending her. It was a shame that he was going to have to cut the long, dark hair that was catching the light as she moved.

He'd requested neighboring rooms so he'd be close by in case Erin needed him. He hoped that wouldn't be the case; she needed no further traumatic experiences.

Erin unlocked the door to her room and went inside. It wasn't the best hotel, but it wasn't the worst, either. It didn't much matter since they would be leaving the next day. She turned around to say something to Win and bounced off his chest. He'd sat her suitcases down and he grabbed her arm to keep her upright.

"Dear God! You're as solid as a brick wall," she said.

He smiled. "Is that a complaint or a compliment?"

"The latter," she blurted.

Letting her arm go, he closed the door and began shrugging out of his coat, which he then tossed on the bed. Picking up his saddlebag, he reached in and pulled out a pair of scissors. They were part of the emergency medical supplies he always kept on hand. He never knew when he might have to cut bandages or suturing thread. "Come over here in the light and I'll get you fixed up."

Erin took off her coat and hung it on a hook by the door. "Ok. I really don't want to do this," she said as she passed by a mirror. In it, she saw the nearly bald place on the side of her head. "Good Lord! Look what he did to me!" Fury took hold of her when she saw that Win was right; she had no choice but to cut it. Even though it would be short, it would be better than looking like she had mange.

He patted the back of the chair he'd moved over into the sunlight. "C'mon. Let's get it taken care of. You'll feel a little better."

She flopped into the chair. "I doubt it, but it's the best thing to do."

"Right. Just hold still so I don't accidently make you look like a rooster."

Having Win cut her hair was one of the most erotic and relaxing experiences of Erin's life. He was very gentle, especially with the sore area of her scalp. His touch was soothing and she noticed that he was very thorough. He moved her head this way and that, making little snips here and there. The shorter her hair became, the more his fingers touched her scalp. A strong shiver of awareness ran through her when his fingers grazed the bare nape of her neck. She didn't want him to guess at the true cause, so she said, "It's so cold without my hair."

Win smiled to himself. "I'm sure it is. Your hair is very thick and also very beautiful."

"Thank you," she said. "It's going to take forever to grow back."

"Probably about a year to get to the length it was, but it shouldn't take it long to reach your shoulders." Win came around in front of her again, looking her hair over in a critical manner. "Just a little more off the left side and then we're done."

When she saw the pile of hair on the floor, she wanted to cry. Keeping her emotions in check, she told herself that it was just hair. She should be thankful that she hadn't been badly injured.

"How much *more* do you have to take?" she asked.

"Not much. I just don't want you to look lopsided and I'm trying to make it a little feminine. I know how you ladies are about your hair, so I want to make it look as good as I can," he said.

As he tilted her chin up a little, she noted the attractive hue of his eyes and the keen intelligence reflected in them. Some people might not have, but she found their shape attractive. Moving her eyes upward, she took in his slightly broad forehead and his thick, jet-black hair, which he kept close-cropped. Her eyes moved downward again and he smiled.

She was already very aware of him as an attractive man, but with his sensual mouth just mere inches from hers, that awareness increased tenfold.

"So what do you think?" he asked.

"I think your hair looks a lot better short than mine will," she replied.

His smile broadened, showing his even, white teeth. "I don't know about that."

Standing back up, he went around behind her again and finished. While cutting her hair, he'd noticed her pretty neck and ears. He had a strong urge to kiss the bare nape of her neck. Refraining from doing that, he put the scissors aside and began massaging her neck muscles. He felt her stiffen under his hands.

"Relax, Erin. I thought your neck might be a little sore from your head being yanked around. This'll help prevent it from getting stiff on you," he said.

That sounds reasonable. She asked, "Is that your professional opinion, Dr. Wu?"

He smiled and said, "Yes, Dr. Avery, it is."

"Well, then, who am I to interfere in your diagnosis?"

Hitting a knot in her neck, he moved his thumbs in small circles, concentrating on loosening it. "Judging by what I'm feeling, I'd say that you haven't been sleeping very comfortably."

"You're right." She sighed as his fingers released more tension. "That feels incredible."

"That's the idea."

Silence filled the room for the next ten minutes as he continued the massage. He noticed that she broke out in goose bumps a couple of times but that she didn't mention being cold. Win thought this was a good sign. He wasn't unaffected by her nearness or the feel of her smooth skin under his fingers and palms. It was encouraging that there was at least a little chemistry between them. When he finished, Erin didn't move, which he found amusing, but not unusual. Most people felt too languid to move quickly after a massage.

"All finished," he said.

Erin didn't open her eyes just yet. "Ok."

"Do you want to look at your hair?" he asked.

"No. I just want to sit here and go to sleep," she said.

He chuckled. "How about you look at your hair and then have a nap?"

She frowned a little. "That means I have to move."

"I guess it does," Win said. "Unless you want me to carry you."

"What?" Erin's eyes snapped open. "No!"

She stood up quickly and began brushing hair from her blouse.

"Crap! Look at me! I look like a shaggy dog."

"No, you're much prettier than a shaggy dog," Win said.

She looked at him and smiled. "You're very sweet."

"My friends would disagree with you," Win said. "C'mon and look. Quit stalling. The sooner you look the sooner you'll get used to it."

Groaning, Erin stepped over to the mirror and looked at her reflection. Her mouth dropped open and she turned her head back and forth. She felt the back of her head, the short strands of her hair feeling foreign under her fingers. The woman in the mirror was also foreign to her. She thought she looked completely different, but not unattractive. Win stood behind her, examining his handiwork, making sure he didn't need to make any more adjustments to her hair.

"You have a very nice shape to your face," he said.

She smiled, but didn't comment. Her reflection fascinated her. She saw what he meant about trying to make the cut a little feminine. He'd added a little tapering here and there, which kept it from looking exactly like a man's cut. The haircut seemed to make her eyes appear larger and made her cheekbones stand out more, too.

"I never dreamed I'd say this, but I really like it. I can't believe it, but I do," she said. Her eyes met his in the mirror. "Thank you, both for saving my life and for cutting my hair."

"You're welcome," he said.

She looked down at all of the hair on the floor and said, "Well, I guess I'd better clean that up."

"I'll do it."

"No, Win. You cut it, I'll clean it up," she said.

He smiled. "Ok. I'll come back in a while and we'll go get something to eat."

Erin watched him pick up his coat from the bed and noted the way his white shirt tightened across his back. He may not have been overly tall, but he was broad and heavily muscled.

"I'll see you in a bit," he said and left the room.

Chapter Four

Traveling with Win was an entertaining experience. He was informative, considerate, and funny. He told her more about his friends and the earthquake. In typical Win fashion, he downplayed his part in rescuing Billy and Josie, who had fallen into the mine when it had collapsed during the natural disaster. They had been hiking near the area when the world had turned turbulent.

Erin was impressed, but sensing that he wasn't comfortable with a lot of praise, she only mentioned it briefly. "So I'm marrying a hero. I already knew that, though. You certainly were heroic back in Cheyenne when you saved me from that robber."

He smiled. "I don't think about myself that way. I just help out whenever I can. I'm just glad that I happened along when I did. I heard you scream, but I wasn't sure where it was coming from at first. Then I came around the side of the depot and found you. I didn't know it was you until you said my name. I knew it couldn't be a coincidence since no one in Cheyenne knows my name. It's not a common one."

"Well, thank you again. No, Winslow isn't a common given name, no matter what race you are. Why did your parents pick it?"

This wasn't common knowledge, but since he was marrying the woman at his side, he had decided that he shouldn't have any secrets from her. "Well, when my parents still lived in China, they met an American businessman named Robert Winslow. Actually, my father saved him from some unsavory characters one night and Robert never forgot it. He and Father stayed friends and, in return for him saving Robert's life, he helped my parents get to America."

"They both sound like extraordinary men."

"My father was and Robert still is. Both of my parents were extraordinary people and despite the prejudice and poor treatment they faced here, they persevered. Everything they did was so I would have a better life than them. I'll always be grateful to them; I just wish they wouldn't have had to work so hard for everything, but they never complained. They just did whatever was necessary to make ends meet," Win said.

"And they helped you through veterinarian school, too," she said. "I would have liked to have met them."

He smiled. "Well, Mother wouldn't have minded too much, but Father was very traditional and I'm not sure he would have approved of me marrying a white woman. He probably would have warmed up to you eventually, though."

"I can understand that. My parents weren't too thrilled that I'm marrying a Chinese man, but I really don't care. So why didn't you advertise for a Chinese bride?"

"Because I wanted a strong-willed woman who could handle living in Echo and most Chinese women are taught to be very subservient to their husbands. I also figured that the chances of finding a Chinese woman who had gone to medical school were very slim," Win replied.

"That makes sense. I'm nothing if not strong-willed. I had to be or I wouldn't have made it through school or my residency, either. A lot of the male doctors did everything they could to make it as inconvenient for me as possible."

"That's another reason that I wanted to marry a female doctor. I know what it takes to work your way through such arduous schooling and I figured if I could find a woman who had, then she was the woman for me," Win said as they left Dickensville, the next closest town to Echo.

Erin replied, "I clawed my way through some days, barely hanging on, but I was going to be damned if I wouldn't make it and show my father that I could do it. I worked two part-time jobs, borrowed money from my grandfather, and saved money any way I could so I could buy books and pay my tuition."

"Tenacity. Another quality I admire in anyone, not just women. My mother was like that in her own quiet way."

"I'm sure she was. It sounds like both your parents were and you inherited that. Did they name you after Robert by giving you his last name?"

His mouth twisted in a wry smile. "Actually, I was supposed to be Robert Winslow Wu, but there was a mix-up with my birth certificate and it was written as Winslow Robert Wu. My parents just decided to leave it at that so that's how I became Winslow."

"That's an interesting story. Whatever happened to Robert?"

"He lives in Mississippi now. I went to visit him after college and stayed there for about three months before coming back home," Win said. "It was because of him that I was even admitted to school. He called in some markers with a few friends who basically browbeat the dean into letting me in."

"You mean because you're Chinese?" she asked.

"Yep. But, like you, I wasn't going to take no for an answer."

"What made you want to be a veterinarian?"

"When I was about nine, I found a fawn in the woods that had gotten caught in a wolf trap and couldn't escape. I was able to get his leg out, but he'd been badly wounded. I wanted to help it and started treating it with some remedies that my parents used for wounds and so forth. It did the trick and he survived. One of the best feelings in my life was watching him scamper away once I released him. That's when I decided I wanted to help other animals."

"That's remarkable," she said. "And it shows that you have a kind heart."

"I guess so. I try to do right by people. As long as they do the same with me, there's no problem."

"Yes, it seems like it's not a good idea to get on your bad side."

"You could say that," he said.

They made Echo by midafternoon that day. Erin thought the town looked nice even though there were many empty businesses along Main Street. Win pointed out Billy's store and the general store. He stopped at the Hanovers', who ran a boarding house in town.

"Here we are," Win said as he jumped down from the wagon.

Erin followed suit, looking the house over. It was a very attractive, well-maintained residence. Win grabbed her bags and led her into the house where they met one of the owners, Arthur Hanover. He was a heavy-set man with a Friar Tuck hairstyle.

Win introduced Erin to him.

"Well, another lovely bride to be, I see," Arthur said in his deep, bass voice. "We're only too glad to have you. Let's get you settled in." He wondered at her short hair and the even shorter patch on the right side, but he didn't mention it.

"Thank you," Erin said. "Win, I just want to put my things in my room. I'd love to see my office, if that's all right."

Win said, "Sure. I'll take these up for you. Which room, Arthur?"

"Second on the left. It has a private wash room, Miss Avery," Arthur said.

"Dr. Avery," Win corrected him.

"Oh goodness. I'd forgotten," Arthur said. "Please forgive me, Dr. Avery."

Erin smiled and said, "It's all right. Please call me Erin."

"Erin it is," Arthur said agreeably.

Win jogged up the stairs and Erin followed him. Her room was very pretty with dark green swag drapes and off-white walls. Several paintings hung on the walls.

Win noticed her looking at them. "This is one of Billy's," he said, pointing to a landscape.

Erin walked closer to examine it better. It had been painted from a high vantage point that overlooked a huge expanse of land. She could make out sheep, dogs, a cabin, and a tipi. It had been painted at sunset and it was beautiful.

"It looks so real, as if I could just walk right into it. Billy is very talented," she said.

Win nodded. "Yes, he is. He's made several people similar paintings, including me and Lucky."

She smiled. "So Lucky really does live in a tipi. It looks like a nice piece of property."

"It is. There's a huge amount of acreage, too. It runs back through those trees, some of which we're planning on clearing out to make room for goats," he said.

"Goats?"

"Lucky wants to sell goat milk and make cheese. I think it's a good way to diversify. The land is perfect for goats, too. They like to forage and they'll eat just about anything," Win said. "Well, why don't we go look at your office?"

"I can't wait," she said with a smile.

Win noticed the way her eyes lit up and once again he thought her a very attractive woman. One whom he wanted to kiss and he wasn't going to wait long to make that happen. When Win wanted something, he went after it and didn't quit until he got it.

"Follow me, Dr. Avery," he said.

Erin was amazed at how well set up her new office was. There was a small waiting room, an office for personnel, which was only her at the moment, and two examination rooms. There was only one examination table and the other exam room was empty. However, there were many standard medical supplies already stocked.

Bandages, several different sorts of medicine, stethoscopes, and other supplies lined shelves in a little closet. The office contained a desk and desk chair. They were older pieces, but Erin wasn't complaining. There was room in it for a filing cabinet and some shelves lined one of the walls. Erin was happy to see that there was also a window in the office.

"This is amazing. How did you do all of this?" she asked.

Sitting a hip on the corner of the desk, Win said, "The town took up a collection so that we could get things started. I also used some of my profits from the business to buy things. As we keep making more money, we'll continue buying the necessary stuff you need and make improvements, too. But it's a start."

Standing close to him, she said, "It's a great start." She was touched by his thoughtfulness and tears stung her eyes. "Thank you for helping me realize my dream."

"Don't thank me yet," Win said with a smile. "We have to start getting some patients in here, but I don't think that'll take too long. You're the only doctor here, so there's really very little choice for them unless they want to keep going to Dickensville. Besides, it's all part of our bargain."

She nodded. "Yes, I remember. You get a wife and I get to be a doctor. A good trade-off, I'd say."

"I think so, too," Win said. "You're really making out better than I am, you know."

"I am?"

"Sure. You get a medical practice, a handsome husband, and free medical care for any future pets you might like to have," he said.

"You really are conceited, aren't you?" she said with a laugh. "Besides, you get a wife and a mother for your babies." She colored upon saying the words.

One of his brows arched. "Hmm. Thinking ahead to having babies, huh? That's a good thing."

"Well, aren't you?" she asked, trying not to become flustered.

The sudden heat in his eyes captured her gaze. "Yes, I am."

Erin's heart beat hard for a moment and her breathing quickened. She stepped back from him a little and said, "That's as it should be since we're getting married."

"I agree." Win let her off the hook. "Are you hungry?"

"Yes," she said, regaining her equilibrium.

"Do you mind meeting some of my friends for dinner? Josie said just to come for supper whenever we got back. I told her it would either be today or tomorrow," Win said.

Erin broke into a delighted smile and Win was attracted to her even more. She was a beautiful woman. He'd gotten very lucky in his search for a wife.

"Let's go then. I'm starving," she said.

Loud laughter reached their ears when they arrived at the Tafts'. Win smiled as he recognized Lucky's robust laugh and he wondered what the Irishman was up to now. It was a force of habit for him to take off his coat and shirt before entering the house.

Evan's Aunt Edna, a sassy woman in her early sixties, had decreed that the price of admission into their home for the men was to come in shirtless. He, Lucky, and Billy played along with her and always complied. He decided that he'd better break Erin in slowly to that, however. Most people wouldn't have approved of that sort of thing and he was sure Erin was one of them.

Win knocked and Billy answered the door. "Hey! There you are! C'mon in. I see you forgot your manners," Billy remarked upon seeing Win still fully dressed.

Win laughed. "Well, we have company," he said as he and Erin entered the house.

Billy said, "Oh, that's right." He sometimes forgot that others didn't know the little game they played with Edna.

Edna's eyes lit up upon seeing Win. "There's my favorite Chinaman. You get better looking all the time."

Win hurried over to hug her. "How are you?"

"Well, I'm not too bad for an old fart," she said.

He kissed her cheek and said, "You're not old, but I did tell you to lay off the beans."

Edna let out a delighted laugh. "So you did. Well, where's your girl?"

Win went back over to Erin. "Everyone, this is Dr. Erin Avery."

Edna saw her short hair and though it very unusual. However, she could see that Erin was a beautiful woman even so. Her large dark eyes were very pretty. As Win took her coat from her, Edna thought that she certainly did have a womanly figure. She stood up and walked stiffly over to Erin, silently cursing the rheumatoid arthritis that plagued her knees and now her ankles.

"My goodness, what a pretty girl you are. It's a pleasure to meet you, Erin," she said.

Erin smiled. "The pleasure is mine. Win's told me a lot about you in his letters and on the way here."

Edna chuckled. "I'm afraid it's all true; the good and the bad."

Erin watched the way Edna moved and thought it was a shame for a woman of her relatively young age. Other than arthritis, it seemed like Edna was in good shape. Her blue eyes were bright and clear, reflecting her sharp intellect and her pretty brown hair was attractively streaked with silver strands. Erin's mind went into physician mode and she began running through possible remedies that might help Edna.

"It was all good, I promise."

"This is my nephew, Evan," Edna said as Evan came out of the kitchen where he and Josie had been cooking. "Evan, this is Erin."

Erin smiled at the strikingly handsome man with black hair and green eyes. "Hello, Sheriff."

Evan held out a hand to her. "Hello, Dr. Avery. Nice to have you with us."

She shook hands with him. "It's nice to be here. I understand you make a mean meatloaf."

"I do all right at it," Evan said with a grin.

Billy stepped forward. "Don't listen to him. He's just being modest. It's the best meatloaf you'll ever eat. I'm Billy. Good to meet you, doc."

Erin blurted, "Dear God, you're beautiful." She could clearly see his Indian heritage in his light bronze skin tone, dark eyes, and chiseled features. His medium brown hair held a few reddish highlights, denoting his white blood.

Billy laughed as his face grew a little flushed. "You're not the first to say that and you won't be the last," he teased her.

As Edna sat down, she said, "Why do you think I want him to come in here without a shirt on?"

Evan groaned. "Will you behave yourself, old woman?"

"If I haven't done it in the past, why should I start now? I'm too old to change," Edna retorted.

Win introduced her to Lucky.

"Pleased to meet ya, Erin. Looks like Win has himself a fine lookin' lass, all right," he said.

Erin was charmed by his merry gray eyes and broad grin; his Irish accent didn't hurt either. His light blond hair was an attractive compliment to his eye color. He was about Evan's six-foot-two height and roughly the same build. "Where did all you handsome men come from?" she asked with a laugh. "And now an Irishman. No wonder you're in your glory, Edna."

Edna nodded. "That's right. Who can blame me?"

Josie came out of the kitchen and Evan introduced the two women.

"Erin, it's so good to have you with us. Be prepared, you never know what's going to happen when they're all around," she said, smiling. "Especially with this one here." She indicated Lucky by poking his arm.

"Now don't be tellin' the fair doctor that, lass. You'll scare her off," Lucky said. "I need her to fix my tooth."

Erin said, "Win mentioned that to me. I'll take care of it first thing tomorrow."

"God bless ya," Lucky said.

Josie said, "Dinner's ready, so come on and eat before it gets cold."

They sat down at the kitchen table and Lucky said the blessing. Erin snuck a glance at Win and noticed that he didn't bow his head or say Amen. *He really meant it when he said that he doesn't have any religious faith of any kind.* Then they started passing plates around and cross-conversations began.

At a lull, Erin said, "I'm sure you're all wondering about my short hair."

Josie said, "Well, it had crossed my mind. I didn't want to be rude and ask, though."

Erin smiled at her and said, "I wouldn't have minded. I'm fairly hard to offend." She went on to tell them what had happened in Cheyenne.

"Bloody hell!" Lucky said. "I hope you gave that mog a clatter or five for me," he added, looking at Win.

Erin stopped chewing her roast beef to say, "What?"

Josie giggled. "You'll have to learn Irish so you can understand Lucky.

"'Mog' means 'fool' and 'clatter' means either, a slap, hit, or punch."

"Sorry about that, Erin," Lucky said. "I forget myself sometimes."

"That's ok, Lucky. I'm very excited to learn how you speak," she said.

Win said, "Lucky is actually tri-lingual. He speaks English, Gaelic, and Cheyenne."

Lucky shook his head. "Actually four if ya count American. Irish English and American English are different, lad. If ya went to Ireland, ya probably wouldn't know half of what was bein' said."

Erin asked, "Like what?"

Lucky thought for a moment. "S'pose I said to ya, 'Tear yer hole off the haggart.' You wouldn't have a baldy notion what I'm sayin'."

"Tear yer hole off the haggart? You're right. What does it mean?"

Lucky grinned. "It means go away, get out of here."

She laughed. "This is fun. I'm going to have you teach me a bunch of stuff and then write my friend Jessica and confuse the heck out of her with it."

Billy said, "It won't take long. He confuses me every day with either Irish or Cheyenne. Sometimes he puts both in the same sentence."

Lucky said, "Just tryin' to keep ya on your toes."

Win had warned Erin to stay away from the topic of Lucky's time spent with the Cheyenne unless he brought it up. Lucky had met and fallen in love with a Cheyenne maiden several years ago, whom he had married. He'd lived with her tribe for three years until the military had forced them onto a reservation. They wouldn't let Lucky go with her and they wouldn't let her stay with him. Before the military dragged her away, she'd divorced him, telling him to go live his life. However, Lucky still felt married to her.

His loss was painful, made more so because she had been five months pregnant at the time. His friends didn't bring it up because it hurt him so much to think about the woman he still loved and the child he'd never laid eyes on.

So although she smiled, Erin refrained from asking him any questions. "Well, I'd say you're a very intelligent man to know so many languages."

"Thanks. So did yer man get ya settled in then?" he asked.

"Well, we dropped my suitcases off and then Win took me to see my office. I'm very impressed. Thank you for all you did to help put it together," she replied

"It was our pleasure," Evan said. "There were a lot of people who helped. They were willing to do whatever it took to get a doctor here."

"I appreciate it very much," Erin said.

Josie said, "Erin, after you take care of Lucky's tooth in the morning, I'm kidnapping you so we can talk about wedding plans."

"Oh, all right," Erin said.

"I'll introduce you to some of my friends who can help, plus Aunt

Edna is a fount of knowledge," Josie said. "We'll help you get things around in time for the wedding."

Edna said, "What she means is I've seen a lot of weddings since I've been around so long, so I know some things."

"Oh, yes. That's exactly what I meant," Josie said with a grin. "You know me so well."

"It's a good thing you're making me a baby to play with or I'd chase you out of here," Edna said.

Josie just smiled back at her.

"Yes, congratulations on your baby," Erin said. "How are you feeling?"

"I'm feeling fine. A little tired some days, but not overly so. I haven't had very much morning sickness," Josie said.

"I'm glad to hear that," Erin said and then changed the subject; she knew that this wasn't the time to ask more thorough questions. She could do that tomorrow when they had more privacy.

The rest of the meal was spent telling Erin stories and filling her in more on Echo and its residents. At the conclusion of the meal, Win said that he and Erin should go so she could get some rest. He needed to get back to the herd and relieve Ross, who had been watching the sheep for Lucky and Billy while they'd come to dinner.

"I'll not be long after ya," Lucky said.

"Take your time," Win said as they went out the door.

Chapter Five

"Your friends are wonderful," Erin said as she and Win mounted the stairs to the front porch of the Hanovers' house.

Win replied, "Yeah, they're some real characters, all right."

"They seem like good people."

"Very good people."

"Thank you for everything, and I'll see you tomorrow at some point," she said as they reached the door.

Win nodded. "Just have Josie bring you out to my place whenever you're done. I can show you your new home and introduce you to the sheep."

She smiled. "I'll do that."

He moved closer and kissed her cheek. "Good night, Dr. Avery."

His lips on her cheek had been warm and soft. "Good night, Dr. Wu."

He gave her a smile and she went inside. Standing in the foyer, Erin took a deep breath to clear away the sliver of desire his little kiss had created. Then she went to bed.

Despite the cold, Marvin Earnest sat out on the porch of the large ranch house in which he lived. His thick frock coat kept him warm. His beautifully handsome features were silvered in the bright moonlight, his blue eyes opaque. The light breeze ruffled his fashionably cut blond hair.

He already knew about the arrival of the new doctor. Marvin always knew everything worth knowing, which he used to his advantage whenever possible. It might not come in handy right away, but it often did later on. Deciding that he would go see the good doctor as soon as she'd opened up shop, Marvin smiled.

Leaning his head against the back of the chair in which he sat, he wondered what excuse he should use to go see her. He was in excellent health, but he would make something up just so he could satisfy his curiosity about what kind of person Erin was. It would be interesting to see if she would even accept him as a patient since Win was sure to have warned her about him.

"Good evening, Marvy."

Marvin looked at his twin. "Hello, Shadow. I was just trying to decide what ailment I should go see Dr. Avery for," Marvin said.

Shadow tapped Marvin's head. "See if she has a cure for insanity."

Marvin laughed and said, "Well, if she comes up with something, I'll let you know since you need it more than me."

Shadow grinned, his features a mirror image of Marvin's. Shadow's long, dark hair and more powerful build were the only ways to tell the two brothers apart. "No Phoebe tonight?" This was a common question between the brothers.

Phoebe Stevens worked as a housekeeper and cook for the Hanovers and she'd been seeing Marvin for a couple of years. She was the only other person outside of Shadow that Marvin loved. In fact, he loved her so much that he was willing to share her with Thad McIntyre, a bounty hunter and long-time friend of the Tafts. Marvin enjoyed knowing Thad had no knowledge of Phoebe's relationship with him. Phoebe accepted

Marvin's dark, twisted personality completely and this was why he loved her. She told him that she needed both him and Thad; Marvin for his dark nature and Thad for his goodness and fun.

Marvin said, "She's been and gone."

Shadow heard the discontent in his brother's voice. "What is it?"

"At the risk of sounding sentimental, just once I'd like her to stay," Marvin said. "Just once."

"Which is exactly why she doesn't. She doesn't want you to get used to it because she doesn't want to commit to either you or Thad," Shadow said.

"I know," Marvin said. "She knows that it gets to me."

"She also knows that you enjoy the torture."

Marvin smiled. "Yes, she does. Next to you, she knows me best."

Shadow said, "Mmm. Better in ways I don't want to."

Marvin's laugh rang out. "I should hope not. So what are you up to now? You're not normally up before dark; I was surprised when you brought me the news about Dr. Avery."

"I had some things to do for my hobby and I needed the light."

Shadow hated the daylight. Nighttime was his preferred time to be out and about, especially because no one in Echo knew of his existence. Marvin himself hadn't known about Shadow until they'd been sixteen.

Marvin sensed his twin's reflective mood. Growing up, the two brothers had always felt that something was missing from their lives, that there was another part of them out there somewhere. Upon meeting, their bond had been immediate and they were often able to tell what the other was thinking and feeling.

"Shadow, don't start that. There's no sense in it," Marvin said.

"There're times I can't help it, Marvy," Shadow said, using Marvin's nickname. "Why didn't Father love me the way he did you?"

A pang of guilt stabbed Marvin's heart. While Shadow had been locked away in the vast basement under the house, Marvin had been given everything: love, wealth, and an excellent education. All of the things that Shadow should have also had. It hurt him to think of the way

Shadow had lived his life until Marvin had accidentally discovered him one day.

Thinking about it infuriated him. "I don't know. He had not one son, but two. He should have been grateful to have not only one, but two sons."

"Don't try to spare my feelings, Marvin," Shadow said. "It's the reason he named me Shadow. I wasn't good enough because I was second born and I didn't look exactly like you."

Marvin's mouth twisted in a snarl. "What does mere hair color matter?"

The cool wave of Marvin's wrath invaded Shadow's mind. "Ok, Marvy. Calm down. I shouldn't have brought it up."

Marvin brought his anger under control. "No, Shadow, it's not your fault. I feel so badly that you had to suffer so much while I—"

"Don't do that. You're right. Thinking about it is pointless. Let's talk about something else."

Marvin exhaled a large breath and said, "Actually, I'm going to bed. How will you spend your night?"

"Oh, I don't know yet. I have a few ideas," Shadow said.

Marvin smiled. "Don't get in too much trouble, brother of mine."

"I won't. Maybe I can find out something interesting."

"You usually do. Goodnight, Shadow."

"Goodnight, Marvy."

Shadow watched Marvin go inside and then set out across one of the pastures, intent on causing some mayhem. It was one of the things he did best.

"Well, you've got a good-sized cavity," Erin said after evaluating Lucky's tooth.

His gray eyes locked on hers. "What're ya gonna do about it?" He was not looking forward to treatment, but if it meant an end to his pain, he'd suffer it.

"I'm going to put in a filling," she said.

"All right. Now?"

Seeing the anxiety in his expression, Erin smiled at him. "Yes. The sooner we get it done, the sooner you'll feel better."

Lucky nodded. "Right. You know best."

Erin readied a hypodermic needle with cocaine and turned towards Lucky, who paled upon seeing it. *Uh oh. I've seen that look before.* "Lucky, it's going to be fine. I'm very good at giving injections. Besides, you're a brave warrior and you can handle a little needle, right?" She'd found that appealing to men's pride was very effective in getting them to sit for injections.

His tooth needed to be fixed and the anesthetic would help accomplish that. He nodded. "Aye. Go ahead then."

Erin quickly delivered the injection, noting the way Lucky's knuckles turned white as he took a death hold on the chair arms. "There. All done. I'll just wait a few minutes to let that do its job."

"That's it?" Lucky sagged with relief. "What the hell was I so scared for?"

"It's very common for people to be afraid of having dental work done. However, if it's done properly, it's not painful," Erin said.

Lucky couldn't feel his tongue on the right side of his face and it made him smile. "It feews stwange," he said and laughed.

She laughed with him. "I'm sure it does. Ok, I think that means we can start now."

Half an hour later, Lucky left her office after thanking her heartily. Erin felt elated over successfully treating her first patient. When Josie came to get her, she was just putting her equipment away.

"Hello, Dr. Avery," Josie said with a grin. "Lucky is already singing your praises. His tooth is much better, thanks to you."

Erin smiled. "I'm so glad. It feels good to help people and I'm happy that I could ease his suffering. He's such a sweet man."

Josie said, "He is. He makes friends easily, too, but he can have a temper. Mainly when Billy annoys him, though."

Erin chuckled. "I can just imagine what they're like together."

"It's certainly never dull. They like to pull pranks on each other," Josie said.

"That must be entertaining. Well, I'm all finished up here."

Josie nodded. "We're going to meet over at Sonya Belker's house. She and her husband Jerry are good friends of ours. You'll like her."

"I'm sure I will. After you, Mrs. Sheriff," Erin said.

Josie laughed. "I see Win told you about that."

"He told me a lot of things," she said with a wink.

"Oh boy," Josie said. "I think I'm in trouble."

Erin laughed as they left the office.

Chapter Six

When Josie arrived at the farm with Erin, Win had a ewe flipped over on its back, pinned between his legs so that he could treat a cut on its underbelly. He checked the herd over on a daily basis for such injuries, knowing infection could quickly set in. The ewe had given up struggling, but still bleated.

Win smiled at the two women as they alighted from the buggy Josie drove, but he kept at his task.

"You look hard at work, Dr. Wu," Erin said, walking over to him.

Her smiling lips made Win want to kiss her. "I am. I heard about the miracle you worked on Lucky's tooth."

"I thought you didn't believe in miracles," Erin said.

Win chuckled as he let the sheep up and sent it on its way with a final pat. "I don't," he said. "Those were Lucky's words, not mine."

Erin could see that he meant it. She wasn't a very religious person herself, but she did believe. Win had warned her that he didn't subscribe to those kinds of notions and she now knew that he hadn't been kidding at all. "I see. What was wrong with your sheep?"

"Just a cut. I keep after small things so they don't become bigger problems," he said. "How'd you ladies make out?"

Josie said, "Very well. We're just about done, unless something else comes up."

Erin nodded. "It'll be a fairly simple ceremony, so I don't anticipate any problems."

"You brought your dress with you, so you don't have to buy one," Josie said.

Win asked, "You brought it with you?"

Erin said, "I didn't know if there was a ladies' boutique close enough that could make the dress in time, so Jessica helped me pick one to bring with me. My trunks should be coming tomorrow."

"I really appreciate how practical you are," Win said. "That's right. You told me about the trunks. Do you want me to bring them here?"

"That would be the logical thing to do," Erin responded.

Josie listened to them. This was the least romantic approach to marriage she'd ever witnessed. They talked about the wedding arrangements as if it was a business deal. Then she remembered that Win had called it a bargain and thought the description fit.

Erin looked past Win at the cabin that stood on the property. "So that's home, huh?"

Win turned to his cabin. "Yeah. C'mon and have a look. I think you'll like it."

She followed him to the cabin. Three chairs sat on the porch. The front door opened into what she gauged to be a ten-by-twelve-foot parlor, which contained a sofa, loveseat, coffee table, and wingback chair. An oval braided rug in cheerful colors covered the floor.

One of Billy's paintings of the sheep herd hung on the wall behind the sofa. Green checkered curtains adorned the two windows. Further on was the kitchen area, which was equipped with a four-plate cook stove and a sink with a pump. Cupboards over the sink provided storage for cups and dishes. A nice table and chair set and small china cupboard rounded out the room.

Win was anxious to see if she liked the place, but he kept calm. As he took her into the master bedroom, Erin saw that it was large and the bed looked comfortable. A very pretty quilt covered it.

"I know how you ladies like plenty of room for clothing, so we built a big closet," Win said, opening its door.

Erin walked past him to look at it and he caught the floral scent of her perfume. It was tantalizing and he again thought about kissing her.

Not only was there space for her clothing, but there were shelves behind where his clothes hung and one over top of the clothing rod. "Goodness. I'll say that's a nice closet. There's plenty of room."

"I'm glad you think so," Win said. "The other room is for the nursery. I didn't get any furniture because that'll be something we'll pick out together when the time comes."

In his eyes, Erin saw the same heat in them as the day before. It made it hard not to think of the act of making babies. "Yes. That's a good idea."

Win gave her a knowing smile and moved away. "Right this way, Dr. Avery."

As she followed him, she asked. "Do you have any objections to me keeping my maiden name for professional purposes?"

Josie sat on the sofa. She perked up upon hearing Erin's question. It was strange for a woman to keep her surname and she was curious about Win's answer.

"Of course not. Having two Dr. Wu's around would be confusing, especially since they're going to get used to calling you Dr. Avery," he said as the entered the other bedroom.

There would be plenty room for a crib and dresser. He'd built shelves along one wall. "This is very nice," she said. "You've built a very nice cabin, Win."

"I had a lot of help, especially from the Irish Indian," Win said with a wry smile.

She chuckled. "I just can't picture him living with Indians."

"It must have been interesting," Win agreed. "I have one more thing to show you."

"Ok."

Back in the kitchen, Win opened a door by the sink. "I got the idea from the Hanovers. They have a big tub in their bathhouse. Lucky loves it. Of course now he bathes in the stream a lot and so do I, but during the winter, this is much better."

Erin saw a large metal tub situated in the middle of the room. A shelf with various toiletries stood in a corner and a stack of books sat close to the tub.

"Do you read in the tub?" she asked. Instantly she regretted her question because it conjured imagines of Win sitting naked in the tub.

"Yep. I get the cook stove good and hot and open the door for about an hour. It gets nice and toasty in here and between that and the hot water, it stays warm a long time."

"Remarkable. This is going to be a very nice home," Erin said. She would have lived almost anywhere if it had meant she could practice her profession, but the excellent designing and construction of the cabin showed her that he paid attention to detail. Another good quality in a husband.

"I'm glad you think so. If there's anything you'd like to change, let me know," Win said. "It's only right that you should have things the way you'd like them since it's your home, too."

His thoughtfulness touched her. Looking in his eyes, she said, "You're something else, Win."

"A good something else?" he asked.

"A very good something else."

The look they exchanged was filled with awareness of each other and Win knew that if Josie hadn't been present, he would have kissed Erin. However, he merely smiled.

"Would you ladies like a cup of coffee? I'll put a pot on," Win said.

Josie said, "I'd love a cup."

"Me, too," Erin said, joining Josie in the parlor.

Win readied the pot and put it on the stove. As he came to join them, someone knocked on the cabin door. He opened it and felt an immediate shaft of hatred stab his abdomen.

"Earnest? What are you doing here?" Win asked. Then he noticed that Marvin held his bulldog, Barkley, in his arms.

Marvin said, "I need your help. Barkley tangled with a porcupine and I don't know the first thing about extracting the quills."

Barkley whimpered, but he didn't struggle in his master's arms. Despite Marvin's failings, he loved animals and children and he treated Barkley as though the dog were his child.

"You shouldn't have moved him," Win said, motioning for Marvin to enter. The thought of having the man in his home disgusted him, but Barkley was his first concern.

"I wouldn't have, but he wouldn't stay still and he didn't want me to leave him. I had Travis bring us over in the buggy so he wouldn't do any more damage to himself," Marvin said, sitting the dog down on the floor gently. He surprised the three occupants of the cabin by sitting right down on the floor with Barkley, who whimpered and pressed himself against Marvin.

"It's all right, Barkley. Dr. Wu is going to get rid of those nasty quills," he said, stroking Barkley's head.

Win couldn't believe he was same man who terrorized people and caused trouble whenever he could. He gathered the tools he needed along with a special salve Lucky had made for wounds.

Joining Marvin and Barkley on the floor, he started examining Barkley. There were fifteen quills and several were deeply imbedded in Barkley's flesh.

Win looked at Marvin and said, "It was good thinking for you to bring him here. If he was that agitated, he might have started biting at them and gotten them in his muzzle or tongue."

Marvin asked, "Can you get them out?"

"Yeah. This might take a while. You're gonna have to hold him still," Win said, noting how different Marvin's blue eyes looked at the moment. The usual cold malevolence in them was replaced by a fatherly concern.

"I'll do whatever it takes to help him," Marvin said.

"Ok. I'm going to start now."

It took close to an hour to extract the porcupine quills from Barkley. Win had done it as quickly and gently as possible. He admitted that Marvin had done a good job keeping Barkley as calm as possible. Win put salve on the two worst spots and wound long strips of bandages around the dog's midsection.

"Take this salve with you. Tomorrow, clean the wounds and put more on. You'll need to watch for infection."

Marvin asked, "Can't you come do it? I've never taken care of anything like this before."

Win regarded Marvin for a moment. He didn't want to set foot in Marvin's house, but Barkley's welfare was more important than his feelings. "Fine, but it's going to cost you."

Marvin nodded. "Whatever you want." He kissed Barkley's head and then stood up. Marvin stretched to get rid of the crick in his back. "I don't know how Mr. Quinn constantly sits on the floor in his tent."

Win smiled in spite of himself. "Tipi. Lucky lives in a tipi, not a tent."

Marvin rolled his eyes and pulled his wallet from his coat. Opening it, he took out a fifty-dollar bill and handed it to Win. "Does that cover today?"

Win blinked at the large sum. "Sure."

Marvin nodded. "Thank you very much, Dr. Wu. What time will you arrive tomorrow?"

"Around two."

"Very good. Josie, good to see you again. And you must be Dr. Avery," Marvin said. "I'm afraid Dr. Wu was remiss in introducing you."

Erin saw Win's face tighten as Marvin extended his hand to her. Win had warned her about Marvin, but she couldn't understand why.

She shook hands with him. "It's nice to meet you, Mr. Earnest."

"Please, call me Marvin. It's wonderful to know that Echo now has medical care. I'll have to stop by to see you. I'm overdue for a physical," he said.

Win's hands tightened into fists and Erin grew concerned. "All right. That'll be fine. Stop by the clinic tomorrow around nine and we'll get it taken care of."

Marvin gave her a bright smile and she was entranced by the beauty of it. *This man is the one Win says is a holy terror? I just don't see it. Of course, he says that's the way he works.*

"I'll be there. Thank you again, Win. Josie, give my regards to Edna," Marvin said, gathering Barkley into his arms again.

Win opened the door and closed it once Marvin exited the cabin. To Erin he said, "I don't want you treating him."

She said, "I can't refuse to treat anyone, Win. He's no different."

"Yes, he is. I don't want you alone with him," Win said. "He's nothing but trouble."

Josie nodded. "Marvin is trouble, but if you know how to handle him, it's not so bad. I learned that from experience."

Erin looked at her. "I can't believe that he's the evil man you've told me about. He seems so nice."

Josie said, "Don't let him fool you. He's very good at making himself seem likable, but there's something cold underneath it. It's hard to describe."

"I understand what you're saying, but I can't turn him away. He's not going to do anything to me. It'll be fine," Erin said.

Win stepped towards her. "No, I don't think you understand—"

Erin stood up and looked him square in the eye. "I might be marrying you, but you won't tell me who I can and cannot treat, Win. We need to get that straight right now."

Win saw that she wasn't going to budge on this. As a physician himself, he knew that the oath she had taken was sacred to her. He said, "You're right, but watch yourself around him. If he does anything you don't like, tell me and I'll deal with him."

"Agreed," Erin said, with a nod.

Josie left shortly after Marvin. Win asked Erin to stay for supper; he would take her home later on.

"What are you going to make?" Erin asked.

Win smiled. "It's a surprise. Why don't you go down and see the Irishman while I make supper?"

"Are you trying to get rid of me?" Erin said.

"Yes, but only for a while," Win said.

Erin put on her coat. "All right. I'll play along."

"Scratch on the tipi flap. That's how you knock on one," Win said. "You'll have a good time."

Erin smiled at him and left the cabin.

Lucky looked up from what he was doing when someone scratched on his tipi flap. "C'mon in."

Erin pulled the flap back and said, "Hello. Win said I should come see your tipi, so here I am."

Lucky grinned. "I'm glad to have ya, lass. Come sit next to me. The fire will keep ya plenty warm. No need for yer coat."

It was very warm indeed in the tipi, which surprised Erin. She took her coat off and laid it to the side. Looking around, she noticed that there was a bow and quiver of arrows, a few wicker containers that had been woven out of some sort of plant, and what she assumed was Lucky's bed. She also saw a few deer hide bags hanging from support poles.

Lucky watched her examine everything. He got a kick out of educating people about tipis and Cheyenne culture in general. "What do ya think?"

"I've never seen anything like it. It's wonderful. You're right; the fire feels good."

He nodded and went back to work on the small bow he was making. Erin asked, "What is that?"

"Pauline Desmond wants to learn how to shoot a bow and arrow, so I'm makin' this for her. She can't learn on mine since it's too big, so I'm makin' it and the arrows her size. All Indians do this for children, mainly lads, but there are a few young ones who like to hunt."

"Young ones?"

"Girls. Her pa said it was fine with him, so I started makin' it yesterday. It can take a while to work the wood into the proper shape," Lucky said. "If it's not spot on, you won't be able to shoot accurately."

"It must have taken you a while to learn this stuff," Erin said.

"Aye. I was terrible at all of it at first, but I decided I was going to do it even if it killed me," Lucky said.

Erin watched his strong hands bend and shape the wood. "It seems like you learned it well. I wouldn't know the first thing about making a weapon."

"I had good teachers. My friend, Wild Wind, could make just about anything. He's a character if I ever saw one. Quick witted and always has a comeback for everything."

Erin heard the wistfulness in his voice. "You miss him."

Lucky nodded. "I do. We became like brothers even though he's an Indian and I'm white. None of that mattered to most of the tribe after I was there a while. I made a lot of good friends and we had a lot of fun together. But there was heartache, too."

Erin didn't feel comfortable asking him questions about it, so she just nodded.

Lucky laughed and said, "We went on a raid this one time and stole thirteen ponies. I wanted to go back and get another one so that we didn't have bad luck. Wild Wind told me that if I did, I was on my own."

Erin asked, "What happened?"

"I went back and got not only another one, but two more. That's how I ended up with enough horses to give my wife's father so I could marry her."

"I don't understand," Erin said.

"Well, you see, in a lot of Indian cultures, when a man wants to marry a woman, he has to give something to her father. The more respected the maiden is, the higher the bride price. It might sound disrespectful to say that you're buyin' a bride, but it's not. The more yer willin' to part with, the more ya hold her in … esteem, I guess you'd say. She knows ya want to marry her very badly if ya give as much as ya can," Lucky said.

"Oh, I see," Erin replied. "So how much did you give?"

"Well, my friends knew I wanted to marry Avasa, that's her name, and since I was only there for about a year, I wasn't very wealthy. So they took me on that raid to get some ponies. I gave sixteen horses, three knives that I had bought, and a revolver. He took Avasa's feelin's for me into consideration and since the gifts were good quality, he gave us permission to marry," Lucky said. The memories were bittersweet for him.

"Sixteen horses and all those weapons," Erin said. "I'd say you held her in very high regard."

Lucky stopped working and said, "I did. I do. She's the most beautiful woman I've ever seen and so sweet and kind. Funny, too. Not a day goes by that I don't miss her and I can't tell ya how much it hurts not to be with her and to know my child."

Erin put a hand on his knee. "I'm so sorry, Lucky. Isn't there anything that can be done?"

"There will be," Lucky said, his face settling into hard lines. "Come hell or high water, I'm going to get her and our baby. If we'd been married in a church, all legal-like, they wouldn't have taken her from me, but because we were married by a shaman, it's not considered valid. One way or another, we'll be together again, though."

Erin looked at the fierce expression on his face and was impressed by the strength of his resolve. She hoped Avasa could somehow feel his love, even from this great distance. "I think if anyone can do it, you can."

"Thanks. It means a lot."

She nodded. "How's the tooth doing?"

His grin was infectious. He put an arm around her and gave her a sideways hug. "Wonderful, God bless ya. I owe you. What do ya charge?"

"For you, nothing," Erin said.

He frowned. "You can't go around doin' that all the time."

"Oh, I'll charge other people, just not you," she said with a wink.

They laughed together before he said, "Don't tell Win that. He'll get jealous."

"We don't have to tell him," Erin said.

"Another lusty lass; just my kind," Lucky said.

"That's right. Now, tell me how you make a tipi," she said.

"Well, ya see these poles...?"

Chapter Seven

While Erin was at Lucky's tipi, Win was hard at work making a nice meal for them. He knew the diner in town wouldn't make the sort of meal he wanted, so he'd had Evan and Josie, who were excellent cooks, show him how to make several dishes.

To most people, Win didn't seem very romantic, but he hid that side of him. His mother had loved reading romance books. Curious as to why she liked them so much, he'd picked one up, and soon he was hooked. He'd been fifteen at the time and he'd been reading them ever since.

While he and Erin had been practical in their relationship thus far, he wanted to show her that he had another side to him. He felt that romance was very important to a marriage. His mother and father had been romantic in their own way, and he wanted his own marriage to have that same quality.

So he covered the table with an attractive burgundy cloth, put a nice vase in the center of the table, and used the pretty china he'd bought several months back. His mother had been adept at many crafts and she'd taught him the art of creating artificial flowers from crepe paper, even though boys didn't normally do such things. Since it was still winter there were no wild flowers to pick; the homemade flowers were his answer to that problem.

He'd found out through their letters that she liked mutton, so he'd made a shepherd's pie with it, thinking the irony of it would amuse her. He'd made cherry tarts that morning and had left a bottle of good red Bordeaux outside to chill. Lucky had tasted the tarts for him and pronounced them excellent, so he was confident that Erin would like them.

Still, he was nervous since he'd never made dinner for a woman before and impressing her was very important to him. He'd put a lot of thought into the dinner and he wanted them to have a nice time together. Shortly before the shepherd's pie was due to come out, he went down to Lucky's tipi to retrieve his future bride.

He heard Lucky and Erin laughing as he neared the tipi. Erin's laugh was rich and pleasant to the ear. Win was thankful to his friend for entertaining Erin so well. His scratch on the tipi was answered in the affirmative and Win entered the tipi.

The two were engaged in a game of knuckles, a common Indian game played with animal bones. Win enjoyed the game himself, as did the rest of Lucky's friends. Josie was a good player, but Evan wasn't, which greatly annoyed the sheriff.

"Who's winning?" Win asked.

Lucky said, "She is. Beginner's luck."

"He's just mad because I'm beating the pants off him," Erin said.

"I'm sure he is. Josie usually beats him, too. Us men don't like being beaten by girls," Win said.

Erin said, "Too bad. Are you here to collect me for dinner?"

"I am."

"What about Lucky?" she asked.

Lucky shook his head. "I've got other plans, love, but thanks for thinkin' about me."

"Where are you going?"

"Over to see Ross to talk to him about some business. His sister is making supper," Lucky said.

"You know she has a crush on you," Win said, smiling.

Lucky made an annoyed face. "I know."

Win let it go, knowing that Lucky would never start another relationship when he was still married to Avasa in his heart. "Well, let's go have dinner. I don't want it to get dried out. Have fun, Lucky."

Lucky grunted and then said to Erin, "Thanks for comin' to see me. Have a good night."

"I will. You, too," she said with a pat on his shoulder.

As they walked to the cabin, Erin saw the warm light that glowed within it and she became excited that it would soon become her home. The handsome man at her side would become her husband and that prospect also excited her. Win stopped her at the door and said, "Close your eyes."

"What?"

"Close your eyes. Please?"

Erin smiled, but gave him a suspicious look before doing as he'd asked.

Win opened the door, guided her inside, and stopped her in the parlor. "Stay here and keep your eyes closed."

"Ok."

She listened to him moving about the cabin and tried to figure out what he was doing.

"All right. You can open your eyes now," Win said.

When she did, she saw a beautifully set table, complete with tall candles and wine glasses. She looked at him in astonishment then back at the table. Walking closer, she saw the plates were real china and the silverware was of good quality. Tantalizing aromas reached her nose and she inhaled them.

"Let me take your coat, madam," Win said playfully.

Erin unbuttoned it and slipped it off. Win took it and hung it by the door.

"You did all of this for me?" Erin asked, truly touched.

Win said, "Yes. Do you mind?"

Her eyes grew wide. "Mind? Why would I mind? It's the most romantic thing anyone's ever done for me."

Her answer pleased him. "No man has ever made dinner for you before?"

"No. Most of the men I know don't cook," she said.

Win smiled. "Most of the men I know don't, either. Lucky and Evan are the exceptions."

"Why did you do this? I already agreed to marry you," Erin said.

Win trailed a hand down her arm and took her hand. "Erin, just because we've already agreed to marry doesn't mean I can't do nice things for you. You're a beautiful, intelligent woman, and I appreciate you."

Erin didn't blush often, but her cheeks grew warm. "You think I'm beautiful?"

Win said, "Yes," and raised her hand so he could kiss the back of it.

The warmth in Erin's cheeks spread through her body and she couldn't look away. "Thank you," she said, somehow remembering her manners.

"You're welcome," Win said, just as captivated as she was.

Erin came back to herself. "Something smells delicious."

"Come sit down and I'll get it out of the oven," Win said.

Erin was charmed by the way he helped to seat her as though they were dining in a fine restaurant. While he was busy at the oven, she looked at the flowers in the center of the table. "Where did you find fresh flowers at this time of year? They're beautiful."

"I didn't. I made them," Win said.

"Made them? They're not real?" She pulled the vase over closer and softly traced a fingertip over one. "You made these from crepe?"

Win smiled at the wonder in her voice. "Yeah. Mother taught me. She was a master at it."

Erin was impressed. "If you hadn't told me, I wouldn't have known they weren't real."

He came back over to the table and sat a large pie dish on it. Erin's stomach growled as she looked at the golden brown crust on top and smelled the fragrant dish.

"That looks incredible," she said as he poured wine in their glasses.

He smiled as he sat down. "Thanks. I hope it tastes good. I've never made it before, so I guess we'll take a chance on it together."

Erin gave him a coy look. "I like adventure."

"I thought you did since you came all the way here to marry a man you don't know just so you can practice medicine," Win said. "You're very courageous, Erin. It's not every woman who would do that."

"My goodness. You're just full of praise tonight," she said, putting her napkin on her lap.

Win served the shepherd's pie. "I'm just telling the truth."

Erin took a forkful, blew on it, and put the bite in her mouth. The savory blend of potatoes, mutton, and vegetables was heavenly. After swallowing, Erin said, "You can consider your attempt at this dish a huge success, Win. It's delicious."

Win had to admit that he'd done a good job at it. "I can't tell you how relieved I am that it turned out well. I'll have to thank Josie for showing me how to make it."

Erin looked at the man across the table from her and asked, "You had someone teach you how to make this just so you could make it for me?"

Win nodded. "I wanted to do something special for you."

Erin lowered her gaze and said, "No one has ever done anything like this for me, Win. You put so much thought into everything. You've been holding out on me. In our letters you never mentioned that you could do these things."

"Not many people know this side of me, but since we're getting married, it's important that you see beyond what other people do," Win said.

Erin took a sip of wine and said, "You mean no one else knows how romantic you are?"

"No, they don't, and if you told them, they'd never believe it," Win said.

"You don't let many people in. I'm the same way," Erin said. "It's more trouble than it's worth sometimes."

Win heard the bitterness in her voice. "Yeah. Something like that. I see I'm not the only one who's ever had a broken heart."

"Someone broke your heart?"

"It was right after I graduated. We met at a friend's wedding, actually. We hit it off really well and things developed from there. I proposed a few months later and she turned me down. She hadn't realized that my feelings for her were that strong."

"So your love was unrequited."

Win nodded. "That's right. She had fun with me, but that's all it was to her. We would go out and so forth, but nothing more."

"You were never intimate?"

"No. I wanted to be, but I never pushed. I found out later on that she was using me to make another man jealous," Win said. He'd long ago gotten over the shame and anger of the situation, but it still wasn't pleasant to talk about.

Erin gave him a smile. "I think my former beau and your former lady must have known each other. I was nothing more than challenge to him and once he'd gotten me into bed, he was through with me."

The bite of shepherd's pie he'd just taken stuck in Win's throat at her remark. He took a swallow of wine to get it to go down. "Was he an idiot?"

Erin laughed at his response. "He was very intelligent."

"No, he wasn't," Win promptly said. "He couldn't have been. Obviously he didn't know what he had."

"Yes, he did, and apparently he didn't like it," she said, meaning it as a joke.

Win didn't laugh, though. "Again, he was apparently a jackass."

"Be that as it may, I put men aside after that. I had more important things to think about. Did you see other women?"

"Yes, I did, but nothing ever developed into a relationship again," Win said. "I never met anyone I thought was worth taking a chance on."

"Then why me?" Erin asked.

"I could ask you the same thing," Win said. "Your letter impressed me and we seem to have the same approach to a lot of things. But I'm pretty good at reading between the lines and I figured we'd both had things happen in the past that kept us from trying again. I felt that because we both knew what that was like, we'd be considerate of that."

Erin saw the sense in what he said. "We'd be compassionate toward each other."

"Right. Do you agree?"

"Completely."

Win finished his pie. "More wine?"

"Just a little. I have to work tomorrow," she said with a little smile.

He poured some and sat the bottle back down. "I'll say this one last time and then I'll let it go. Just watch yourself around Earnest."

She smiled at him. "I will. I promise."

"I'll be right back with dessert," he said.

"Dessert, too? You're going to spoil me, Win."

"You deserve to be," he said, retrieving the tarts and returning to the table.

They were the perfect accompaniment to the pie. "Mmm. Fantastic."

Win was pleased with them, too. "I guess Lucky was right. He was my taste-tester."

"I agree with him. Feel free to cook like this whenever you like," she said, taking another tart.

"That's the biggest compliment you could pay me."

He watched her tongue catch a crumb and fought groaning. Their eyes met and held again. Win got up and went to her, unable to stay away any longer. Pulling her to her feet, he wrapped his arms around her and settled his lips firmly over hers. She tasted sweet and he wanted more of her.

Erin had no objection since she felt the same way about him. His hard chest felt wonderful under hands and she rested her arms on his shoulders, running her fingers through his thick, soft hair. She hadn't wanted to kiss a man like this since Garrett and Win's desire for her heightened her own. It would be so easy to stay with him, but she wasn't quite ready.

Slowly, she pulled back, looking into his dark eyes. "Thank you for dinner." It was the only thing she could think of to say.

Win's mind wasn't any sharper than hers at the moment. "You're welcome." Then he smiled. "Does your brain feel as fuzzy as mine right now?"

"A brain? You just assume that my brain is connected to my body at the moment?"

"I think we're in the same boat."

"At least we're in it together," she said.

Win laughed and moved away a little. "Yes, we are." He plucked one of the flowers from the vase and handed it to her. "This is for you."

She smiled and took the flower. Looking down at it, she saw something glimmer inside it. Upon closer inspection, she saw a ring nestled in the crepe petals. She withdrew the ring from the flower and looked at Win in amazement.

"Wonder how that got in there. Well, since you found it, I don't want to waste it," Win said. "Dr. Avery, will you marry me?"

Erin didn't bother to attempt to stop the tears that sprang into her eyes. "I didn't expect … I mean, it wasn't … You never …" She stopped at that point, took a deep breath and said, "Yes, Dr. Wu, I will marry you."

"May I borrow that for a moment then?" he said, indicating the ring.

"You may," she said.

Win took it from her fingertips and slowly put the ring on her finger. It was something he intended to do only once and he wanted to savor the moment he became an engaged man. Seeing his ring on Erin's finger was very satisfying to him and he gave her hand a squeeze.

Looking in her eyes, he saw the same desire in them that he felt. Cupping the back of her head, he kissed her, taking his time about it. It was a novelty to feel the short strands of her hair against his palm, but he liked it. He also liked when she moved closer and put her hands on his back. Lingering over her lips, Win loathed ending the kiss, but he did.

His voice was slightly husky as he said, "That man in your past was the biggest fool in the world, but it's lucky for me he was."

Erin saw that he meant it. "It's lucky for me that that woman was only using you."

"We're a couple of fortunate people then aren't we?"

"We are."

Win held her for a few moments and then said, "I guess I should get you home. You have a busy day tomorrow."

"I guess so," she said, but she was enjoying his embrace. Forcing herself away from him, she said, "I'll help you clean up."

"No, you won't. I'll take care of that," Win said.

She gave him a dubious look. "Are you sure?"

"Positive. C'mon. We'll get you home before it gets much colder," Win said. "Besides, I need to get Sugar from Billy. He's babysitting her tonight."

"Oh! Your burro. I forgot about her," Erin said.

"I'll introduce you tomorrow," Win said. "I didn't want her to interrupt tonight, so I had him watch her for me. He's the only other one she'll stay with."

"Babysitting a burro. Now I've heard of everything," she said as they put on their coats and left the cabin.

Chapter Eight

As he was about to open the door to the outside of the passageway, Shadow heard a commotion. An angry man yelled and the frightened cries of a woman reached his ears. Although he listened intently, he couldn't make out what they were saying. Cracking open the door, his excellent night vision allowed him to see a man who was hitting the woman. Shadow growled under his breath.

The man was large in stature and the woman was of average size. Shadow enjoyed fighting, but this man had chosen a much weaker target than himself. What challenge was that? Slipping unnoticed from the place between the large boulders, Shadow made sure the door was shut before creeping up behind the enemy and grabbing him from behind.

With practiced movements, Shadow made quick work of the man, snapping his neck in a matter of seconds. The man fell heavily to the ground. Shadow then turned to the woman.

"Are you hurt?" he asked.

"Who are you? Where did you come from?" she asked after several moments.

"Don't worry about who I am. Are you hurt?" Shadow could smell her fear and see it in her wild, dark eyes.

She didn't know what to do or what to say. Should she simply run away? Should she answer him? Looking behind her, she knew that she couldn't stay here. Turning back, she gazed at the lifeless form of her tormentor and then at the dark figure before her. She couldn't make out his features, but she knew that he must be powerful to have killed her assailant so easily.

"Answer me!" Shadow demanded.

"Shh!"

Shadow's eyebrows rose. How dare she shush him?

"There are others," she whispered urgently.

"Others? Who?"

"I don't have time to tell you. I have to get away from here. It will be worse when they find him," she said.

Shadow's keen hearing picked up movement in the trees. Making a risky decision, he said, "Not a word or you'll end up like him."

His hand clamped around her arm and he dragged her behind him before propelling her through a door of some sort. It closed behind them and he slowly slid the bolt home so that it made no noise. Shoving her against the wall behind her, Shadow put his lips against her ear and whispered, "Do not make a sound. Not one."

She nodded her head vigorously. The place they were in was devoid of light and she couldn't see his features. His deep voice held a rough timber. They heard voices on the other side of the door. She felt and heard the stranger growl softly against her ear since he hadn't moved away from her. Neither had he released her or eased his weight from her.

"What's your name?" he asked.

"Bree," she whispered, knowing if she didn't answer him, he would inflict pain on her.

"Who are they? Why are they chasing you?"

"I escaped from them," she said.

"Why did they have you?"

"Because I made them money."

"Doing what?"

"I'm good at making counterfeit money," she said.

This tickled Shadow's funny bone and he laughed. "A crook. I just saved a crook. Excellent."

She'd expected him to be outraged and haul her off to the sheriff. Bree hadn't expected approval or humor.

The voices grew louder and shouts of alarm were heard as they discovered their fallen comrade. Shadow's teeth ground together in annoyance. "You've inconvenienced me."

"I'm sorry," she said hastily. "I didn't mean to."

Shadow heard her fear and it bothered him. "I won't hurt you as long as you listen to me and do exactly what I tell you to."

"All right."

Her immediate obedience also bothered him. He recognized it all too well. "How long have they had you?"

"A long time."

"Why did you decide to leave?"

Bree said, "Why does anyone want to leave? Freedom."

Freedom. Shadow understood that. "I'm going to take you somewhere until morning. You will not ever speak of your time there. You will be blindfolded the whole time. I'll be watching you every second. Tomorrow, I'll bring you back here and set you free and you will never talk about me. I do not exist. Do you understand me?"

Desperate, Bree grabbed his cloak. "No!"

Shadow gripped her hair and pulled it hard. "Either you agree or I'll throw you out right now!" he whispered.

"You don't understand. I have nowhere to go!" she responded. "No money for food. Nothing! They'll find me and kill me!"

"What makes you think I won't?"

Bree took a risk and said, "If you were going to, you would have done it already."

Shadow growled again. "I have no wish to kill you, but if you don't do as I say, I won't have a choice. I don't like killing women, but sometimes ..."

She understood and nodded. "Yes. I'll do exactly what you tell me to. I swear."

"Good girl," Shadow said and spun her around. "Forward. Don't worry I won't let you run into the wall unless you give me a reason to."

"Ok."

As they walked, Bree tried to see where they were going, but she couldn't make anything out. She didn't understand how her new captor could see anything in the blackness. Although he kept a tight hold on her upper arms, she sensed that this was more to guide her than any ill intent on his part.

Then he jerked her to a stop. "Stand still."

Her taut nerves stretched further when he blindfolded her with some sort of cloth.

"Forward."

Bree moved her feet again, expecting at any moment to trip over something. However, he kept her from hitting anything.

"Stop."

She heard a door open directly in front of her and then he moved her through the opening. Blessed warmth hit her and she could have cried with relief. She shivered, not realizing how cold she'd been until then.

"Stop. Take off your coat."

She was surprised when he helped her with it. Bree expected him to want her to take off more, but he said, "Forward."

He guided her along again and then halted her. "Bend down. There's a bed in front of you."

Bree found it.

"Sit down and stay still."

Immediately she obeyed and felt her boots being unlaced and removed.

"Lie down. You'll sleep here tonight. Remember, I'll be watching you." She did and he covered her up. "Go to sleep."

"Who are you?"

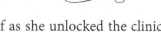

"No one. I'm just a shadow. Now sleep."

Humming to herself as she unlocked the clinic, Erin was ready to start her first official day as a doctor in her own practice. After starting the woodstove in the waiting room, she readied some charts and made sure the fully equipped exam room was completely ready. Excitement had kept her awake until late the night before. Looking at her ring, she realized that she was as excited to be engaged as she was about beginning her career.

Thoughts of Win filled her mind and she wondered what he was doing right then. Most likely seeing to the herd or whatever else he and Lucky had gotten up to. She'd like to be invisible and watch them during the day. She was sure it would be very entertaining, especially when Billy was added to the mix.

The bell over the waiting room door jingled and she left her office to see who it was. She smiled upon seeing Evan.

"Hello, Sheriff," she said. "How are you?"

"I'm good, thanks. I brought you a present," he said and held out a thermos and a coffee cup.

"Oh, you're a godsend. I hadn't given much thought to that sort of thing," she said as she took them from him.

"Well, that's what friends are for. I also came to make sure the wood stove is going, but I see you got it already."

"Yes, but thanks for thinking about me," she said. Narrowing her eyes, she said, "You wouldn't be here to check on my safety, would you?"

Evan smiled a little, his green eyes shining. "I'm always looking out for the safety of Echo's citizens, Dr. Avery."

"I don't suppose my fiancé put you up to this, did he?"

Evan looked chagrined. "It's not out of the realm of possibility. Well, I won't hold you up, but I'll be around if you need me. Congratulations on your engagement. Win's getting himself a good woman."

She blushed. "Thanks for the coffee and everything else, too."

"You bet," Evan said before leaving the clinic.

It wasn't much longer before Marvin showed up for his appointment. He'd seen Evan riding up the street, but hadn't paid the sheriff any mind. There was time to aggravate the sheriff later, but he had another source of entertainment in mind at the moment.

Entering the clinic, he noted that it looked clean and orderly. It was sufficiently warm and he detected the scent of coffee. Erin came out of the office and he broke into a broad smile.

"Dr. Avery, how good to see you again," he said.

His smile was disarming and Erin couldn't reconcile him with the monster everyone kept telling her about. "Good morning, Marvin. How's Barkley?"

Marvin's smile disappeared. "He's in quite a bit of pain, I'm afraid. I was up with him during the night. I kept him in my room so he wouldn't roam; he couldn't seem to get comfortable, even up on the bed with me."

"I'm so sorry to hear that," she said. "I'm sure Win will be able to do something for him when he comes to see him today."

Marvin nodded. "Yes, I'm sure he will. Thank you for asking."

"Certainly. Well, shall we get started?"

"Of course. You need a nurse," Marvin said.

Erin led him into the exam room and shut the door. "I hope to be able to hire one at some point, but for now, I'll be fine. How long has it been since you've been to a doctor?"

"About a year, I think. I'm a very healthy individual. This is just to establish care," Marvin said.

"I understand. However, since I've never treated you, I'm going to have to gather a history from you," Erin said.

"Of course." Marvin noticed the ring on her left hand. "I see that things are official with you and Dr. Wu now. Congratulations."

She smiled. "Thank you. Yes. I'm very happy about it."

"I can tell. So, I imagine that Win and his cronies have been bending your ear about what a horrible person I am," Marvin said.

Erin paused as she moved to listen to his heart. Looking into his azure eyes, she said, "They mentioned a few things."

Smiling, he said, "I'm sure they did. I expected no less."

Erin didn't respond to that. Instead she listened to his heartbeat. It was very strong and regular. "Your heart sounds perfect."

For the next several minutes, Erin asked him questions and he answered them. He enjoyed having her off-kilter. Skilled at finding out what annoyed people, he didn't expand on his previous statement. Although she was trying to hide it, he saw the wheels turning in her mind and he enjoyed knowing she was expending so much brain power on him.

"Well, Marvin, you're a very healthy individual indeed. I'm glad to see it," Erin said.

"Thank you. I look forward to seeing you again and it's very comforting to know you're in Echo," Marvin said as he stood up from the examination table.

"Thank you. Let me know if there's anything you need," she said, deciding to ignore the earlier discomfort.

His genial smile reassured her. "I'll do that, although I'm surprised that Win is allowing you to treat me."

Erin bristled at that. "My fiancé doesn't decide who I see, Marvin. I do. As long as you don't give me one, I won't have any reason to not treat you."

He looked offended. "I can assure you that I have no ill will toward you, Dr. Avery. How much do I owe you?"

"Since it's your first visit, it's on the house," she said. "Marvin, your history with other people isn't any of my business. As far as you and I go, I don't have any bad feelings toward you, either."

He smiled, looking relieved. "I'm glad to hear you say that. Well, I've taken up enough of your time. Have a good day, Dr. Avery."

"You, too, Marvin," Erin said.

Out on the street, Marvin smiled to himself as he walked along in the cold March air.

When Bree awoke, she was surprised that she had fallen asleep given the circumstances. She was still blindfolded, but she sensed that even if she took it off, it would still be too dark for her to see anything. She had no idea what time it was or how long she'd slept.

"Hello?" Her voice was tentative.

"Good morning."

His voice startled her. "I didn't know if you were there."

"I told you I would be watching you," he said.

"Yes, you did. I'm sorry."

Shadow watched her sit up. "Are you hungry?"

"I don't want to cause you any more trouble than I already have. You said you would release me," Bree said.

"And you said you have no money or friends. I don't mind letting you go, but are you sure you want me to?"

"I don't know what to do," Bree said. "They could be out there waiting to grab me again."

"I could get you to Dickensville. You could either find work and stay there or you could keep running," Shadow said.

Bree's hand fisted as anger set in. "I still wouldn't have any money or anywhere to stay."

"I suppose I could make a donation to your cause," Shadow said.

"A donation?" she asked.

"I'll pay you to leave and never mention me. Would that be acceptable to you?" he asked.

Bree was puzzled. "Why would you do that?"

"Because I greatly value my privacy."

"Why are you so secretive?"

"Enough questions! Do you agree to the arrangement or not?"

"What choice do I have? If I don't agree, what will you do with me?" she asked, fighting tears. Crying would serve no purpose and most likely anger him.

Shadow decided to put it back on her. He was enjoying their conversation. "What other solution do you see?" He hadn't spoken to anyone outside of Marvin since he'd been to Cheyenne for one of his secret karate training sessions. The women he went to see in Dickensville never saw his face and he never spoke to them.

"They might look for me in Dickensville. I'm not safe anywhere, really."

"You need to leave Montana. Go to a larger city where you can get lost and change your name," he said. "Then you can be free."

"I don't know how to be free," Bree blurted. "I want to be, but I don't know how to be. Not anymore."

That intrigued Shadow because he knew how that felt. Sudden freedom after craving it for so long was a scary thing. "How old are you?"

"I've lost track. Somewhere in my mid-twenties."

"How old were you when they took you?"

"Eighteen. That much I remember. All I've known since then is counterfeiting. Day after day, figuring out how to make fake money look real. Working with inks, designing plates, all of it."

Shadow growled, not out of annoyance with her, but out of anger and resentment towards the men who'd held her. There was a tiny bit of compassion in Shadow, mostly for his brother, but he found himself identifying with Bree in many ways.

"I understand," he said. "But that still doesn't solve the problem of what to do with you."

Bree clenched her hands at her sides as tears began falling from her eyes. "Just kill me. Please just kill me. I know you can do it. You have the strength. I don't want to go on like this!"

Oh, how I remember praying for that very same thing. I used to beg him to put my suffering to an end, but he wouldn't. He should have. It would have been the smarter thing for him to do, but he ended up paying for his stupidity.

"Quiet! I'm not killing you. There's already one body to deal with and I don't want to be inconvenienced with another. There will be too many people alerted and I can't risk that," Shadow said. "We're both prisoners; each in our own way."

"You're not a prisoner," she said. "You can move about freely and do as you like."

"That's true to a certain extent."

"Why do you have to hide?"

"I'm no one and that's the way I want to keep it," he said.

Abruptly she said, "I have to take care of my personal needs."

"All right. I'm giving you a chance to make me trust you. If you make a wrong move, or try to escape, I *will* kill you. Understand?"

"Yes. I'll behave."

"Good."

She flinched when his large hand settled on her shoulder, but he was gentle in removing her blindfold. She'd been right about not being able to see anything. Blackness met her open eyes. Bree felt his body heat and knew that he still stood in front of her. She shied away when his fingers brushed a lock of her wavy brown hair from her face.

"You're a beautiful woman, Bree. Stand up."

She did and heard him move away. He took her arm and began guiding her. Soon he said, "There's a doorway right in front of you. Go through it and stand still."

Bree complied and then heard a match being struck. The flame created dim light. She saw a candle on a small table in the room. As he lit it, she looked at his hands, discovering that they were as large as they felt and she could see the strength in them.

"When you're done, blow out the candle and open the door."

He withdrew then, closing the door behind him. Bree gave her eyes a chance to adjust. She was astonished to find herself in a beautiful toilet. A bit on the masculine side, but that made sense given her—what was he? Captor? Savior? Bree didn't know. There was no window in the room. Was she in a house? She couldn't tell.

She saw that it contained a large, ornate porcelain tub and an actual flush toilet, something that only the very wealthy had. It was odd that they were in the same room since that generally wasn't the practice, but perhaps things had changed during her captivity.

Not wanting to keep the man waiting, she hastened to take care of her needs. She blew out the candle and opened the door again.

"Come out," he said.

She was getting used to him guiding her and she went where he silently directed her.

"Sit here," he said, pushing her down into a chair. "Keep your head down."

"All right."

He lit another candle and stepped back out of her line of sight. Bree gazed around her, agog at the elegant room before her. The drawing room was well appointed with fine furniture and artwork on the walls. There were no windows, but she could see where the room would be beautiful enough to distract from that fact.

"You must be very wealthy," Bree said.

"Mmm, you might say that," Shadow said. He enjoyed her amazed appreciation of his home. He also liked the way the flickering candlelight caught the red highlights in her brown hair. "Are you hungry?"

"Yes."

"I will once again give you the benefit of the doubt. If you move from this chair before I return, I'll know it and things will become very unpleasant. Can I trust you?" Shadow asked.

"Yes."

Bree stayed put, not doubting that he would be able to tell if she didn't. She occupied herself by looking at her surroundings more and trying to figure out who this man could possibly be.

Chapter Nine

"Oooff!" Billy said. "Sugar, knock it off! How am I supposed to aim when you keep butting me like that?"

He was taking a break from his shop to do some target practice with his bow and arrows. Lucky had set up a target range at the lower end of the property away from the sheep and several people used it on a regular basis.

Lucky chuckled. "Come now, Sugar. Let Billy alone so he can shoot. He needs all the advantage he can get."

Billy's dark eyes narrowed as he looked at Lucky. "I think I'm doing well, thank you very much."

"True, but it's like anything else—there's always room for improvement. Of course, I don't have to work very hard at it since I'm nearly perfect now, but you're still catchin' up."

Billy groaned at his egotistical statement. "Your conceit knows no bounds, I see."

"Not conceit; confidence. Besides, ya need to fix your grip, lad," he said. Getting behind Billy, he adjusted the way Billy was holding the bow. "There. Now pull back, keep your tension steady, and take aim."

He grabbed Sugar's halter and kept hold of her until Billy took his shot. He didn't hit the bull's eye, but it was close.

"Good, lad. Now we have to get you shooting faster," Lucky said.

"I'm never gonna do it the way you do it," Billy said.

Lucky smiled. "Well, you're probably right about that, but you'll get close, I imagine."

"Again, your ego is boundless," Billy said as he watched Lucky take aim.

The Irishman had no sooner let his arrow fly until he had another notched and sent it after the first one. Billy watched his friend rapid-fire six missiles at the target, each of them piercing the target close to the others. He'd seen Lucky do it hundreds of times, but it never got old. He made it look so easy, but Billy knew it took incredible skill.

"I'm never gonna be able to do it like that," Billy said.

Lucky eyed Billy and said, "Keep tellin' yourself that and ya won't. Half of learnin' anything is bein' positive."

"Says the man who gave up on trying to paint a sheep," Billy said.

Lucky scowled as his barb hit home. "That's different. That's a creative talent and that's not where my creative talents lie. This is a technical ability. Maybe ya won't be able to shoot like that, but maybe ya will. Ya don't know until ya try your hardest."

Billy hadn't meant to anger Lucky, but he could see that he had. "Ok, I'll keep practicing. Sheesh. Simmer down."

"Ya know what your problem is, Billy? Ya just expect things to come easy for ya. Well, they don't in this life and the sooner ya learn that the better of ye'll be," Lucky said. "So quit your whining, notch up another arrow, and shoot the damn thing the way I taught ya!"

"Fine!" Billy said.

Incensed by Lucky's sharp remarks, he became determined to make Lucky shut up. He took aim, fired, and notched another arrow. He shot until his quiver was empty. His shots weren't as good as Lucky's, but they were darn good.

Lucky grabbed him and clapped him on the back. "Look at that!

See? I knew ya could do it. That was fine shootin'."

Billy looked into Lucky's gray eyes. "That was an act, wasn't it?"

Lucky grinned. "'Twas, and it worked, too. There's nothin' like anger to give ya a push to do better. Ya channeled that anger into concentration so ya could shoot more accurately. Well done, lad."

"You're such a plonker," Billy said, using the Irish word for idiot.

With a laugh, Lucky ran down to the target to retrieve their arrows. As he did, he noticed that the ground was disturbed about five yards into the woods from where he stood. Most people wouldn't have noticed it, but Lucky wasn't most people. Living with the Cheyenne had trained him to always be observant of his surroundings and look for anything out of the ordinary since it could save your life.

He sat the arrows down before walking over to it. It was a large area and the earth was fresh. "Billy! Come here!"

Billy jogged down to him and looked at the ground. "What is it?"

A shiver ran through Lucky as he asked, "Does that look sorta like a grave to ya or am I imaginin' things?"

Billy's eyes rounded as he looked at Lucky and then back down at the oval mound of fresh dirt. "I hate to say it, but, yeah. It looks like a grave. I guess there's only one way to find out."

"I'm not diggin' it up," Lucky promptly said.

"Don't look at me," Billy said.

"Well, someone's got to dig it up," Lucky said.

Billy shook his head. "Not me."

"Me neither."

Win opened his cabin door to find Lucky and Billy standing on his porch.

Without preamble, Billy said, "We think we found a grave, but we need you to dig it up."

"A grave? Where? What kind of prank are you two pulling on me now?" Win asked. "I'm getting ready to go to Earnest's to take care of Barkley."

Lucky said, "Well, go ahead. You can dig it up when you get back."

"I'm not digging anything up. It's probably not a grave anyway," Win said as he grabbed his bag from the table next to the door and stepped onto the porch.

Billy gathered his courage and said, "Ok. Can I borrow your shovel then?"

"Sure. You know where it is," Win said. "I'll see you later."

Billy and Lucky watched with dismay as Win mounted his horse and trotted away, followed closely by Sugar.

"Well, I'll get that shovel and start digging, you scaredy-cat," Billy said.

"Ya can call me all the names ya want, but I'm not doin' it."

They argued the whole time they retrieved the shovel and walked back to the pile of dirt.

Screwing up his courage, Billy plunged the shovel into the earth.

In the sheriff's office, Josie sat on Evan's lap, her head resting on his shoulder and his laid on her growing stomach.

"I can't wait until our baby comes," she said. "I'm glad Edna finally let us switch rooms so she doesn't have to go upstairs at night."

Evan said, "I know, but it's only so we can be on the same level as the baby. Of course, we'll have him or her in our room for a while anyway, but she insisted we do it now."

"She's as excited as we are," Josie said. "It's so cute when she pats my tummy and tells the baby to grow big and strong."

Just then, Lucky burst into the office, cutting off Evan's reply. Josie let out a cry of surprise and Evan held onto her so she didn't fall off his lap.

"What the hell's the matter with you?" Evan angrily demanded.

"I'm sorry, but ya have to come with me, Evan. Billy and I found a body!"

Josie gasped and stood up. Evan did the same and put on his hat. "A body? Where?"

Lucky's face was pale. "Not far from the shooting range. We found it when we were target practicin'. I noticed it and Billy dug it up. We didn't take it out of the hole but we saw him."

Evan kissed Josie and said, "Don't wait supper on me if I'm not home. God only knows how long this is going to take. All right, Lucky. Let's go."

Lucky gave Josie a quick squeeze and then the two men were gone.

Evan smiled as he looked at Billy and Lucky. "I can't believe you two are afraid of a dead body. It's not going to attack you, for Pete's sake. Now c'mon and help me get this guy out of here so we can see who it is."

Billy frowned, but he removed more dirt from on top of the body until he and Evan were able to get a hold on the man and pull him free of the shallow grave in which he lay.

Evan said, "This was done in a hurry and they didn't do a very good job at it. They should have buried him out in the woods further."

As soon as they laid the body on its back, Billy let go and rubbed his hands on his jeans. "God that's a horrible feeling. Am I going to have to touch him again?"

"Well, you're gonna have to help me get him in the wagon so I can take him to Erin. I want her to tell me the cause of death. I'm guessing a broken neck, but I'd like her to confirm it," Evan said.

"It takes a lot of strength to do somethin' like that," Lucky said. "T'wasn't a woman who did it in that case."

"I agree," Evan said. "I don't recognize him so he can't be from around here. Someone passing through, I guess."

Billy said, "Yeah. I don't know him, either."

Evan crouched and began searching the man's pockets. Billy and Lucky cringed, glad that Evan was the one performing the task instead of them. The sheriff pulled out a wallet, a set of keys, and a piece of paper from various pockets on the man's clothing.

Evan looked through the wallet. There was a large sum of money in it, but no form of identification at all. The keys could go to anything. The piece of paper didn't provide any clues either since there were only monetary figures written on it. None of the contents of the dead man's pockets helped them figure out the man's identity or that of his killer.

"It wasn't robbery. There's a lot of money here. I'm guessing close to three hundred dollars. Who would leave that behind?"

Billy said, "Someone who didn't care about it. Seems like they only wanted to hide him and get out of town."

Evan looked at Lucky. "Can you track where they came from? I can get Homer to help you."

Lucky nodded. "Aye. I can. Billy and I will get started now and I'll send him to ya if I get stuck."

"Thanks. I appreciate it. Take a gun, just in case," Evan said.

"Right." Lucky jogged off to his tipi to retrieve his revolver.

Billy asked, "Why do I always get roped into doing this sort of thing?"

"Because you're good at it. You should be my deputy," Evan teased him.

"No, thanks. I'm a lover, not a fighter," Billy said. "I don't mind helping out, but it's not something I want to do all the time. You need to find someone with your kind of personality."

"You're right about that. Hopefully I'll be able to hire someone after a while," Evan said as Lucky returned.

"Billy, help me get him in Lucky's wagon before you two leave," Evan said. "I hope you don't mind me borrowing it."

"Not at all," Lucky said.

Once the body was loaded, Billy set off with Lucky into the woods.

"They obviously don't know how to cover their tracks. It's as clear as day which way they came from," Lucky said.

With his newly acquired tracking skills, Billy could also see it. "It looks like there's more than one. Maybe three of them."

"Right. And you can see that they were carrying something because the impression is a deeper," Lucky said as they moved along.

They were silent for a while as they followed the trail. They had gone roughly three miles before they found the spot where the killing had occurred.

"There's no blood," Lucky said, examining the ground closely. "He wasn't stabbed or shot. I think Evan's right; someone snapped his neck."

"We're on Earnest's land now," Billy informed him.

"We are?"

"Yeah. I know all of the properties around here and this is his land."

Lucky and Billy looked at each other. "Do ya think he's involved?"

Billy ran a hand through his hair. "It's a possibility. Evan will have to talk to him."

"I don't envy him that chore," Lucky said. "The trail leads away from here. C'mon, we might be able to tell where they came from. Look how far apart some of these tracks are. They were runnin'."

Billy squatted to take a closer look at a single print he saw. "I think one of them was a woman. Look at this print. It's small and the boot isn't the right shape for a man."

Lucky examined the print and patted Billy on the shoulder. "You're right. Good job. You've learned well."

"Well, let's get going. We've only got a couple hours until dark. I don't wanna have to go all the way back for Homer," Billy said.

"Right."

They began moving quickly through the forest in search of more information to report back to Evan.

Barkley panted and licked Win's face as he finished changing his dressing. "It's coming along just fine. Give it a couple more days and I won't have to bandage it any longer—he'll be able to keep it clean on his own."

Marvin sagged back in his chair, relieved that his beloved canine was all right. "Thank you, Dr. Wu."

Win watched Marvin and saw that his concern for Barkley's welfare was real. "You really love him, don't you?"

Marvin smiled as he picked up the bulldog and put him on his lap. "Yes, I do. Very much. Surprised?"

"Yeah. You're such a son of a bitch otherwise, but when it comes to Barkley you're a completely different person."

Sobering, Marvin said, "Has it ever occurred to you that I've been wronged as much as I've supposedly wronged others?"

"No," Win said promptly as he put his tools and supplies back into his bag. "I don't believe you're misunderstood at all, Earnest. I think you're exactly what everyone thinks you are. I'll be back tomorrow. Oh, and if you try to pull anything with Erin, I won't hesitate to take your head off. Are we clear on that?"

Marvin laughed and Win was hard pressed not to deliver a lethal blow to the man's larynx that would drop him dead in seconds.

"Win, why would I do anything to our new doctor? She's a competent physician and a lovely woman besides. It would be idiotic to cause trouble where she's concerned," Marvin said. "And, it certainly wouldn't behoove me. I have a business proposition for you and doing anything to cause more negative feelings toward me wouldn't be good business sense."

"Not interested."

Marvin said, "So opening your own official practice isn't something you want to do?"

"Not if you're involved."

"Hmm. That's a shame. I was just thinking of all the furry friends you could help the way you have Barkley. And, I was thinking about putting you on a retainer for our horses and cattle. However, if you're not interested, you're not interested. I'll see you tomorrow, then?"

Win said, "See you tomorrow," and left Marvin's parlor.

As he mounted his horse, he cursed Marvin. The man knew people's weaknesses and wasn't afraid to prey on them. Riding into town, Win fought an internal struggle; he didn't want to be under Marvin's thumb, but the man had enough money to help Win get properly set up with an office. Win rejected the temptation that Marvin had dangled in front of him. He didn't want to become one of the people Marvin kept at his disposal.

Travis Desmond, Marvin's ranch foreman, was just such a person. Jobs were scarce in Echo and Travis only retained his employment with Marvin so that his wife and child could eat. Travis hated Marvin, too, and couldn't wait for the day when he could tell Marvin that he quit. Only a few people knew about his involvement in the sheep farm and they would keep that secret until Travis was ready to quit his job.

Win turned his mind away from all of that as he thought of his fiancée and smiled. His idea was working out in many ways. Echo was getting a good doctor, he was getting a beautiful wife, and Erin was getting her dream. Yes, life was good.

Arriving at the clinic, Win tied up his horse, made Sugar wait outside, and entered the waiting room.

"I'll be right there," Erin called out from her office.

Win didn't wait for her. He stepped into the office and shut the door. "Hi," he said with a smile as she looked up at him.

An answering smile spread over her face. "Hi, yourself."

"You're a sight for sore eyes," he said, coming around her desk.

She saw the hunger in his eyes and hers responded in kind. He bent and pressed his lips to hers in a firm kiss of greeting. When he would have pulled back, she slid a hand around his neck and held him in place. In response, he pulled her out of her chair and wrapped his arms around her, holding her close.

Erin was surprised that she was so attracted to Win, especially after avoiding men ever since her involvement with Garrett. Was that why? Was it just the lack of male companionship that made her relish Win's attentions? No, it was Win himself. He was everything she could ask for in a man and yet much more.

He was grounded, determined, kind, straightforward, and handsome. She'd never thought about marrying a man from another race besides her own, but his dark, exotic eyes and dusky skin were extremely appealing. The power in his muscles thrilled her.

"Hello? Erin?"

They broke apart upon hearing Evan's voice. She caught her breath and straightened her clothing quickly. Giving Win a smile, she opened the office door and went into the waiting room.

"Hi, Evan. What can I do for you?" she asked.

"I need you to look at a body to confirm cause of death."

"A body?"

Win had joined them. "Who is it?"

"We don't know. Lucky and Billy found him."

"So they weren't kidding?" he asked.

Evan and Erin looked at him. "What do you mean?" the sheriff asked.

"They told me they thought they'd found a body, but I thought they were trying to pull some prank on me. They always are. I swear sometimes that Lucky isn't any more grown up than Billy. Anyway, I had to go to Earnest's to take care of Barkley, so I left. I didn't know they were serious," Win said, feeling badly that he'd left his friends that way.

Evan gave him a small smile. "I can understand why you'd think that about them. They are always up to something."

Erin asked, "Where is he?"

"Out back. I didn't want it to become a spectacle," Evan said.

They went out the back of the building. Win recognized Lucky's wagon. He helped Erin up into it and climbed in after her.

After examining the man, Erin concurred with Evan's assessment. "I don't think there's any need to perform an autopsy. The only thing I see wrong with him is his broken neck. Whoever did this is right-handed. See the bruising on his left cheek? This is where the killer grabbed him and pulled from. Whoever did it is very strong."

Evan nodded. "Yeah. That doesn't tell us much, though. There're a lot of strong men around here who could've done something like this."

"Not necessarily. It takes someone with a certain mindset and experience to do something like this," Erin said. "Do you know how to snap someone's neck?"

Evan shook his head. "No, actually. I don't."

"I do," Win said. "Erin's right. It takes someone who's been trained to be able to do it effectively."

"You know how to do something like that?" Erin asked.

Win said, "Yeah. I'd only ever do it in an extreme circumstance, though."

"Someone wanted this guy dead for a reason. Maybe to keep him quiet about something or just to get him out of the way. I don't have much to go on, but I'll figure it out," Evan said.

Erin heard the steel in Evan's voice and she knew that he wasn't a man who gave up easily. "I'm sure you will," she said.

"Well, I'll get him over to the undertaker. I'll tell Sam, too, since he'll need to have a funeral for him. Not much else to do about it. I'm gonna have Dan take a couple of pictures of him before he's buried. I can show them around and maybe someone will recognize him," Evan said.

Win nodded. "Good idea."

"I have Lucky and Billy following the trail to where this guy came from. Hopefully it'll lead to somewhere that'll give us some more answers," Evan said. "I was hoping we wouldn't have a murder this year. This one looks like it's gonna be a lot harder to solve."

Win said, "Well, when will your helper be back?"

"Thad? Who knows? I can't count on him all the time," Evan said. "I need help. Real help. Well, no sense in wasting time with that. I'm gonna get going so that I can go home at some point tonight."

Win said, "If I can help at all, let me know."

"Thanks, both of you," Evan said.

Helping Erin out of the wagon, Win replied, "No problem."

They watched Evan drive away and then went back into the clinic to clean up after handling the dirty body.

Win noticed how quiet Erin was and he felt badly that something like this had happened after she'd only been in town two days. "It's not like that all the time, Erin."

Erin snapped out of her thoughts at the sound of his voice. "Hmm?"

"We don't have very many murders around here," Win said. "So you don't have to be worried about that."

She smiled. "I wasn't. I was just thinking about his family. They won't even know what happened to him. What if he has a wife and children? It's very sad."

Win nodded as he dried his hands on a towel. "You're right. It is."

She also dried her hands and sighed. "Well, I was having a good day up until now."

"I didn't even get a chance to ask you how it went. Why don't we go have supper at the diner and then go to Spike's for a while? Like I told you, it's a quiet little place. You'll like it."

"I think that's a fine idea, Dr. Wu," Erin said.

"Shall we, Dr. Avery?" Win said, playfully offering her his arm.

She chuckled and took it, letting him lead her from the clinic.

Chapter Ten

Lucky and Billy met up with Evan at his house later in the evening. The two men were cold, tired, and hungry. Josie made them some eggs and sausage while they filled them in their findings.

"'Tis a real mystery where this fella came from. We hiked for miles until we got to the main road. Looked like there was some sort of scuffle, but there was nothin' else," Lucky said and then took a bite of toast.

Billy said, "So, we figure they must have been in buggy or wagon. They might have been holding this guy and he escaped, but we can't figure out where a woman fits into it all."

Edna perked up at that. "A woman?"

Lucky nodded. "Aye. One of the prints looks like a woman's boot. It's too small for a man and it's not the right shape for a man's or boy's."

Billy was too busy shoving food into his mouth to answer, but he nodded his agreement. Lucky looked at him with dismay. He hated it when Billy ate like that. "Ya know, even my Cheyenne friends didn't eat like that and they eat with their hands."

The young man just shrugged and continued eating. Lucky glowered at him a moment before saying, "The place where that bloke was killed is on Earnest's property."

"It is?" Evan asked.

Billy nodded. "Mmm hmm," he said as he chewed.

Lucky wanted to smack Billy, but refrained from doing so. "Aye. Ya might want to pay the devil incarnate a visit to see if he knows anything."

"You better believe I will. First thing tomorrow," Evan said.

After handing coffee around to everyone, he and Josie sat down on the sofa together.

He let out a tired sigh. "So now we have a woman added to the mix. We've got a foot chase that resulted in the death of a man. The woman and other men have disappeared. There was nothing on the guy that tells us who he was or what he was doing in the area. And he was killed on Earnest's land. God only knows what that means, if anything." Evan took a swallow of coffee and then sat up straighter. "I'm gonna go to Spike's for a while. If I see any strangers there, they could be part of all this. I'll also ask Spike to be on the lookout for anyone suspicious."

Josie hated to see Evan go back out, but she knew that it was part of Evan's job. "All right. Please be careful."

He kissed her cheek. "I'll try not to be too long."

She sighed as he left the house. Edna reached a hand over and patted her arm. "I know how you feel, honey. I was married to a lawman for a good many years, so I know how hard it can be. Take comfort in how good he is at his job and enjoy every second you can when you're with him."

Josie took her hand. Edna was a tremendous source of comfort to her at times like these. She was still unaccustomed to being a sheriff's wife and she missed Evan when he couldn't be home at night. She smiled at Edna and said, "You're right. I'll be fine."

Lucky's heart went out to her. It wasn't the same thing, but he knew what it was like to miss a spouse with whom you were deeply in love. "Don't worry, lass. We'll keep ya busy. How 'bout some cards?"

Josie brightened. "Yes! I want to beat you again," she said, grateful to her Irish friend for the distraction. As she had many times since meeting Lucky on the train to Echo, she thanked God for bringing him into her life.

Billy grunted and said, "Count me out. I'm too tired to play. I hear my bed calling me from here. I'm gonna stop over and see the folks a little and then go home."

Billy's parents lived next door to the Tafts. He took his dishes to the kitchen, came back into the parlor, and kissed both women goodnight. Shrugging into his coat, he asked Lucky, "Are you and Win doing any butchering tomorrow?"

He couldn't stand blood and he didn't like to go out to the sheep farm when they were butchering.

"We're not. Will we see ya then?"

"Yeah. I want to do some sketches of the farm from a different angle. Spike wants a painting of it, but I want to do something a little different," Billy said.

"All right, then. Goodnight."

Marvin was pleasantly surprised to see Phoebe ride up his driveway. His eyes devoured her as she walked over to him. She was the type of woman who preferred wearing jeans or trousers and she had a very fine form. Even though she wore a heavy cloak, he knew what she looked like under it and that image filled him with hunger for her. As she joined him on the porch, she kissed his cheek before sitting in the chair next to him.

"To what do I owe this pleasure?" Marvin asked the woman he loved.

She trailed her hand along his leg. "I was lonely."

He grabbed her hand in a crushing grip. "You mean I'm good enough because your old man is out of town, is that it?"

Phoebe winced but smiled at him. "It wouldn't matter whether he was in town or not. I was lonely for *you*."

Appeased, Marvin loosened his hold and kissed her palm. "I suppose I believe you."

Phoebe's brown eyes searched his beautiful face. "I don't lie to you, Marvin. I promise."

"But you lie to him. Why not me?"

"Because he doesn't understand me the way you do. He could never accept me the way you do," she said. "You know all about that."

His wicked grin flashed and she thrilled at the sight of it. "Yes, I do. Which is why I love you. Why can't I be enough for you?"

Phoebe always felt a little guilty when Marvin asked her this type of question. "I've told you."

"Yes, I know. I'm the dark and he's the light and you need both," Marvin said impatiently. Suddenly, he stood up and hauled Phoebe up with him. "If it's darkness you want, then it's darkness you'll get. I have plenty of that. Plenty that you haven't seen yet."

Phoebe was suddenly fearful of Marvin. She'd never heard him talk like this before. Usually there was an element of teasing in his voice, but not now. The look in his eyes was downright savage and his face was devoid of any humor.

"Marvin, you're hurting me. I'm not kidding. What's the matter? Why are you so angry?" she asked in a frightened voice.

Muttering an oath, Marvin loosened his hold on her arms slightly. "Do you see how crazy you make me? How long will you continue to torment me this way?"

With trembling fingers, Phoebe touched his face. "I'm sorry to cause you pain. Do you want me to stop coming?"

Marvin wanted to tell her not come back, but he couldn't. He craved her and needed her. Even as much as he hated the fact that she wasn't faithful to him, to not have her in his life at all would be even more torture. With a growl, he kissed her, giving her his answer. Then he turned her around and took her inside the house.

Shadow heard them coming and ducked back into the parlor out of sight. He sighed, knowing that he would have to wait for a while to talk to Marvin. It was probably for the best. If he'd talked to Marvin before Phoebe had come, it would have made his brother even more agitated than he was that night.

Going into Marvin's office, Shadow entered the closet and pressed the hidden button that opened the panel in the back of it. He slipped through and made sure the door clicked shut behind him before descending the stairs into the basement. Needing no illumination, he strode through the space until he reached the other secret door, the one behind a large shelf that held various jars of jelly and canned vegetables.

Releasing the latch holding it shut, Shadow opened it and went through, once again making certain that it was entirely shut before continuing on his way into his "lair" as it was called. This lair was actually a very beautiful underground house. Shadow hadn't asked for it, however. It had been Marvin's idea. After Shadow had tried to argue with Marvin about it to no avail, he let his twin do what he wanted, knowing it would help ease Marvin's guilt.

Shadow didn't think it was necessary since Marvin had been as much of a victim as he had. Still, he did enjoy it to some extent, although he only used a third of the vast space: his bedroom, the bathroom, small kitchen, and the smaller sitting room. He had no use for the large dining room, drawing room, or study. There was one other place he went and looked at, but not too often. The cage. This was where he'd spent the first sixteen years of his life. Sixteen years of misery, degradation, and nightmares. Loneliness, rage, despair, and bitterness had been his constant companions.

All that had changed when Marvin had found him, though. Shadow paused outside the small sitting room as he remembered the first time he'd seen Marvin's face. *His face.* They'd stared at each other, neither one believing what they saw. No sooner had Marvin found him than they'd heard their father coming.

Marvin had hurried over to the cage, whispering urgently, "I'll be back. Be quiet. I'll be back."

Shadow closed his eyes as tears threatened at the sweet memory of knowing that he wasn't alone in the world anymore. He had hidden his joy, burying it deep lest their father see it and become suspicious. That joy had given Shadow the strength to go on, to face whatever might come. And Marvin, God bless him, if there was a god, he'd come back repeatedly and they'd come up with a plan. And it had worked, right down to the last detail. *Perfection.*

Shaking off the memories, Shadow got on with the business of dealing with the present and the woman who waited for him in his sitting room. Entering, he saw that she hadn't moved from the sofa where he'd made her sit. Skirting around the area of light the candle on the table next to the sofa made, he sat in one of the other chairs.

Bree looked at the broad expanse of chest and the powerful arms, but that was all she could see of him. He always hid his face, but his body was another matter. She felt this was deliberate so that she understood that she was no match for him physically.

"What am I going to do with you?"

Bree ground her teeth together. "I don't know."

Shadow smiled at her irritated tone. It had been his intention to get a rise from her. "Let's approach it from a different angle, shall we?" he asked.

She sighed. "Ok."

"Ask yourself this question; what do you desire the most? If you could do anything you wanted to, without any obstacle, what would it be?"

"To learn how to live again."

A chill washed over him. He'd uttered very similar words to Marvin once upon a time. *Show me how to live like you do, Marvy. I don't know how.* His brow puckered as he thought about her statement.

"And you want me to teach this to you?"

"I don't know anyone else."

"You don't know me, either," Shadow reminded her.

"I know that you saved me and that you haven't killed me or hurt me," Bree countered.

He laughed. "Trying to appeal to my sense of decency, are you? I don't have much of that and what I do have I've reserved for someone else."

"Then just kill me and get it over with."

Shadow sighed and pulled a face. "I find myself in a strange place, Bree. I don't seem to be able to kill you. I've considered it. I should kill you if I knew what was good for me and killing you would be better for me. Yet, I don't want to. Yes, there's the inconvenience of burying you somewhere where they'll never find you, but that's not why. I know some very good places for getting rid of bodies and I would have put your former captor in one of them if he hadn't already been taken away from where I killed him."

"You're not the only one who's in a strange place. Can't you at least tell me your name?"

"Hmm. I suppose it is rude of me to withhold it since I know yours. It means nothing to anyone anyway. You can call me Shadow."

Bree smiled. "Are you joking?"

"No. It's my real name."

"Why did your parents name you that?"

"That's not important. So you want to learn how to live a normal life again. I don't live a normal life. Normal for me, but not for other people. They like to live in the daylight, but I prefer the nighttime," Shadow said.

"I see."

"I doubt it. I'm sure you're used to being up during the day, correct?"

Bree nodded. "Yes, but I could learn to live as you do." The thought of being her own terrified Bree more than death. "I'll beg if you want me to. I'll do anything. Just don't throw me out."

"Anything?"

"Anything."

Shadow began running scenarios through his head and he could see where having more eyes and ears around might be advantageous for him and his brother. He would gain her complete loyalty and devotion first and then let her loose for short forays upon which he would follow her. Marvin could do the same. Yes, it could work. He grinned at the prospect.

"Bree, what I will want from you—no, *demand* from you—is your complete allegiance to me. In return, I'll teach you how to live as others do. I'll show you how to have freedom, at least a certain amount. I'll take care of you. You'll want for nothing, but you must never cross me, or I'll make you suffer. Death will seem much more preferable than what I'll do to you. If you agree, say so or you may leave. It's your choice. Would you like some time to think about it?"

Bree shook her head a little. "No. I don't need any time. I agree to everything you just said."

"So you'll do whatever I say without objection?"

She heard humor enter his voice and smiled a little. "I'm not sure about never objecting, but I'll do it."

Pleased with her answer, Shadow laughed. "There's a little spirit in you. Good. I don't want you to be a complete pushover."

She sobered. "Do you expect me to ...?"

"Warm my bed?"

She gave him a nod. "Yes."

"Do you want to?"

The humor was still present in his voice.

"Maybe."

"Maybe?"

She gave him what she knew was considered a flirtatious look and said, "You might be ugly. You said I was beautiful, but I don't know what you look like. Why should I want to be with an ugly man?"

Her answer amused him. "I assure you that I'm not ugly."

"I don't believe you. You won't show me."

"Ah, yes. I think you have more spirit than I first thought." Again, Shadow figured that it couldn't hurt anything since she had no knowledge of who he or Marvin was. "Ok. You win."

Leaning forward, he picked up the candle and brought it closer to him. Bree watched the candlelight flicker over the most beautiful male face she'd ever seen. Vivid blue eyes stared back at her. They were set in a chiseled face framed by dark hair that fell to his shoulders. His dark brows rose in a questioning manner.

"Well?"

She couldn't speak for a moment and he smiled at her. She wouldn't have thought it possible, but his beauty increased. "No. You're not ugly."

He laughed again. "Well, so what about warming my bed?"

She looked down at the floor and said, "If you wish."

Going on instinct, Shadow asked, "What did they do to you?"

Her gaze returned to his, surprised that he'd been so insightful. Bree had the distinct impression there was nothing he didn't know. She also felt that he had experienced tremendous suffering. Bree saw a flicker of kindness in his eyes.

"Terrible things."

The force of the rage Shadow experienced shocked him. Not since his parents had been alive had he felt anything close to it. Anger, annoyance, and frustration, but not true, pure, hot rage like the kind that coursed through his veins at that moment. Needing release, he slammed a fist down on the stand where the candle had sat. It cracked under the great force behind his action.

Bree cried out in fright and pulled her legs up onto the sofa, hiding her face against her knees. As he watched her, something within Shadow shifted. It was a strange sensation, one he had only ever felt towards Marvin. He'd never felt compassion for a woman before. Lust, amusement, and pity, but never compassion.

Sitting the candle on the coffee table in front of the sofa, Shadow moved to sit next to her. She shrank away from him and the compassion grew a little more.

"Bree," he said softly. "Look at me."

She didn't want to, but she was afraid of what he would do if she didn't. Slowly raising her head, she gazed into his eyes, trying not to flinch.

"I won't hurt you and I won't ever take you against your will," he said. "I'm trying to trust you, something I've only done with one other person. If you betray my trust, there will be consequences. That's the only way I'll ever hurt you. Do I have your word that you'll obey me?"

Seeing that he meant every word, Bree nodded and said, "Yes. You have my word. I promise to obey you."

"Good. You should sleep," he said.

"I'm not tired."

"There's something I have to go do," he said.

She didn't want to be alone, but she didn't have a choice. "I'll stay right here on the sofa."

Shadow moved off the sofa and walked over to a candelabra, which he proceeded to light. "There's no need. You've given me your word and I have to trust you at some point. Feel free to explore, but do not leave. If you leave, well, you understand ..."

Bree was very curious about her new residence. "Yes, I understand."

Shadow gave her a hard look and said, "Behave. I'll be back."

Chapter Eleven

Spike sat a beer down in front of Evan. The bar owner was a white-haired man in his early sixties who'd lived in Echo all his life. He'd lost his wife a number of years ago and he'd been so in love with her that he'd never desired another wife. Spike was content to run his bar and spend time with his friends when they came in.

"Where's your crocheting?" he asked Evan.

Evan had some strange pastimes for a man. He liked to crochet and wasn't afraid to do it at the bar where everyone could see. Anyone who made a nasty wisecrack about it came to regret it. Edna had taught him when he'd been a boy and he'd stuck with it. He was talented at the craft, too, and he made baby blankets and afghans for various people around the community. Josie had also been teaching him some embroidery and he was happy with how skilled he was becoming at it.

He smiled. "I left it at home. I'm here on official business. I need to know if you've seen any strangers in here."

Spike wiped down the bar and thought about it. "A couple nights back there were a couple of fellas who came in, but they didn't stay long and they didn't cause any trouble. Why? What's goin' on?"

Evan loved Spike like an uncle, but the man couldn't keep a secret to save his life. "I'm not ready to divulge that yet. Describe them to me."

"Well, let's see. The one fella was about your height. Brown hair, a little on the long side. Average build, I'd say. The other one was gettin' kinda thin on top, but he had blond hair. He was shorter and pretty hefty. Somewhere in their thirties, I'm guessin', but I'm not always a good judge of age," Spike said.

Evan didn't let on, but Spike's first description sure sounded like the dead man.

"What was the taller guy wearing? Do you remember?"

Throwing the bar towel over his shoulder, Spike said, "Hell, I don't know, Evan. Uh, now wait. He had on a brown duster and he was wearing fancy boots, too. Does that help you? What did this guy do?"

"I'm not sure yet. If you see anyone else you don't know, let me know, ok?"

"Sure. You're really not gonna tell me what's going on, are you?"

Evan shook his head. "Nope. I'm still investigating and it's sort of sensitive."

Spike sighed, his blue eyes narrowing at Evan. "You just like to torture me that way. You get me all curious and then leave me hangin'."

"Yep. That was my plan." Evan grinned at him and took a pull of his beer. He became quiet as he tried to fit the pieces of the puzzle into place.

Recognizing the look in Evan's eyes, Spike let him alone. He'd known Evan long enough to tell when Evan's mind had gone into sheriff mode and that it was best to not bother him at those times.

Evan closed his eyes and pinched the bridge of his nose. The puzzle pieces just wouldn't come together in any way that made sense. When he opened his eyes again, he found Thad McIntyre sitting on the stool next to him.

"Welcome back," the grizzled bounty hunter said with a grin. "You were gone a little while." He, too, was familiar with Evan's habit of retreating deep inside his mind when he was mentally working on a case.

Evan returned his grin. "Did you just get back today?"

Thad nodded, downed a shot of whiskey, and then said, "Yep. Just a bit ago. I stopped in Dickensville today and got cleaned up."

Whenever he was on the road, Thad didn't pay much attention to personal hygiene. He had bigger worries like catching murderers and robbers so he could cash in on the rewards. Stopping to clean up would cost him valuable time and the vermin might escape or be caught by another bounty hunter. Usually when he returned, Thad stunk to high heaven and no one wanted to be around him until he'd bathed and changed.

"Thank you," Evan said. "I appreciate it."

"Sure. So what are you pondering?"

Evan glance pointedly at Spike and said, "Oh, nothing much."

This was the code phrase they used between them that told each other that something major was happening.

"Oh, ok," Thad said casually. "Let's go play some cards then."

"Sounds good."

They found a table off to the side and Thad began shuffling a deck of cards that he'd taken from an empty table.

"So what's goin' on?"

Evan picked up his cards and said, "Lucky and Billy found a body buried on the farm today."

Thad's dark eyes met Evan's. "Who is it?"

"No one we know. He had a bunch of cash on him, but no identification of any kind. There were a set of keys and a piece of paper in his pockets, but that was it. I'd never seen him before and neither did Lucky, Billy, or Win. No one knows about this and that's the way I want to keep it. I don't want the killer, or killers, to be tipped off."

Thad nodded. "Good idea."

Evan made an annoyed face. "The only problem is that Earnest may be involved."

"Good. Arrest his evil ass," Thad said.

"I said 'may' be involved. Lucky and Billy followed the trail from the grave and found where the guy was killed. It's on Earnest's land, but not close to the house. I'm gonna have to question him about it and there's no guarantee that he'll keep his mouth shut if I tell him to," Evan said.

"So when you're done askin' questions hogtie him and gag him."

Evan laughed. "If it was that easy, I'd have done that long ago."

"You should just let me kill him. I can make it look like an accident," Thad said.

Cocking his head, Evan replied, "You just incriminated yourself."

"You wouldn't arrest me, anyhow."

"I wouldn't want to, but unless it was self-defense or in defense of someone else, I'd have to."

"You're too much like Reb and your old man. Too upstanding. It would be in defense of the whole town if I did it, so I'd say that you wouldn't need to arrest me," Thad said as he threw down his bad cards.

Evan chuckled. "I always love the way you bend the law to suit your needs."

"How do you think I've been so successful all this time? I'm creative. Now, how're Josie and the baby doing?" Thad asked.

"Great." A big grin spread across Evan's face.

Thad looked at the younger man, who was like a nephew to him. He was glad to see Evan so happy. He deserved it after all the hell he'd gone through in his lifetime, starting with the murders of his parents and sisters.

"Good to hear, my friend. Other than finding dead bodies, how are Irish and the Indian doing?"

"Good. Billy's been working on his artwork and helping with the farm whenever Lucky and Win aren't butchering."

Thad laughed. "That boy has a sensitive stomach about that stuff. Poor kid. How's his wounded heart doing?"

Evan smiled. "He's fine now. It took a while, though. I think it had more to do with all of the stuff about his heritage that made it worse."

Thad nodded. "Yeah. I think you're right."

The previous summer, a woman in Dickensville, whom Billy had been seeing, had ended things, telling the then eighteen-year-old that he was too young and she'd never marry him because he was an Indian. It had cut Billy to the quick and he'd become bitter and depressed.

Gradually, he'd pulled out of it, concentrating on his art and the sheep farm instead of the heartache. He'd also leaned on his friends and parents to help get him through. Before his split with Shelby, Billy had carried on with the girls around Echo, but since then, there'd been no such rumors, which told Evan that Billy hadn't been bothering with girls.

In a way, Evan thought this was good, but it also concerned him because he was afraid it meant that Billy had given up on women because he feared rejection. He'd wanted to talk to the boy about it, but he was afraid he'd open up the old wounds.

"He'll be all right, Evan. Give him some time. He's had a lot to deal with. It can't be easy being him," Thad said. He knew that Evan loved Billy like a little brother and that he worried over him. "He's strong, though. He'll show all those narrow-minded idiots that he's just as good as they are. Better than them, if you ask me."

Evan's temper flared as he thought of the racism that Billy had to endure. "He shouldn't have to! He's a sweet kid and—"

"Easy, sheriff," Thad said. "You don't have to convince me. I agree, but getting riled up about it right now won't do any good."

Evan crumpled the cards he was holding in his fist and threw them on the table.

"Evan," Thad said. "This isn't about Billy. You're always testy when you got a tough case on your hands. Not to mention anything involving Earnest. Put those two things together and your state of mind becomes a powder keg."

The sheriff's green eyes glittered with suppressed anger. "You're right. Maybe I should just let you murder him. God knows we'd all be better off for it."

"That's what I'm telling you, but you'd never sleep again if you did that. No, I won't shoot Earnest unless I have just cause," Thad said.

"Now, tell me the rest of what's going on with this case."

Evan gave Thad all of the information he had, but Thad couldn't put it together, either.

"I'll figure it out," Evan said.

Thad nodded. "I know you will. You always do. But I'll be around for a while, so I can help out. In the meantime, you need to go home to your wife and I might have some other plans, too."

Evan laughed at the wolfish grin that Thad flashed at him. "I'll just bet you do. How is Phoebe these days?"

"I don't know, but I aim to go find out," Thad said as he stood up.

Evan was the only one who knew that Thad and Phoebe were seeing each other. "Have fun," he said as he also got up.

Thad thumped his shoulder and said, "I always do."

However, Thad was disappointed to find that Phoebe wasn't home. She had a private entrance to her small suite of rooms and she always answered the door for him. They had come up with a special knock a while back so that she'd know it was him. It was late at night so Thad wondered where she could be. She didn't frequent either Spike's or the Burgundy House, the disreputable saloon on the other end of the canyon.

Phoebe only had a couple of friends and she certainly wouldn't be at any of their houses at this late hour. There was only one other place she could be: with another man. That thought angered Thad, but he told himself that he had no right to be. Their relationship was a casual one with no demands on each other.

They'd started seeing each other about three years ago. It had been a surprise to Thad when Phoebe, who was over twenty years his junior, had flirted with him. Things had developed from there and whenever he was in town, they saw a lot of each other. Not out in public, though. Phoebe didn't want that sort of relationship. She wasn't looking for commitment.

Thad had come to love Phoebe and although he knew that he wasn't expected to be, he stayed faithful to her. She had no clue about that, however, and he wasn't going to enlighten her. The idea of her with someone else filled him with hot jealousy, but he couldn't just go accusing her, especially when they'd never mentioned becoming exclusive.

He had his ways of acquiring information, though, and he knew how to find out what he wanted to know. Lighting up a cigarette, he sat down on her stoop and settled in to wait for her.

Phoebe was very tired when she arrived home. She usually was after an evening with Marvin. He'd been rather erratic that night and she'd been scared of him a couple of times. Usually, he walked her out to her horse in a very gentlemanly fashion, but tonight he'd merely kissed her goodnight and told her she knew her way out.

Phoebe figured he was punishing her for her continued unfaithfulness. This confused her because until now, her bad behavior had always amused Marvin. It seemed as though he was growing weary of sharing her. Maybe it was time to end things with him, but Phoebe loved him and she didn't want to stop seeing him.

Because she was so preoccupied with her thoughts, she didn't notice Thad right away. She jumped when she heard his voice.

"Hi, sweetheart. Miss me?"

Phoebe's heart thumped against her ribs in surprise. "Thad! You scared the hell out of me. When did you get in?"

He chuckled and said, "Not long ago. Where have you been?"

Although she was happy to see him, Phoebe knew she couldn't endure any more lovemaking that night. She let him pull her into his arms and kiss her, but she wasn't as enthusiastic as normal.

Thad felt it and drew back. "What's the matter?"

Phoebe smiled at him. "It was a long day and I couldn't sleep. I went for a ride, but now I have a headache."

"I have a cure for that," Thad said with a chuckle.

She laughed, but said, "Not tonight, lover."

He said, "Not that. C'mon. Let Thad make that headache go away."

This was what she loved about Thad. His goodness and fun were infectious and she guiltily thought about how much she missed him when he was gone. Yet, she yearned for Marvin at times, too. It made no sense to her.

Unlocking her door, she led him inside and lit a lamp. Thad helped her out of her wrap and took off his coat, hanging both of them on the coat rack by the door.

"Now, sit down here and let me work some magic on you," he said, patting the back of one of her kitchen chairs.

She smiled and sat on the chair. Giving massages was something Thad was good at and he usually always gave her one. His talented hands began moving over her shoulders and she sighed as he worked out the kinks in her muscles.

"So how's things around here been? Arthur says you have a few boarders besides me right now," Thad said as he shifted his focus to her neck.

"Yes. That's why it was a long, busy day. It's good for business, but it means more work for me," Phoebe said.

"That's why you should let him hire someone to help you."

She smiled at the concern in his voice. "I don't want anyone else in the kitchen messing things up."

"Ok, but what about to do the cleaning? Then you could just do the cookin'. Arthur's told you he'd be willing to do that," Thad said as he sank his fingers into her thick, golden-brown hair and started massaging her scalp.

Phoebe said, "I know, but I'm territorial."

He chuckled and said, "I know you are." As he finished the massage and bent down to kiss her neck, he caught a whiff of what he knew was a man's cologne. In her ear, he said softly, "You're not the only one who's territorial, Phoebe."

Phoebe pulled away from him and smiled. "Since when? You've never been territorial. Thank you for the massage. My head feels better."

"Sure," Thad said. "Maybe I'm becoming territorial, Phoebe. Has that ever occurred to you?" He remembered his earlier advice to Evan about keeping a handle on his anger.

Not you, too, Thad. Phoebe stood up and said, "This is the first time you're saying anything like this."

Thad said, "It must be because I'm pretty tired myself." He forced himself to smile. "Well, now that I've treated my patient, I'll let you get some rest and go do the same. We'll catch up tomorrow, ok?"

Phoebe nodded. "That sounds good. Come around eight and I'll make up to you for tonight."

Thad took his coat from the rack and looked at her. Spite made him say, "Make sure you don't smell like the other guy by the time I get here."

His remark was so unexpected that Phoebe couldn't hide her surprise and she knew that guilt was stamped all over her face. "Thad..."

He held up a hand and said, "Phoebe, you don't owe me an explanation. I know that we're not committed or anything. Don't get excited. Get some sleep." He opened the door, smiled at her, and stepped outside, pulling the door shut behind him.

Phoebe sat back down on the chair, her fingers trembling as she pressed them against her mouth. Stupid. That's what she was. Hadn't she known that this would happen eventually? She'd been playing with fire and now it seemed as though it was all going to go up in an inferno. It was time to end things with one of them, but which one?

If she ended things with Marvin, he'd destroy her. He loved her, but he wouldn't hesitate to seek retribution. Thad, however, wasn't like that. He would be hurt and angry, but he wouldn't be revengeful. Tears sprang into her eyes at the thought of not seeing him anymore, but it was the only logical choice. She cried the whole time she got undressed and crawled into bed.

In his room on the second floor of the boarding house, Thad sat on his bed, taking long pulls from the bottle of scotch he'd brought with him home from Spike's. He had a decision to make and he didn't like having to make it. Could he share Phoebe? Until that night, he'd never had any reason to suspect her of being with anyone else besides him. She was always so happy to see him and ready for fun and passion.

Maybe she'd just finally gotten tired of being with a man who was so much older than her. Somehow that didn't ring true to Thad, though. Phoebe became annoyed whenever he brought up their age difference. When had she started seeing this other man? He realized that it could have been going on for God only knew how long since he was out of town so much.

Thad was surprised by how much it bothered him to think that he'd possibly been sharing her for a long time without even knowing it. It infuriated him, actually. In that moment, Thad knew that it was over between him and Phoebe. He couldn't stomach touching her again now that he knew she'd been with someone else. On one hand, he wished that he didn't know, but on the other, he supposed it was good that he did.

Putting down his bottle, he pulled off his boots and tossed them to the side before stretching out on the bed and trying to sleep.

Chapter Twelve

By the time Evan had shown up at Spike's, Erin and Win had already gone. They'd had a nice supper together and after a couple of beers, they were ready to pack it in for the day.

"Thank you for such a nice evening," Erin said.

"You're welcome. I'm glad you had a good time. I did, too."

Erin had borrowed a horse from Arthur so they could go to Spike's, which was on the other side of the canyon. Looking over at Win, she thought how fortunate she was that she actually liked the man she was going to marry in just a few days. While she'd been willing to marry anyone in exchange for her own practice, it was definitely a relief that she and Win got along well.

Thinking about his kisses made her warm inside and she couldn't deny that she was very attracted to him. His incredible physique wasn't the only thing that drew her to him. His intelligence, quick wit, and compassion for others were also characteristics that would make being married to him very pleasant.

"Are you nervous about getting married?" she asked him.

Win smiled at her. "No, I'm not. You would think I would be, but

I'm not. Are you?"

"A little, but mainly because I don't want to disappoint you as a wife," Erin said. "I'm not all that domesticated since I've been mainly concentrating on school so much."

"I understand that. I wasn't looking for a housekeeper and cook. I wanted a professional woman because I wanted to share a lot of the same interests with her. We'll figure out all that domestic stuff together," Win said. "I knew that what I was after isn't very traditional, but I really don't care about what other people think."

Erin chuckled. "I can tell that."

Win said, "I decided at an early age that I was going to do what was right for me and not be concerned with what society tried to dictate was appropriate behavior. As long as I'm not hurting others, I don't see where it matters what I'm doing with my life."

"You really do march to the beat of your own drum," Erin said. "You're an atheist, for one thing. Why?"

Some people might have shied away from the subject, but not Win. "I've never seen any evidence that some force greater than us is at work. My parents worshipped and prayed on a daily basis and their lives never improved. When my father became sick with miner's lung, my mother prayed so hard and yet he still died. When I was younger, I did follow their religion, but when my prayers were never answered, I knew that there was nothing watching over us. We're on our own to make our own destinies and happiness if possible."

Erin thought his outlook was very bleak and it bothered her. "So you don't believe that there is a benevolent God?"

"No, I don't. He's never interceded in my life in any way. I've always had to take care of myself and make my own way. Yes, Robert helped me, but that wasn't an act of God. It was just a friend helping another friend. I'm not like Lucky; I don't see mystical forces guiding every decision or action we take," Win said.

"I'm not very religious myself, but I do believe in God," Erin said. "What if I wanted to raise our children as Christians?"

"You're more than welcome to, but don't expect me to encourage it or become one," Win said. "If they grow up believers, I won't think any less of them or try to discourage them. However, I will make it understood that I don't believe."

Erin thought that sounded fair. "I think that's a good approach to it. So you don't celebrate any religious holidays?"

Win laughed. "Oh, Evan and the rest force me to come to Christmas dinner and I exchange presents, but it isn't in the name of any deity. It's just a fun time with my friends. Does that bother you?"

Erin shook her head. "No. It doesn't influence my decision to marry you, if that's what you mean."

"That's good," Win said. "I would hate for it to become a problem later on."

"It won't," Erin assured him.

He brought his horse over closer to hers. "Did I tell you today yet how beautiful you are?"

His praise made Erin blush. This wasn't something she was used to having men tell her. "No, you didn't."

"Well, you are. I can't wait until we're married to show you just how beautiful I think you are."

Her stomach quivered inside as she met his smoldering gaze and her lungs wouldn't expand for a moment. That look alone showed her how attractive he found her and she marveled at it. Erin didn't normally wish her life away, but she found herself wanting Saturday to come very quickly. She knew that Win didn't feel the need to wait for his sake, but he was being respectful of her.

Although she was no longer a virgin, she'd made a vow not to be intimate with another man outside the bounds of matrimony. She wanted that level of commitment so that she knew that the man really cared about her and that he wasn't just after a fling. It was another reason she'd liked the mail-order-bride idea—the man was obviously looking for a meaningful relationship.

Staring back at Win, Erin couldn't deny that she wanted him to kiss her and it seemed as though he read her mind. When he leaned towards her, she met him halfway, their lips meeting as both of them stopped their mounts. It wasn't a long kiss, but it was passionate and one that made Erin feel hot inside.

Win couldn't remember ever wanting a woman more than he did Erin and he could tell that being with her was going to be like nothing he'd ever experienced before.

They smiled at each other and started their horses again. Sugar had been trotting in a circle around the horses and now she trotted in between them, nipping first at Erin's boot and then Win's.

Erin laughed at her. "She's so funny, Win. I can't believe Billy lets her in his apartment."

"Seeing a burro inside a house isn't something you see every day," Win agreed. "I let her in the cabin sometimes. She likes to lie on the rug in the parlor."

"Has she ever pooped in the house?" Erin asked.

"Nope. I think she thinks she's a dog," he said. "She knows how to open doors, so when she has to go out, she lets herself out and closes the door behind her, too."

Erin laughed and leaned down so she could pet Sugar. "And she goes everywhere with you?"

"Pretty much. If I have to go somewhere she can't, I leave her with Billy. I'll tell you something; she's a good guard burro, too. I'd hate to be the one she was mad at. She's quick and bites hard. She's small, but mighty," Win said.

"She's a guard dog?"

"Yep. You'll have to see her in action. When someone knocks on the door, she stands at attention and her tail swishes back and forth like crazy. If they come in without being told to, she'll rush them until she sees whether they're someone she knows. If she does, she just wants to be fussed with. She nailed Thad one time though because she hadn't met him yet. He just walked in and she bit his arm bad. I patched him up, but it was funny. Even he laughed. He said he was going to take her with him the next time he went out on a job."

Erin laughed at that image. "I can't wait to meet Thad. He sounds very entertaining."

"He is. I like hearing his stories about his job. He's fearless and creative in tracking down criminals. Definitely a man you want on your side," Win said.

"Sounds like it. Of course, I hear that you're quite talented in the fighting department yourself," Erin said.

"You could say that."

"Josie says that you once choked a man with Evan's yarn."

Win laughed. "I did. If I don't have a weapon on me, I create one with whatever might be lying around. That night, it just happened to be a ball of yarn sitting on the bar. A single thread of yarn isn't all that strong, but when you use around ten or so strands together, they make a pretty good garrote."

"Remind me not to make you mad," Erin said.

"It takes a lot to make me really angry," Win said. "I've learned how to control it and look at things from all sides before letting my temper get the best of me. Because of my skills, I usually prefer to walk away if possible."

"I can understand that. I think that's smart."

They'd arrived at the boarding house and rode around back to the stable. Win put Erin's horse away while she played with Sugar. When he was done, Win walked right up to Erin and kissed her without any preamble. Win wanted to keep on holding her, but he didn't want anyone to happen upon them. With so many boarders at the Hanovers', it was a good possibility that someone would.

Erin realized this, too, and the kiss ended by mutual consent. "Goodnight, Dr. Wu."

"Goodnight, Dr. Avery," Win said.

He walked her to the back door and waited until she'd gone inside before going back to his horse and mounting up. "C'mon, Sugar. Time to go home." He sighed and wished he wasn't going home alone.

—◦—

"Have you gone completely mad?"

Shadow smiled at his twin's question. "I think you know the answer to that."

Marvin wasn't amused in the least. "This isn't funny, Shadow!"

Shadow stretched his long legs out in front of him and crossed them at the ankles. Slouching down a little in the wingback chair in which he sat in the parlor, he said, "You haven't let me finish."

"Why should I? You've told me that you've killed a man, kidnapped a woman, whom you're holding downstairs, shown her your face, and told her your name. What more do you need to tell me?" Marvin said. Anger turned his eyes to blue ice.

"She doesn't know where she is, who I am, or how to get out of where she is. As far as my name? She only knows my first name, not my last. There's nothing she could tell anyone that would lead anyone to me. I don't exist, remember?" Shadow asked.

"Of course I remember!" Marvin shouted. "I'm the one who's kept you safe all these years, aren't I? Away from all of the ridicule and scandal, just as you wanted it. Are you ready for your existence to be known? Is that it?"

Although Shadow felt his temper rise, he knew the best way to handle Marvin was to stay calm. "No, I don't want my existence known. That won't serve our purposes at all and frankly, I don't want anything to do with people on a 'normal' level."

"What then? Do you intend to keep her as a pet?"

Shadow snarled in response to his question. "No. I am not keeping her as a pet. I'm keeping her because she can be useful to us."

Marvin scoffed. "I fail to see how. She's nothing but a liability."

"Marvy, why do you think I'm loyal to you?"

His twin sighed. "Because you love me."

"Yes, I do. We understand each other. No one else understands me but you. And she'll be loyal to me for the same reasons by the time I'm done with her," Shadow said.

Marvin couldn't control the mirth that bubbled forth. The parlor rang with it and Shadow smiled at him.

"You're going to make her fall in love with you?" Marvin asked. "Am I drunk? Drugged? None of this is making sense to me."

"It's simple. I'm going to become everything to her. I'm going to teach her how to live the way you did for me. She doesn't know how to live a normal life. I remember what that was like. She's scared to death that I'm going to throw her out. She begged me to kill her if I didn't intend to keep her," Shadow said.

"Begged you to …" Marvin's amusement turned to curiosity. "How unusual. You say she's been held captive for a number of years?"

"That's right. She's more scared of the men who had her than she is of death or me," Shadow replied.

Marvin smiled again. "That's only because she doesn't know you like I do."

"I tried to explain that to her, but it didn't seem to bother her. Another set of eyes and ears won't hurt anything, Marvin. In fact, she'll be able to do something that neither you nor I could ever do."

"What's that?"

Shadow said, "Become friends with the women in town."

"If she becomes friends with them, won't she want to run away?" Marvin asked. "I don't think you're thinking very well, Shadow. All it takes is one little slip and it's all over. Not only that, but what information do you think will be useful?"

"We don't know what's useful or not, do we? Women talk freely when there are no men around. Who knows what she could find out for us? For example, she would be able to get close to the sheriff's wife and find out about any investigations that could involve us," Shadow said. "That's something that's hard for me to do and you certainly can't do it since he hates you."

Marvin had to admit that Shadow had a point, but … "It's still too risky. She's a wild card and we can't afford that. We have big plans ahead of us and we don't need anything to foul them up."

"I'll tell you what; I'll start my ... training, so to speak, and then you can meet her and judge for yourself. If you still feel that way, I'll kill her and get rid of her," Shadow said. "Give me two weeks."

Marvin closed his eyes and leaned his head back against his chair. "Fine. Two weeks, Shadow, but you'd better make sure that she doesn't get out. If I don't agree, be prepared to get rid of her."

Shadow smiled. "Agreed. Now, would you care to tell me what's going on with you?"

Marvin sighed. "Phoebe. I find that I'm wearying of sharing her and yet I can't let her go."

"It's a conundrum," Shadow said. "I don't know what to tell you to do about it, though. What would you do if she were yours alone? Marry her? She doesn't want to get married. You've proposed to her enough."

"I know. Maybe it's time to move on somehow."

Shadow felt his twin's pain in his heart and he wished that there was something he could do to ease it. "I'm sorry, Marvin."

Marvin inhaled deeply, burying the pain down deep and opened his eyes to look at Shadow again. "Don't be. Well, I'm going to bed and you have a woman to train."

Shadow smiled. "Ok. Goodnight."

Marvin left the parlor and Shadow blew out the lamp before descending to his lair again.

Chapter Thirteen

Early the next morning, Evan lay in bed with Josie, holding her close. She still slept and, even though it was time for him to get up, he didn't want to move and wake her. A light snore came from her and he smiled. She didn't like it when he told her she snored, but he thought it was cute.

There wasn't a day that went by that he didn't thank God for giving him Josie. She brought joy to his life in so many ways, big and small. Just seeing her smile was enough to make him happy and he knew that it would always be that way. Moving his hand to rest on her stomach, he felt awed by the thought that they'd created life together and he couldn't wait for the day their baby entered the world.

Josie stirred and put her hand over his. "Good morning, Sheriff."

He grinned. "Good morning, Mrs. Sheriff. You were snoring again."

She swatted his hand. "I was not."

"Yes, you were."

This earned him a kick in the shin.

"Ow!" they both said at once.

"You have hard bones," Josie said, rubbing her heel on her other leg to soothe it.

Evan laughed. "I hope they are. I'd look pretty strange walking around with wobbly legs."

Josie giggled and rolled over to face him. "You're going to have to help me do that after a while and rub my feet, too. I'm going to be pregnant in the summer heat."

"I know, honey," he said, smoothing back a lock of hair from her face. "I'll rub your feet and flip you like a pancake when you need it. And I'll even rub your back for you."

Looking into his emerald eyes, Josie said, "You are the most wonderful husband in the world."

"Well, I don't know about that, but I have my moments," Evan said. "What are you doing today?"

She kissed him and said, "I have to go to the store and I'm going to stop and see Erin. Not because I need to, but I just want to see how she's doing. And then later on I have to go clean for Mr. Leonard."

"That's right. You told me about cleaning for him today. I forgot." He pulled her closer and said, "I wish we could stay right here all day."

"Me, too. Wouldn't that be wonderful?"

"Mmm hmm." He nuzzled her neck.

She smiled. "Don't you start that. Edna will be ready for breakfast soon."

"She can wait a while longer or else make some toast. That much she can do," he said against her ear.

"Shame on you," Josie said, even as she shivered against him.

"We'll make it quick," Evan said. "It'll put me in a better mood so that I don't kill Earnest."

She laughed at his reasoning.

"I'll make it worth your while," Evan said, feeling that he was gaining ground.

"Evan," Josie started pushing against his shoulder. "You have to let me up. I'm going to be sick."

Immediately, he released his hold on her and helped her out of the bed. She ran to the washroom and shut the door. Evan got up and pulled on underwear, padding downstairs in his bare feet. He went into the kitchen and started making tea for Josie to help settle her stomach. When it was ready, he mixed in a little sugar and some ginger, which was good for relieving nausea.

Taking it back upstairs, he found Josie sitting on their bed.

"Thanks," she said as he handed it to her. "Sorry."

He sat down by her and said, "Don't worry about it. You haven't had morning sickness for about a week now. I'm glad it's slowing down for you."

"Me, too. Mmm. That's good," she said.

"Good. Well, I guess I'll get dressed and go feed the old woman," he said.

Josie chuckled. "I'll be along after a bit."

He kissed her temple. "Why don't you lay back down a little? I don't think you're gonna want to venture downstairs until we're done eating."

"I think you're right," Josie said. "Are you sure you don't mind?"

"I'm sure, honey. I'll stop by at lunchtime, ok?"

"Ok. I'll be ready to eat by then."

"Don't I know it?" He quickly moved out of her reach.

She made a face at him. "Here I am, the mother of your child, and you're making fun of me."

He pulled on his pants and said, "I'm not making fun of you. I'm having fun *with* you."

"No, you're making fun of me," she said with a comical pout.

Evan greatly enjoyed Josie's silly sense of humor. Going over to her, he kissed her forehead and said, "I would never make fun of you."

"Sure, sure," she said.

He chuckled and kissed her forehead again. "Finish that and lie down. I'll see you for lunch. I love you."

"I love you, too. Be careful."

"I always am."

Watching Evan riding up his driveway, Marvin smiled as he started down the veranda steps. He assumed the sheriff was coming about the man Shadow had killed and he was going to enjoy toying with Evan.

"Good morning, Sheriff Taft," he said genially. "Travis is around here somewhere."

"I'm not here to see Travis. I need to talk to you," Evan said.

"Oh. All right. Do you want to come in?"

"No. Here is just fine. Yesterday a body was found near Lucky's farm. Do you know anything about that?"

Marvin's eyebrows rose. "A body? Whose body?"

"A man I don't recognize," Evan said. "What do you know about it?"

"Why would I know anything about it? I'm many things, Evan, but I don't go around murdering people. I'm assuming that you believe he was murdered?"

"Yes, he was. He was killed on your property," Evan said.

Marvin appeared genuinely shocked, but as Evan knew from personal experience, nothing was ever as it appeared with him.

"Where on my property? Do you mean close to the house?"

"No. Out in your woods on the north side of the property. I deputized Lucky and he followed the trail back there."

Marvin's expression darkened at the thought of Evan and any of his friends traipsing around on his property. They'd hidden the entrance to Shadow's lair well, but it still wasn't good for anyone to be in that area.

"Well, I can assure you that I know nothing about any dead man and I certainly don't like that someone committed such a crime on my land. I'll ask Travis if he or any of the other men have seen anything suspicious and have them come to see you if they know anything," Marvin said. "I wish you luck in finding the culprit," Marvin said. "Was there anything else? I'm going to Dickensville for the day and I'd like to get on the road."

"Earnest, know this: if I find out that you're somehow involved in this, there'll be hell to pay. I'm very good at ferreting out the truth, as you know."

Looking in Evan's eyes, Marvin didn't take his threat lightly. Although Evan was young for a sheriff, he'd been trained by Rebel Taft, one of the best sheriffs in Montana, and Marvin knew his investigative skills were top notch. "I understand, but the simple fact is that I had nothing to do with killing anyone." *At least in quite a while.*

"Don't worry about talking to Travis and the boys, I'll do that," Evan said.

"Fine," Marvin said dismissively. "Damn. I forgot something in the house. Good day, Evan. I hope you find out who did this. It makes me very uncomfortable to think that someone could be lurking about." Inside Marvin laughed.

Evan didn't answer him; he just gave him a hard look and rode towards the barn. Marvin walked calmly back into the house, went to his office and closed the door. Opening the closet, he pressed once on a hidden button that was connected to a bell system and then waited. Soon the secret panel slid open and Shadow stepped into the light. He winced as it stabbed at his eyes.

"What?" he asked, putting up a hand to block out the bright sunlight.

Marvin informed him of Evan's visit and that the sheriff was still on the premises. "Keep your pet with you. We don't need her to get out."

"She's not my pet, but she'll stay with me. Don't worry. She doesn't know how to get out anyway," Shadow said.

"She'd better not," Marvin said. "I'm leaving now to go buy her some necessities."

"Ok. Thanks."

"Sleep well, brother dear," Marvin said, exiting the office.

Shadow smiled and went back downstairs.

When Shadow entered his lair again, he found Bree waiting anxiously for him.

"What is it?" he asked.

Bree crossed her arms over her stomach and asked, "Is he mad? Does he want you to get rid of me?"

Shadow smiled. "No. He's going shopping in another town today. I told you not to worry."

Bree nodded. "All right. Good."

"Now, I know you might be a little bored, but I'm going to sleep for a while," Shadow said.

"There are books," Bree said quickly. "I'll be fine."

Shadow knew she was trying to placate him to stay in his good graces and while he'd enjoyed that with women in the past, he didn't with Bree. "Ok. If you need anything, let me know."

She nodded and left him to go to the sitting room. Following her in, Shadow gave her a small smile and then continued on to his bedroom. He undressed and lay down, but stayed on the alert in case Bree tried to pull anything. This was merely a precaution; he didn't really believe she'd leave.

Bree sat on the sofa, a book propped on her knees that she'd drawn up, but she couldn't concentrate on the story. Her mind kept going back to the enigmatic man in the other room. Who was he? Why did he choose to be up at night? What did he want with her? Had she stepped into a worse situation? It relieved her that he hadn't hurt her or demanded anything sexually from her.

He'd fed her, given her free rein of his home, and sworn to protect her. What about his brother? Could he be trusted? Would he try to hurt her? Bree didn't know what to think about it all. Why did she feel safer with a total stranger than the men she'd been with? She supposed she was trying to optimistic.

She looked around the sitting room and, although it was beautiful, she would like to see some sunshine, even for a short time. She couldn't do anything about that right then, however, so she settled back more comfortably on the sofa and tried to read again. It was no use, though. The lines of text on the page meant nothing to her because she just couldn't focus. She felt lonely and wished that Shadow would come talk to her, but he was sleeping.

Shadow had fallen into a light doze when he sensed a presence close to him. Opening his eyes, he saw Bree standing uncertainly by the bed.

"What is it?"

"I'm sorry. I just ... I don't know—"

He cut her off by grasping her arms and pulling her over him onto the bed. Rolling over, he looked down at her, chuckling at her shocked expression.

"Is that better?"

It took her a moment to be able to speak, but she nodded. "I guess so."

"Good." He rolled back over onto his back. "Sleep. You'll be busy later on and need your energy."

"Ok."

How was she supposed to sleep lying beside him? She gnawed on her lip, wondering what it was that she would be busy doing. Shadow's behavior was strange to her. He wasn't expecting anything from her. He'd scared her, but he hadn't hurt her. She shifted into a more comfortable position and began relaxing.

It wasn't something she'd planned on doing, but she suddenly needed some human contact. Sliding her hand over, she found his and put hers in it. Inwardly she cringed and waited for his reaction. His much larger hand closed around hers and a feeling of security filled her, something that hadn't happened since she'd been a teenager.

"Sleep, little one," Shadow said.

Smiling, she closed her eyes and did just that.

Chapter Fourteen

Erin heard a commotion out in the waiting room including a loudly banging door, a clanging bell, and a man uttering a lot of curses. Then hoof beats sounded on the wooden floor. Erin was just rounding her desk when Sugar poked her head around the doorframe and pricked her ears at Erin.

She let out a happy little squeal and walked over to Erin just as Win caught up to her. Erin noticed he was limping a little.

"Are you ok?" she asked, trying not to laugh.

Win glared at the burro. "Fine. She stepped on my foot coming in here. I'm sorry. I tried to keep her out, but she's stronger than you'd think."

Erin scratched Sugar's ears and the burro grunted with contentment. "It's all right. There's no one in here and even if there were, I'm sure they would have enjoyed the entertainment."

"Yeah, I'm sure they would have," Win said, smiling. "I came to see if you wanted to go to lunch before I have to go out to Earnest's to see Barkley."

"I would love to," Erin said. "I don't have any patients until later on."

"How is business? Slow?" Win asked.

"Not this morning. I should give Lucky a commission," Erin said. "Almost every person that came in said that Lucky told them what a good job I did with his tooth and that he'll never go to another doctor."

Win laughed as he began moving Sugar back into the waiting room so that they could get by her. He held Erin's coat for her and said, "Everyone likes Lucky, so I'm sure an endorsement from him will go a long way to helping get more patients in here. Although, they were pretty excited about getting a doctor in the first place." He opened the door and motioned Sugar through it. "Get out of here."

The burro trotted outside and then turned around to make sure they were coming.

Erin locked up and then Win took her hand. She smiled and said, "Are you making sure I don't get lost?"

"That and keeping your hand warm," he said.

"I have gloves on."

"I don't care," he shot back with a smile.

She laughed and looked around town, noting the various people who walked along the streets on the cold March day. "What were you up to today?"

"Looked the herd over like normal and did some target shooting with Lucky. Nothing exciting," Win said.

"Sounds idyllic."

"It was. You know, if you ever need any help, I'd be happy to do it. I can treat a lot of human conditions, but I'm not an expert like you are," Win said.

She bumped his arm playfully. "Are you offering to be my nurse?"

He sent her a roguish grin. "Only if you give me an examination, too."

Erin shook her head. "Nope. Not unless you present with some sort of ailment."

"What if I have a fever?"

By the gleam in his eyes, Erin could believe that he might be burning up. She was surprised that the air around them didn't warm up.

"I suppose that might warrant an examination."

"We'll explore that at a future date."

They reached the diner and made sure that Sugar didn't get inside with them. She wasn't happy and stood with her ears back and her head down. Erin chuckled at her sulking.

"She really is attached to you."

Win sighed. "I know. Sometimes it's inconvenient, like right now."

"But's she's very cute," Erin said as they took a table.

"She's something, all right," he said.

They spent the next forty-five minutes exchanging stories about their college days and laughing together. Win loved the way Erin's face lit up when she smiled and he liked her laugh. There was nothing fake about it.

When they finished their meal and went back outside, they found Evan fussing with Sugar. It looked like he was measuring her.

"Sheriff, what are you doing?" Win asked.

Evan smiled at them. "Hi, Erin. Win. I think Sugar needs a sweater."

The couple instantly began laughing.

"You're going to make her a sweater?" Win asked. "Is that part of your duties as a lawman?"

Evan grinned. "Nope. This is a gift for my furry friend here." He hugged Sugar's neck and she grunted with delight.

Win looked at Erin. "Do you see how spoiled she is? I don't know of any other burro who's going to get their own sweater." He turned towards Evan and added, "Just do me a favor and don't make it gaudy colors."

Appearing affronted, Evan asked, "When have you ever known me to make something ugly? It'll be something very fitting of a lady."

"This I gotta see," Win said.

Sobering, Evan said, "I talked to Earnest this morning and he said he knew nothing about our dead man."

Win said, "Even if he did, he's not going to tell you. It's probably just a coincidence that they ran onto his land, but who are they and what were they up to?"

"Those are questions I aim to get answers to," the sheriff said.

"Well, if anyone can, it's you," Win said.

Nodding, Evan said, "I'll let you two go. I'm going home for lunch. Have a good rest of your day."

They bid him farewell.

Erin asked, "Do you really think Marvin is mixed up in this?"

Win said, "When it comes to Earnest, I don't put anything past him. C'mon. I'll walk you back to your office and then I have to head out to his place to take care of Barkley."

"Ok," she said. As they walked, she responded to Win, but in her mind, she kept trying to reconcile the man everyone kept warning her about with the one she'd met.

That evening, Erin went out to the sheep farm for supper. She was very curious about Lucky's Indian cooking since she'd never had anything roasted in the ground before. When she arrived, she heard laughter coming from Lucky's tipi and headed in that direction. She scratched on the flap and Lucky told her to enter.

"Hello, gentlemen," she said upon seeing Billy, Win, and Lucky.

Win smiled at her and Erin's pulse rate rose. "How was the rest of your day?" he asked.

"It was good. I had three patients and got a few other things done."

"Good to hear, lass," Lucky said. "Make yourself comfortable. We'll be ready to eat soon. I just have to go dig it out."

"Oh! I want to see," Erin said.

Lucky smiled. "Well, c'mon then and I'll show ya."

Erin followed him outside and over to a pile of coals. Lucky crouched down and moved the coals aside with a long stick with a fork on the end of it. Then he fished around in them until he found the handle of a large roasting pot and lifted it out of the ground. He set it down, moved to another spot, and did the same thing.

"Now we hafta see what they look like," he said, lifting the lid off one of them.

The aroma that wafted out of the pot made Erin's mouth water. Lucky was satisfied with the appearance of the turkey.

"And now we eat," he said.

He'd brought a couple of buckskin cloths with him and he used them to put around the hot pot handles so he could safely carry them.

"Can I trouble ya to hold the flap open?" he asked.

"Certainly." Erin hurried ahead of him so she could help him.

Once inside the tipi, Lucky put down the pots and went over to another pot that he had hanging over the fire. He lifted the lid and stirred the contents and Erin's stomach rumbled as more delicious scents filled the tipi.

"What is that?" she asked.

"Tubers, corn, and turnips that I made into a soup using some of the turkey stock. I made fry bread to dip in it," Lucky said.

"What's fry bread?" she asked.

"Well, a lot of Indian tribes make it. It's a sort of flat bread. You'll see. You can use it for during a meal and as a dessert. We'll do both tonight. I made enough so we can have it with some mixed berry dressin'."

Billy said, "Wait until you taste it. It's one of the best things I've ever had."

Win said, "It's delicious. Now, when Lucky cooks we don't use utensils. You eat with your hands."

Erin thought he was joking. "You're very funny."

Billy said, "No, he's right. The Cheyenne eat that way. You have to do it like that to get the full experience."

Seeing they were serious, Erin said, "All right. I'm all for the full experience."

She sat next to Win and watched Lucky dole out large portions of food onto plates and into bowls, which were then passed around until everyone had theirs. Lucky said a prayer in Cheyenne and then Erin watched how the men ate. She was too hungry to care about using utensils and followed their example.

The turkey was incredibly tender and flavorful. She attacked it and it wasn't long before it disappeared. The soup was a little trickier, she found.

Win said, "Dip your bread in the broth and eat that first. Then drink the broth. After that, just tip up the bowl and the vegetables will slide right into your mouth and what don't, just dig out with your fingers."

Erin laughed when Billy finished drinking his broth and burped. He went right on to eating the rest of it, barely taking a breath in between bites. Lucky just sighed and shook his head.

Win said, "You might as well give up, Lucky. He's not going to stop eating that way."

Erin thought it was funny that Lucky was so concerned with table manners and asked him why.

"My ma, God rest her soul, woulda smacked him upside the head for eatin' like that," he replied. "She drummed manners into us from the time we were little. I asked his ma if she did that and she said she tried hard, but it did no good."

Billy just smiled as he chewed and Lucky scowled at him.

Erin enjoyed the byplay between the two men. It reminded her of a brotherly sort of relationship and she thought it was sweet that two men who'd been strangers a year ago were so close now. Looking at Win, she saw that he also fit into that category and thought it a remarkable thing.

She asked, "Did you two know that Evan's going to make Sugar a sweater?"

Billy almost choked on his food. "What?"

Win laughed. "Yep. We came out of the diner at lunchtime and Evan was measuring her."

Lucky said, "Now I've heard of everything. A sweater for a burro. It'll be entertainin', that's for sure."

By the time they'd eaten the rest of the fry bread with the fruit dressing Lucky had made, Erin was ready to burst, but she had no regrets about eating it all.

"Lucky, that was a fantastic meal," she said. "I hope you'll invite me again sometime."

"You're always welcome, lass. No invitation needed. Besides, you'll be livin' here soon, so you'll have plenty of my cookin'. So who's for a game of knuckles?"

The game began and they all lost track of time as they played and laughed. Finally, Erin said, "I think it's time for me to go home, boys."

Win said, "Why don't you just stay here tonight? I'll sleep in here with Lucky and you can have the cabin. It'll be better than riding home in the cold."

Erin thought it sounded like a good idea and it would give her a chance to see what living there would be like. "Are you sure?"

"Absolutely," Win said.

"Ok. Well, in that case, I guess I'll turn in. Thanks for a wonderful evening, Lucky," she said.

"Don't mention it. Sleep well," he said.

She said goodnight to Billy, too, and stepped out into the night air. It had turned frigid and the idea of staying in Win's warm cabin was a very welcome one.

"Billy should stay, too," Erin said as she and Win walked to his cabin.

"Oh, he will. If I know him, he'll be asleep before I get back to the tipi. Lucky, too, most likely. Lucky falls asleep in a matter of minutes most of the time and Billy's not far behind him," Win said.

"What about you?"

As they walked up the porch steps, he said, "It takes a little longer for my mind to shut down."

"Me, too, sometimes," Erin said.

Win shut the door after they'd gone in and went to his room. "The bed is comfortable."

Erin colored a little bit at that as thoughts of them sharing the bed rose in her mind. "That's good."

He lit a lamp and said, "I'll build up a good fire in the fireplace and you'll have heat all night. There are plenty of blankets on the bed, so you'll be nice and snug."

She nodded. "Thank you very much."

"You're welcome."

After seeing the desire in his eyes, she was surprised by his brief goodnight kiss.

He noticed her reaction and said, "Erin, unless you want me to stay with you tonight, that's all I'm going to allow myself with a bed only a couple of feet from us."

Erin smiled. "No, I don't think you staying is a good idea."

He returned her smile. "Ok. Sleep well. Come get me if you need anything."

"All right. Goodnight."

Once he was gone, Erin stripped down to her chemise and got into the bed. It was very comfortable and it smelled like Win, she noted. In a couple of days, this would be her home and she would be sleeping in this bed with him. She smiled at the excitement that surged through her at the thought of that.

In the space of a couple of months, her life had completely changed and definitely for the better. She blew out the bedside lamp and watched the moonlight stream in the windows as she grew accustomed to the way the room looked in the dark. Still full from dinner and surrounded by warmth, Erin soon succumbed to sleep.

Chapter Fifteen

The next couple of days were a whirlwind of activity for Erin. She was busy at the office and with the last-minute wedding preparations. The night before the wedding, she was too excited to sleep and lay awake thinking about all the next day would bring.

She was about to become a married woman and the thought both thrilled her and terrified her. Being a good wife to Win was very important to her and she didn't want to disappoint him in any way. He was a good man and so handsome and she had the feeling that being married to him was going to be wonderful.

Thinking back to his romantic proposal, she smiled as she thought about that unexpected side of Win. Most of the time, he seemed well grounded, but that night, he'd shown her the softer part of his personality. Looking at her ring in the moonlight as she lay in bed, Erin couldn't wait until dawn came.

Win was doing much the same thing. It was the last night that he'd be the sole occupant of the cabin and the prospect filled him with happiness. He was very lucky to have found a woman like Erin. He couldn't imagine a more perfect woman with whom to spend the rest of his life. Evan, his best man, had thrown him a bachelor party at Spike's and they'd had a great time playing cards and drinking.

He laughed over how drunken Billy had gotten, which made him extremely silly. It had also severely hampered him in placing bets and he'd given up after a while, blaming Lucky for his inebriated state. Win knew that the boy would have one heck of a hangover in the morning.

Their wedding day dawned cold and snow flurries swirled through the air. They were planning on going to Dickensville for a couple of days and they hoped that the weather held.

The ceremony had been planned for late morning so that they would have more time away. With Erin just opening her practice, going on a long honeymoon wasn't a good idea, but they would come back on Monday so she could reopen the office on Tuesday.

Since the wedding was during cold weather, Erin had chosen a long-sleeved satin dress with a lace overlay. She was happy that no alterations had been needed. Josie would be her maid of honor and she'd asked Lucky to give her away. The Irishman had been honored that she'd asked him. He'd said that since he'd performed the duty for Josie, he would do a good job because he was experienced.

Josie had helped her get ready but since her short hair didn't require much styling, it didn't take very long.

"Were you nervous on your wedding day?" she asked her.

"On our original wedding day I was, but not on our actual wedding day, I was chomping at the bit to marry Evan. I wanted to marry him so much that I think I forgot to be nervous."

Erin smiled. "I thought I'd be more nervous than I am. I know that some women panic on their wedding day, but I don't feel panicky at all."

Josie hugged her. "I think you and Win are very well suited for each other. I'm sure you'll be happy together."

"Thank you," Erin said. "He's certainly a very handsome man. My friend, Jessica, thought I was crazy for doing this. She's not prejudiced, but she was concerned because I'm marrying a Chinese man. It doesn't bother me at all. I find him very attractive and exotic."

Josie grinned. "Yes, he is. He's also a good man and he'll be a wonderful husband and father, when the time comes."

Erin looked at Josie's growing waistline and smiled. "You and Evan are going to be wonderful parents."

Josie put her hands on her belly and said, "I can't tell you how happy we are. When we first found out, Evan cried right with me because we were overjoyed that we'd conceived so quickly. It may have happened on our honeymoon or soon after." She blushed and giggled.

Erin said, "That's wonderful. I wouldn't be upset if that happened with Win and me."

Josie's expression turned sly. "I see the way he looks at you. I don't think that will be a problem."

It was Erin's turn to blush. "I think you're right."

"I was surprised that you asked me to be your maid of honor since pregnant women are supposed to be hidden away."

"I don't care about that. I've always thought that was ridiculous. Besides, your dress hides your little belly. If some of the British nobility can go to balls while their pregnant, it's all right for you to be my maid of honor. If someone doesn't like it, they can leave."

A knock on the office door made them jump.

Lucky's voice came through the door. "Is there a lass in there who's lookin' to get married today?"

They both laughed and Josie opened the door for him. "Come in, lad," she said with a smile.

He chuckled at her mimicry of him. "Well, now. Ya look like an angel, Erin, ya do."

"Thank you. I just wish I hadn't had to cut my hair."

Lucky looked her hair over. "I don't know as I've ever seen a woman with such short hair before, but it suits ya well. You're a beautiful woman, short hair or not."

"You're good for my ego," she said.

He smiled at her. "Are ye ready?"

Erin took a deep breath as she suddenly became nervous. "Yes," she said, shoving away her anxiety.

He offered her his arm. "Come then. After you, Josie. Ya look lovely."

"Thank you."

Lucky waved her out the door and followed with Erin.

Win stood at the altar with Evan beside him. The normally steady man was a wreck inside. He knew that this would be one of the most important days of his life and he was suddenly worried that he wasn't going to measure up to Erin's expectations. He knew it was unreasonable to feel like that when she was obviously looking forward to marrying him as much as he was her.

If she'd had any objections or last-minute concerns, she would have come to him with them. Wouldn't she have? He hoped so.

Evan knew Win better than anyone else did and he sensed his inner turmoil. Win was very good at hiding his feelings, but when he became so quiet, there was usually something going on in his mind.

"Erin is a wonderful woman," he said. "You're a lucky man."

Win smiled at that. "I know."

"You're going to be very happy and if you work real hard at it, I'm sure it won't be long until you have little Wu's running around," Evan said with a wink.

Win laughed. "That's the plan."

"So you have nothing to be worried about. I know it can be nerve-wracking, but everything will be fine. Don't be afraid of the ceremony. You'll do great. When you told me about your plan, I had some pretty big doubts, but almost as soon as I met Erin, I knew you'd made the right decision."

"Really?"

Evan looked Win in the eyes and said, "Yes. I'm not just saying that. It's obvious how much you have in common and, so far, you get along really well. It doesn't hurt that she's real nice to look at, too."

Chuckling, Win said, "You're right about that."

Evan patted his shoulder and said, "So don't be nervous."

Win did feel better. "Thanks. You're a good friend."

Pastor Sam Watson, a huge man who stood six-foot-seven and weighed in around two hundred and thirty pounds, took his place at the altar.

"We'll be starting in just a moment," he said, his brown eyes shining at Win. "Are you ready?"

The veterinarian nodded. "Yes, I am."

"Good. Nothing to be nervous about."

Sam's wife, Bea, began playing "Wedding March" on the organ and the men grew quiet. Evan watched Josie walk down the aisle first. He knew she'd been worried about how she looked in her dress because she was starting to show more, but he thought her even more beautiful than on the day they'd married because she carried new life within her.

She took her place at the altar and Erin and Lucky appeared at the entrance to the sanctuary. Lucky looked down when Erin's hand tightened on his arm. He raised an eyebrow at her, but she smiled and nodded that she was all right. They began moving forward and Erin looked at Win. He looked incredibly handsome in his tuxedo and her pulse began to rise.

It wasn't the largest wedding congregation, but it wouldn't have mattered if there were three hundred people present because all she saw was the man who was about to become her husband. His dark eyes never left hers and she saw desire in them and the high regard in which he held her. That there was no love there didn't concern her very much. There was time for that.

As Win watched her near the altar, his nerves calmed and all of his focus centered on her. He thought that her dress was beautiful, but not nearly as beautiful as she was. From her luminous brown eyes to the delicate slippers she wore with her dress, she was a study in feminine beauty. His eyes missed none of it and the closer she came, the harder his heart seemed to beat.

Lucky performed his duty with aplomb, handing Erin over to Win with the utmost seriousness, except for the wink he sent Win. Leaving them, he sat with Edna and Billy.

Erin and Win smiled at each other as Sam began the service. Holding each other's hands, they recited their vows to each other, promising their devotion and fidelity to one another. Neither one of them stumbled over the word "love" in the vows, feeling that it was highly likely that such an emotion would come in time. For now, they were content with the feelings that did exist between them and the bright outlook they shared about their future.

Billy heard sniffing next to him and looked over at Lucky. He watched the Irishman and Edna taking turns with her handkerchief and had trouble quelling his laughter. He turned frontward again and tried to get the image out of his mind. He caught Evan's eye and saw that the sheriff had also seen this. Evan smiled at him and Billy actually bit his tongue to hold his mirth in check.

The time came for the couple to kiss and Win cupped Erin's face, smiling at her before pressing his lips to hers. The church ceased to exist for Erin at that moment. His kiss was sweet, yet potent, and she didn't want it to end. When it did, she saw that his eyes were smoky with the same passion she felt.

Thad sat on the other side of Billy and whispered, "Looks like Win was right; seems like it's easy to kiss her since they're almost the same height."

Billy chuckled quietly and grinned.

The congregation clapped and a couple of the men present whistled while the newlyweds smiled and laughed. They held the reception in the church basement and several of the women went downstairs to take care of the last-minute preparations as Dan Griffith, a young man in town who was handy with a camera, took their pictures. That accomplished,

Win and Erin went down to the basement.

The decorated tables were very pretty and they were very touched by all of the hard work everyone had put into the celebration. The women preparing the meal had outdone themselves and even Evan had helped with a couple of dishes. Bea Watson had worked her baking magic and the wedding cake was a lovely creation.

Evan's toast was heartfelt yet brief because he knew that Win wasn't comfortable with a lot of public sentiment.

"I first met Win when he saw that my horse had thrown a shoe. I didn't know him from Adam, so when he walked over and said, 'Mister, let me take a look at your horse,' I didn't know what to think, but I let him. He told me that it was ok to go ahead and shoe the horse again since there was no swelling or tenderness.

"I thanked him and we introduced ourselves. When he heard that I was the new sheriff in Echo, he said, 'I've never seen such a young sheriff before.', and I said, 'I've never seen a Chinese veterinarian, but here you are.' We became friends right then and I'm proud that we still are. He's a great man, a great vet, and Echo is lucky to have him.

"Erin, Win's getting himself a good woman. You're smart, you have spirit, and you're brave as heck for coming to Echo to marry him. You're perfect for each other and I know everyone here will join me in wishing you many years of happiness."

The guests clapped and joined their voices together in echoing Evan's sentiments. When the food was served, Win was surprised to find that a couple of Chinese dishes had been made.

Erin said, "I wanted to do something to honor your culture, too."

Win sampled the wonton soup and udon noodles with a black pepper sauce. He hadn't had the dishes in a while and, although it was evident to him that someone inexperienced in Chinese cuisine had made them, they were still very good. "Who made these?"

"Evan. I found some Chinese recipes and brought them with me," she said. "I'm glad they're all right."

Win complimented Evan on the dishes and thanked Erin for being so thoughtful in including them in the reception menu. She'd even gotten enough chopsticks for everyone so they could experiment with them while they dined. They ate with zeal, laughing when Erin couldn't keep her noodles in her chopsticks.

Win tried to show her how to use them, but she just couldn't master it. Everyone else had fun with them, too, some having more success than others with the unfamiliar utensils. Billy had no trouble in using his whatsoever. He ate the way he normally did, shoving big amounts of noodles into his mouth at one time.

His mother, Arlene, laughed when Lucky reprimanded him for his poor table manners.

"You might as well give up, Lucky," she told him.

"This is a special occasion, boyo," Lucky said to Billy. "Boyo" was a term Lucky only used when he wasn't happy with someone.

Billy just slurped noodles into his mouth and smiled at Lucky, making the Irishman glower at him. When it was obvious that Erin wasn't going to catch on to the chopsticks, Win fed her noodles to her. It became an intimate thing for them and the air became charged between them.

With the meal finished, they moved on to cutting the cake, feeding each other a bite before they were to begin dancing.

As Win took her over to the dancing area, Erin said, "I am a lousy dancer, just so you know."

"You're just telling me this now?" he asked, smiling.

"It's embarrassing."

"Don't worry. Follow my lead. We'll keep it simple, ok?"

Josie was a talented guitar player and singer. The previous year, she'd taught Billy how to play and he'd bought his own guitar. The Indian youth also had a beautiful baritone voice and he and Josie liked to play and sing at Spike's sometimes.

He'd had a couple of bad experiences with prejudice when performing, but he'd developed a thicker skin since then and he'd learned to ignore them. They set up a couple of chairs and Arthur joined them in singing, his bass voice mingling perfectly with theirs.

Erin was scared that she would trip, but Win guided her through the simple waltz, keeping her on track and upright. He was amused to find that she had no sense of rhythm at all. Erin wasn't surprised that Win was light on his feet since his movements were graceful, even when he was just walking.

She was very relieved when other people joined in the dancing since it would take a lot of the focus away from her. They danced to a couple more songs before she gave up and they left the dance area.

As they sat down, Erin said, "I hope you don't mind that your wife is a horrible dancer."

"I don't mind, as long as you don't mind that your husband snores."

"You snore?" she asked.

He nodded. "It's true."

"You're just telling me now?" she asked.

Win grinned. "Well, I wasn't going to tell you before you married me. You might have backed out of the deal."

"No. I'll just kick you every time you wake me up."

He laughed. "I guess we'll both be tired a lot."

She giggled at his remark. "I guess so."

It wasn't long after this that they left so that they could make Dickensville before dark. Thad had brought the horse and buggy that Win had borrowed from Jerry and it was ready outside for them. They'd packed light since they were only going to be gone for a couple of days and their luggage was already stowed inside it. As they drove away, well wishes were shouted after them.

Although it had seemed that the weather would hold steady, they'd barely left Echo when it began snowing heavily.

"I don't like the looks of this," Win said. "It could quit anytime, but I don't want to get stuck on the road in it."

Erin was disappointed, but she said, "Well, Dr. Wu, let's do the practical thing and go home instead. I think as long as we're together, we'll have just as nice a time as going to Dickensville. We can go another time."

He smiled and started turning the buggy around so that they could go to the farm. "Dr. Avery, I think that's a fine idea. That practical side of you is just one of the reasons I married you."

"And what are some of the other reasons?" she asked.

"Are you fishing for compliments?"

"Yes," she said, making both of them laugh.

As they drove to the farm, they exchanged silly virtues about each other that had convinced them that they would make good mates. They didn't really notice the poor weather. Thick snow coated their hats and outerwear by the time they arrived.

Win made Erin wait on the porch while he unhitched the horse and put it in the barn that had been erected on the property. He finished quickly and ran back to the cabin, jumping up onto the porch. He carried their luggage, and set it down.

After opening the door, he scooped Erin up and said, "I don't really believe in luck, but just in case, we'll honor the tradition just the same."

She laughed. "That's fine with me. I do believe in luck."

He carried her through the doorway and put her on her feet. "I'll get a fire going; it won't take long to warm up in here."

Once he'd done that, he went out onto the porch and retrieved their suitcases. He took them into the bedroom and said, "Here, pull up a chair to the stove. It's starting to get hot. I also made a fire in the bedroom."

She did as he'd suggested and smiled. His considerate actions charmed her and she was suddenly glad that the weather had turned bad. Spending two days alone in the cabin with Win seemed like the perfect honeymoon to her.

Sitting down next to her, Win saw her smiling and asked, "What?"

"I was just thinking that I'm not disappointed that we couldn't go away. I think we'll have just as nice a time here, don't you?"

Looking into her eyes, Win said, "Yes, I do." Leaning closer to her, he kissed her and said, "I'm glad you don't mind."

She shook her head a little. It became warm in the cabin and they moved their chairs back to the table. Erin took her coat off and hung it up by the door.

"I'll be right back," she said and went into the bedroom, closing the door after her.

Win loosened his tie and shed his tuxedo jacket, hanging it over a chair. He sat down on the sofa and relaxed. When Erin stepped out of the bedroom, she wore something Win had never thought he'd see her in. She wore a red traditional Chinese Hanfu dress embroidered with butterflies that sipped nectar from a peony. This was a symbol of lovers tasting the joys of passion. Win saw that there were also ducks, which symbolized marital bliss.

As his eyes traveled over her, he noted how perfectly she had done up the garments that consisted of the traditional skirt, tunic top, and robe that wrapped around her body and was tied with a sash.

Standing up, Win went to her, taking her hands. "*Ni zhen mei*," he said. "That means that you're very beautiful."

Hearing him speak Chinese was enchanting. "Thank you. Did I do it right?"

"You did it perfectly."

"Good. I'm assuming that you also have the men's version of this."

He nodded. "Yes."

Giving him a saucy look, she said, "Go get it on, *zhangfu*."

Win smiled at her use of the Chinese word for husband. Her accent needed a little work, but he was impressed with how well she said it. "Yes, *nuran*, which means 'wife'."

She chuckled as he walked away. As soon as he closed the bedroom door, she set to work. She found his traditional Chinese tea set, pulled out a pot, and put water on the cook stove to boil. Looking through a couple of other cupboards, she found the table cloth he'd used the night he'd proposed to her and she put it on the table.

Then she pulled out the small pouch of green tea leaves she'd hidden in one of the voluminous sleeves of her robe. She couldn't find a scooper, so she used a wooden spoon to put the leaves into the small teapot.

By the time he joined her, the water had just come to a boil. He grinned when he saw the tea service. "What are you doing?"

"We're having tea," she informed him.

He looked so handsome in his black *shenyi*, the traditional men's robe that was worn over silk pants. She tried hard not to stare, but it was hard not to. The clothing emphasized his broad shoulders and powerful chest. Crickets, which stood for a fighting spirit and a leopard indicating his fighting prowess, were embroidered on it. She hadn't thought it possible, but the outfit made him look even more virile.

She said, "You look very handsome. Please sit."

"Thank you."

He watched her serve the tea. Her technique wasn't quite accurate, but he appreciated all of her effort and consideration for his culture. It told him that she held him in very high regard and he was deeply touched.

Taking a sip, he was pleasantly surprised to find that it was perfect. It was neither too bitter nor too strong. They sipped at it and talked about the wedding and their future plans. They felt comfortable with one another and Erin thought the experience was the happiest in her life. Sitting in traditional Chinese clothing, sipping tea with her very good-looking husband felt natural to her.

When they'd finished their tea, Erin cleared the table and put the cups and teapot in the sink. She turned around to find Win standing behind her. She gasped because she'd never heard him move. The smoldering look in his eyes kindled her desire for him. He put his arms around her waist and kissed her fervently.

She smiled against his mouth as he began backing her towards the bedroom. He chuckled in response, his lips never leaving hers. Erin discovered that Win was good at multitasking. Not only did he guide her backwards, but he began undoing the sash of her robe. It wasn't a hurried action; they took their time undressing each other.

Erin smiled inside as she remembered Jessica asking her if she would have a problem making love with a Chinese man. As Win lay down on the bed with her, she didn't have one single qualm about it. Everything was beautiful about him—his exotic eyes, tanned skin, and hard muscles. How could any woman not want to make love with a man like that?

Win had been with a good many women over the years, but none had fueled his desire the way Erin did and he knew that if destiny really existed than she was his. He felt a true connection between them and it was a heady feeling to discover that she felt the same way.

While the snow fell and the cold wind blew outside, inside their cabin, they created a bond that went beyond the physical. Neither of them was in a rush to put a label on it. Instead, they simply gave themselves over to it, the experience overwhelmingly beautiful and binding.

Chapter Sixteen

Waking up in Win's arms was a surreal experience for Erin. She opened her eyes and saw that he still slept. With his face relaxed in sleep, his appearance was boyish and very endearing. She traced his jawline with her fingertips, unable to stop herself from touching him. He stirred a little and smiled.

She ran her hands through his silky hair and lightly kissed him. His arms tightened around her and he ardently kissed her back. Instantly their passion burned bright again and they didn't get out of bed for a long time.

Later on, they got the fires going again. Not long afterward, there was a knock on their door. When Win answered it, no one was there. Instead, all he found was a large, steaming pot sitting on the porch. Win got a couple of towels and brought it inside. The aroma was delicious and his stomach felt very hollow as he brought it out to the kitchen.

"It looks like Lucky is following some Cheyenne traditions," he said as he sat it on the stove.

"What do you mean?" Erin asked.

"It's a custom that when a newlywed couple is on their honeymoon, their family and friends bring them food and other gifts during that time." Lifting the lid, he discovered that Lucky had made them venison stew with potatoes. "Mmm. His venison stew is delicious. Wait until you taste it."

Erin turned to him with bowls and a ladle. "Dish it up, please. I'm starving."

"Yes, ma'am."

Soon they were sitting down, eating their good friend's offering, which they greatly appreciated. All that day and the next, the only meal they had to cook was breakfast. Lucky and others brought them various meals and desserts, leaving them on the porch. Although there was a knock announcing the arrival of the tasty food, they never saw anyone. They were given complete privacy and they were grateful to their friends for helping to make their short honeymoon so special.

While the newlyweds were experiencing life-changing moments, so were some other people in another part of Echo. Bree thought that she'd been caught up in a wonderful dream and she hoped she never woke from it.

The brothers Earnest showered her with attention and she couldn't ever remember having so much fun. Marvin was having the time of his life bringing home women's clothing for her to wear. He bought it in Dickensville since it would be suspicious if he bought any in Echo. The clothing ranged from very casual to elegant.

Shadow got a kick out of the way Marvin had her put on a fashion show for them. It reminded Bree of when she'd played dress-up as a girl. She would come into the parlor in an outfit, curtsy, and strike various poses while the men laughed and praised her.

It was amazing to her how quickly they were able to get her over her initial shyness. She was growing accustomed to Shadow's schedule and found that she didn't mind it as much as she thought she would. Once the cook, Fiona, was gone for the day, she was given free rein of the house. No one knew of her or Shadow's existence. Marvin watched Bree and Shadow together and he could see a bond forming between the two of them. He noticed that Bree seemed to bring out Shadow's lighter side and he was happy about it.

He began to think that Shadow's idea could possibly work. They would have to wait a while to implement their plan, but they could afford to be patient. After all, being careful and thinking things through was what had enabled them to keep Shadow's existence a secret for so long. Ever since the night Marvin had discovered Shadow, they'd been meticulous in their planning.

While Shadow went off on his nightly sojourns, Bree read or worked on some of the crafts that Marvin had picked up for her. Whenever he returned to the ranch, he came in by way of the back entrance to the large house to unload his purchases so he didn't arouse the suspicions of the ranch hands, who would be working on the other side of the property. These kinds of precautions were necessary and Marvin enjoyed executing them successfully.

Marvin had offered to give Bree one of the bedrooms upstairs, but she'd refused, preferring to stay with Shadow. She still had nightmares and being with Shadow made her feel safe and cared for—something she'd been without for a long time. They hadn't become lovers, which perplexed her. Shadow never pressed that issue. There were times when she would bolt up in bed and he would hold her, but nothing more.

Shadow wanted Bree, but he'd promised her that they would only become intimate on her terms and he was letting it be completely up to her. It was another way he was earning her trust and devotion. Doing nothing more with a woman than actually sleeping in the same bed with her was having a profound effect on Shadow, too. Bad dreams often disturbed his own sleep but since Bree had been with him, his rest was much more peaceful.

She didn't know it, but there were times when he lay awake looking at her beautiful face. His incredible night vision allowed him to see her clearly in the dark. Sometimes he was able to tell when she was beginning to have a nightmare and he gathered her to him to help ward it off. When Marvin had asked about the exact nature of their relationship, Shadow hadn't been offended. They always told each other everything.

This discussion occurred one night out on the porch, which was their favorite place to talk, regardless of the weather.

"Have you ever just slept with a woman, Marvin? Just slept, nothing more?" Shadow asked.

Marvin thought back through the women he'd been with. "No, I haven't. After we were intimate, there were times when we slept, but we never just slept."

Shadow laughed. "Neither did I until Bree came along. It's a beautiful experience. I hope you get the chance to do it sometime."

A frowned marred Marvin's handsome features. "I don't expect that to happen any time soon."

"What's wrong?"

Marvin sighed. "It's time to end things with Phoebe."

Shadow gave him a surprised look. "Why?"

"She broke things off with Thad and she hasn't been the same since then. She misses him and it's affecting our relationship. I don't know what happened between them. She won't tell me. It wasn't so bad sharing her when she was actually with another man, but being with her when she's pining for him? I can't tolerate that. As much as it hurts, the next time she comes I'm going to tell her that it's over."

Shadow put a hand on Marvin's shoulder. The gesture conveyed his sympathy and let Marvin know that he hurt for him. The twins shared a strong bond in that they could often feel what the other was going through. Now was no exception.

Sensing that Marvin no longer wanted to talk, Shadow quietly withdrew, going on his way like usual.

Erin's practice grew steadily busier, which thrilled her. It was gratifying to her to be able to help others who were suffering one ailment or another. She kept her prices a little lower, figuring that when the town's economy improved, she could charge more. However, right now, people couldn't afford high prices. Sometimes they paid her in services instead of money, which ended up helping her save money.

One middle-aged woman, Charlene Harris, had offered to come clean the office for Erin in exchange for healthcare for her severely asthmatic son, Adam. The fourteen-year-old boy's outward appearance was deceiving. He appeared robust and he was a good-looking boy, but he had trouble doing a lot of outside work in the spring and fall. Winter could be hard on him, too. He lived for the summer when his asthma subsided.

Erin had agreed to the arrangement because it meant that she didn't have to pay someone to clean and she knew that it helped Charlene, too. She would have treated Adam for free, but she knew that Charlene's pride wouldn't allow that. Charlene came at the end of every day to clean and straighten up.

While Win never interfered in her practice, Erin valued her husband's advice. He always listened attentively and sometimes came up with solutions that she wouldn't have. It was the same with his veterinary practice. Since their wedding, more people were coming to him for their animal care. With each one of his successes, the practice grew even more.

Their marital relationship deepened and while Erin was extremely happy when she was working, she was always eager to get home to Win. If he was home, he often cooked dinner so it was ready when she arrived. If she arrived before he did, she cooked. Their nights were passion-filled and he always surprised her with his romantic side.

One night when she came in the door, she found the cabin lit with dozens of candles, including the bathroom, where Win was filling the tub with hot water.

"Hello. What are you doing?" she asked in Chinese.

He had been teaching her simple phrases and she was catching on well.

In English, he said, "I thought you might like a nice bath."

With a wicked little smile, she said, "Only if you join me."

"I'd love to."

"Then we should hurry before the water gets cold," she said.

And hurry they did.

There came a night in May when Erin came home to find Win in a pensive mood.

"What's wrong?" she asked.

"Nothing," he answered.

She asked, "Are you sure?"

"Yeah. I've just been thinking about a horse I've been treating, that's all."

Win didn't lie to her, but Erin could tell that something else was bothering him besides a sick horse. She'd never seen him so agitated before.

When they went to bed, no sooner had they blown the lamps out than Win sighed and said, "All right. Do you want to know what's really wrong?"

His irritable tone surprised Erin. "Yes, I do."

Win didn't know how to tell her. "I read books."

This wasn't shocking news to her. "I know."

"I read all kinds of books."

There were several different genres of books in their cabin, so this wasn't a new revelation, either.

"I know."

The man who feared little in life closed his eyes and cringed as he said, "Including romance books."

Erin could feel the tension in his body as she lay against him and it was adorable that her strong, virile husband secretly read romance books. It was also touching that her opinion of him mattered so much to him.

"You read romance books?"

Keeping his eyes closed, he said, "Yes.

She smiled, but kept the laughter out of her voice. "I see. How long have you been reading them?"

"Since I was fifteen. Mother read them and got me hooked on them. She taught me to read and write English and we used to read them and talk about them."

The image of him and his mother discussing romance books did her in. Her laughter started out as a soft chuckle and built from there. She put her arms around him and held him close even while she shook with mirth.

Win wasn't sure what to think, but he figured that if she was hugging him, it couldn't be a bad thing.

Finally, she recovered enough to say, "Now I know where your romantic streak comes from. I think I'm a very lucky woman to have a husband that reads romance books. If you didn't, you wouldn't be inclined to do the nice things for me that you do."

His gaze met hers. "So you don't think any less of me as a man?"

"Of course not. I think that you're very brave to admit that you like those books," she said.

"No one else knows but you."

She rose up on an elbow to look at him. "Really? I'm the only one who knows your secret?"

"That's right. Please don't tell anyone. I'll never hear the end of it."

"I promise not to tell anyone on one condition," she said, running a hand over his chest.

He smiled. "What condition?"

"That you don't ever stop reading them."

Win let out a laugh and said, "It's a deal, Dr. Avery."

"I have one other condition, Dr. Wu."

"Which is?"

She responded with an urgent kiss. There was something very exciting about having a husband who read romance books.

When their lips parted, he said, "It's definitely a deal."

Chapter Seventeen

L ambing time came and all of the little ones that came along kept the
sheep farmers busy. Keeping track of lineages was also important.
Erin was impressed with how methodical Lucky was about it and how
he was able to tell one ewe or lamb from another. He was so many
contradictions rolled into one man that it was hard to keep track of
them all.

He believed in both the Catholic and Cheyenne religions and
practiced various aspects of both of them. He was a white Irishman
living in an Indian tipi who cooked Indian-style food and hunted with a
bow and arrows. He was strong as an ox and yet gentle with women and
children. One minute he'd berate Billy for something he perceived as
bad behavior and the next he'd praise his young friend for something
done well.

Lucky's mood changes never bothered Win though, who usually
just told Lucky off if he irritated him too much. Sometimes it struck
Lucky as funny and sometimes he'd become angry and stomp off. His
anger never lasted long, though. Soon he'd be back to move on to
whatever they were doing next or to strike up a new conversation.

Erin watched Lucky with Josie and saw that they were as close as any brother or sister she'd ever seen. She soon understood why that would be. Lucky seemed to think it was his personal mission to take people under his wing and guide them. He taught her how to shoot a bow and arrows, to cook the way he did, and when Win was busy at night or on the weekends when she was closed, he entertained her—and everyone else, for that matter.

She got to know Billy as well and loved to stop in his shop to see what new paintings he was working on. Lucky wasn't the only who liked to give lessons. One such night, he set up an easel and set of paints for her so she could try her hand at painting. Her cat ended up looking more like a dinosaur, but Billy wouldn't hear of getting rid of her painting.

A week later, he came out to the farm and gave it to her. He'd had it framed and Win promptly hung it in their parlor. Whenever their friends came to play games or just to sit around and talk, at least one person remarked about what a talented artist she was. Josie named the creature in the painting "Dinocat". Erin was happy with the way Josie's pregnancy was progressing and felt confident that all would go well during the birth at the latter part of June.

Although Win and Erin wanted children sooner rather than later, they felt no pressure about it. They were enjoying their time alone together for the moment. She picked up Win's habit of reading romances and they started reading them aloud to one another. They tried to get two copies if they could so they could sit and read back and forth as though putting on a play.

Erin read the women's dialogue and Win the men's, but they would also switch it around. They kept each other in stitches whenever Win said things like, "I can't live without him, Ruby," in a falsetto voice or when Erin said, "She's the only woman I'll ever love," in as deep a voice as she could. Sometimes they went hoarse from laughing so hard.

She could always tell when their new books arrived because, if he could, Win dropped whatever he'd been doing as soon as she got home and came running.

Lucky and Billy watched this happen on several occasions. The three of them had been shearing sheep when Erin got home one night.

Win said, "You boys take over. I have something important to do."

Billy's mouth dropped open when Win streaked across the pasture and leapt up onto the porch. He and Lucky couldn't hear what he said to Erin, but she squealed, hugged Win, and dragged him into their cabin. They watched as Win came back out and put the two large sticks he kept by the porch in an X pattern at the foot of the stairs. This was how many Indian cultures indicated that someone wasn't to be disturbed unless there was an emergency. Lucky had taught this to all of his friends. Then Win hurried back inside again.

The Indian and the Irishman looked at each other and Billy said, "I guess you know what they're doing, huh?"

"Aye, and the way they been at it, it shouldn't be long until they're expectin' their own wee bairn."

They laughed as they went back to work.

"Are you crying?" Win asked Erin.

She shook her head. "No."

"Yes, you are," he said, trying to see her face.

They had been reading in bed and as he'd read the last sentence in their latest book, he'd heard her sniff a little as she'd laid her head on his shoulder.

"It was just such a romantic ending," she said, brushing away a tear.

Win nodded. "It was."

"I know how she feels," Erin said. "She never thought she'd find someone to love and neither did I, but I have." Her eyes met his. "When I answered your ad, I didn't expect to fall in love with the man I married. But from the first moment I met you, you became my hero, literally and figuratively. You saved me from that thief, you cut my hair for me, and you helped me get my practice off the ground."

He would have spoken, but she shook her head, so he stayed silent.

"Every day you do things for me that you don't have to do, things that most men would never think to do. Romantic baths, candlelit dinners, and massages, just to mention a few. I'm lucky to have found a man like you to love. *Wǒ ài nǐ*, Win. I love you."

"*Wǒ ài nǐ*, Erin," Win said without hesitation. "I'd hoped that I'd fall in love with the woman I chose, but I didn't know if it would happen. But here you are and you make me so happy. I love you, too."

The sweet feeling that stole over Erin upon hearing those words was so powerful that it was almost too much to contain. Long into the night, they whispered those words to each other, never tiring of hearing them.

At the beginning of May, Marvin had made it known that he was taking a trip to the train station in Corbin to pick up a couple of family friends. While he actually did have to go to Corbin on business, the rest of it was just for show. He timed his return for late at night so that all the ranch hands would have gone home since none of them lived on the property. Marvin had never built any bunkhouses because of the risk that Shadow would be discovered if anyone else lived there.

He'd stayed away a couple of days longer than he'd told Travis and Fiona he would, but this was also part of the plan. When Fiona had arrived the morning after he arrived home, Marvin sat her down at the kitchen table.

"Fiona, I'm afraid I have some distressing news. I know you don't know my friends, but Mr. Josephson passed away unexpectedly on the trip to Corbin," Marvin had said.

Fiona was shocked. Marvin had been so happy about his friends impending visit. He'd said that Mr. Josephson had been a good friend of his father's and that he'd finally convinced him to come for a visit. Apparently, Mr. Josephson had asked if his daughter Bree could come with him and Marvin had graciously acquiesced.

"I'm so sorry, Mr. Earnest," she said. "What happened?"

Marvin's jaw worked as he warmed to his performance. "They think it was most likely a stroke. I feel to blame. Maybe if I hadn't coaxed him to come here, he would still be alive. He never said that he'd been in bad health or that the trip from California would be too arduous."

Marvin's grim expression had saddened Fiona. "You're not to blame, sir. No one could have predicted such a thing. It could very well have happened even if he hadn't been traveling."

He'd given her a small smile. "Thank you. Now, Bree is here. I'm afraid that she's very distraught, as you can imagine. Unfortunately, the undertaker in Corbin couldn't embalm the body because there had been several deaths he was dealing with, so the body couldn't be shipped back home. Since the weather has been rather warm, the only choice we had was to bury him."

"I couldn't escort Bree back to California on such short notice and frankly, I don't think she would have stood the trip, even if I could have. I had no choice but to bring her home with me. She has no one else. Her mother passed away several years ago and she has no siblings."

As Fiona had listened to him, tears had filled her eyes as she thought about the poor girl's plight. "I understand why you would do such a thing, but, sir, people will talk; she's an unmarried woman living under the roof of a single man."

Genuine anger over one of the proprieties of the time had filled Marvin. "I understand that, but what else am I to do? Who is going to act as a chaperone? Everyone hates me as it is; what's one more transgression?"

Fiona had dropped her gaze. She didn't want to agree with him, even though it was true. She always tried to see the good in everyone and Marvin had always treated her fairly. "I can't do it. I have my parents to look after."

"I know you do. Fiona, you're a single woman working for a single man. Please do not take this the wrong way, but you're a very pretty woman. Have I ever acted inappropriately towards you?" Marvin asked.

Fiona had worked for Marvin for two years and in all that time, he'd never propositioned her or made a pass at her. He'd been kind and friendly, but he'd always been respectful of her.

"No, sir."

"Right. And I never will. It's no different with Bree. She's a grieving woman, for God's sake. Besides, I have my eye on a very lovely woman in Dickensville," he'd said. "I'm not ready to divulge her identity, but I'm hoping that something develops between us."

Fiona had smiled. "I hope so, too. I know you've always said that you'd like to have a family."

"Yes, I would," Marvin had said. "So, as you can see, there's no cause for concern over Bree's presence in the house."

During their conversation, Bree had been waiting on the back staircase that led into the kitchen. She'd been waiting for her cue and as soon as Marvin had given it to her she descended the stairs the rest of the way and entered the kitchen.

"Miss Josephson." Marvin had risen and said, "I didn't expect to see you quite yet. I was going to let you rest longer."

Bree smiled tightly at him and looked over at Fiona. "I couldn't sleep so I thought I'd come for some tea, if that's all right."

Marvin guided her over to a chair and seated her. "Of course, it is. Miss Josephson, this is my wonderful cook, Fiona."

Bree said, "Hello, Fiona. It's nice to meet you." Her anxiety over giving a good performance gave her the pale complexion of a grieving person.

"Thank you, Miss Josephson. It's nice to meet you, despite the circumstances. My condolence on your father's passing," Fiona said. She could see how distraught the young lady was and her heart ached for her. "Now, you just sit right there, and I'll make you some tea and something for breakfast."

"I'm not hungry," Bree said.

Fiona said, "I know you might not feel hungry, but you need to eat something to keep up your strength. Will you try to eat a piece of toast for me?"

Bree gave a slight nod. "I'll try."

"Good. Mr. Earnest, what would you like this morning?"

"One of your delicious omelets would be delightful," Marvin said. When Fiona's back was turned, he'd winked at Bree to let her know she was doing a good job.

They cultivated this story and Marvin introduced Bree around town. Shadow had worked hard on making Bree devoted to him and it had paid off. Gradually, he'd explained to her what his life was truly like, telling her that if she was uncomfortable with it, that she was free to leave at any time.

However, he hadn't counted on was becoming just as devoted to her. However, they still hadn't become lovers because Shadow refused to be the one to move their relationship along. He didn't want to pressure her. She had yet to tell him about her time with her captors and he never wanted to do anything that would remind her of any ill treatment she'd experienced.

Shadow paced back and forth in his sitting room. He wasn't normally up at two o'clock in the afternoon, but today was the day that Bree had taken her first solo trip into Echo and he was worried sick. Not for himself, but for her. She'd gained confidence and understood what they expected her to do, but it didn't make him feel any better.

It had been years since he'd experienced this sort of anxiety. He imagined all sorts of horrible things happening to her without him there to protect her. He would do anything to keep her from harm. With that thought, he came to an abrupt halt. He would do the same for Marvin. When had Bree become so important to him? He didn't know.

The sound of the secret door opening interrupted his train of thought.

"Shadow! Shadow!" Bree called out.

He was startled when she ran into the sitting room and threw her arms around him.

Shadow returned her embrace. "What's wrong?"

She drew back a little, her eyes shining with glee. "Nothing! I did it! All by myself!"

Relief and pride flooded his being, bringing a grin to his face. "Of course you did."

The way she bounced up and down a little was amusing. "I went into the store, bought my things, and talked to Tansy. She's a very nice lady. I finished there and came right home, just like you said to."

"I knew you could do it," he said.

A knowing gleam entered her eyes. "You were worried."

"Yes, I was, but not because I didn't think you were capable. It's what other people might do that worried me," he said.

"Well, you can stop worrying." She hugged him again. "What's my next assignment?"

Her eagerness pleased him. "Ready for another so soon?"

"Yes! Do you want me to go to the store again? Talk to someone in particular? What?"

When he laughed, she shook him and laughed, too. Her comfort level with physical contact with him had grown and now she didn't hesitate to take his hand, hug him, or playfully grab onto him. He had come to crave her touch, but he never let on.

"I'll have to think about it," he said.

"Think fast!" She danced away from him and came back. "It's been so long since I did anything like that on my own. It feels incredible!"

Shadow said, "I remember what that was like. When Marvin let me out of my cage the first time, I didn't know what to do. I'd longed to be freed, but I'd never stepped outside of it until then. It felt like a huge accomplishment when I did, so I understand what you mean."

It pained her to hear about the things he'd gone through, but she always listened to him. "I'll never understand how people can do such cruel things."

Shadow always skirted around these statements because she didn't know that she was living with a monster. Not yet. "Enough of that. Let's not ruin your big day."

"You're right." She surprised both of them when she gave him a brief kiss. Her eyes widened and her cheeks turned pink. "I'm sorry. I shouldn't have done that."

That one small bit of contact ignited the desire he'd held in check for so long. "You probably shouldn't have, but don't be sorry. I'm not."

Fright filled Bree, but not because she was afraid of Shadow. She backed away from him. "You don't understand."

"Stay still." He took a step towards her.

"Shadow, no." She retreated again.

His expression darkened. "Stand still!"

His sharp words froze her in place. Her heart hammered inside her chest as he closed the distance between them.

"I've always promised you that I would never hurt you, Bree, and I make that same promise to you again now," he said. "But I've been waiting for you to do something just like you did now. All I want is one kiss. Just one and nothing more."

Bree shook her head and lowered her gaze. "No."

"Haven't I proven that I'm trustworthy? Haven't I shown you that I'm capable of great restraint?"

She nodded but couldn't speak.

"Bree, I've laid beside you every day when we slept and I've never done anything more than hold your hand or hold you when you've had a bad dream. I could have overpowered you and done what I wanted with you, but I promised that I would never do anything like that. I won't hurt you any more than you already have been. Those days are over. I trusted you to go into town, even though I knew you could tell someone about me. Can't you trust me just a little?"

She was silent for a few moments and then nodded. "Yes."

Her timid response intensified his resolve to be as gentle as possible with her even though he wanted her like no other woman he'd ever known. Gently, he cupped her face in his hands and enjoyed the smoothness of her skin against his palms. Her eyes were squeezed shut.

"Bree, look at me. Please?"

The softness in his voice gave her the courage to open her eyes. His soft smile increased her confidence. His beauty was mesmerizing to begin with, but when he smiled, she could hardly take her eyes off him.

He lowered his head and pressed his lips to hers. The fire inside him blazed into an inferno, but he kept the contact brief and released her after a few short moments.

Bree had never been kissed so sweetly before and it was a profound experience for her. Here stood a man who had committed brutal acts of murder and yet he'd given her a kiss that was only a little more than chaste. At any time, he could have forced her, but he hadn't. She was surprised to feel disappointed that he hadn't kissed her more.

She surprised herself further by saying, "Is that it?"

Shadow arched an eyebrow. He wasn't sure if she was pleased or disappointed. "What do you mean?"

"I just didn't expect you to be done so quickly."

She definitely didn't sound pleased. He kept from smiling. "I kept my promise. One kiss and no more."

She blushed again and avoided his gaze. "It's because I'm ugly, isn't it?"

"What?" He'd spoken a little more loudly than he'd intended. "Why do you think you're ugly?"

"I don't want to talk about it."

He saw her change back into the scared woman she'd been when they first met and it was very important to him to draw her out again. "Bree, I can assure you that you are a very, very beautiful woman."

She looked at him for a short moment. "No, I'm not."

"Yes, you are. You don't know how many times I've wanted to make love to you or the way I burn for you. But I made a promise to you and I won't risk making you fear and hate me by crossing that line."

"You have? You do?" she asked.

"I have and I do."

Shadow's praise didn't change her opinion of herself, but it made her happy that he found her beautiful. It also amazed her.

157

"Why haven't you said anything?"

"Because I know that, even after all this time, any hint at further intimacy still scares you."

He was right. She was perfectly comfortable sleeping in the same bed with him, but if he'd tried to do more than hold her hand or embrace her, she would have been terrified.

"I've left it up to you," he said. "I didn't know how you felt about me, so if anything was going to happen between us, it would be because you wanted it to."

She saw that he was telling her the truth. "I believe you, but I'm sure that you have other women you could go to who are eager to be with you. I'm sure they're not afraid of you."

He took her face in his hands again. "You're right. I could see other women, but I don't want to. I haven't been with another woman since the night we met."

A jolt of surprise shot through her. "Why not? I don't understand."

"Because I think that I have a chance at something I never thought I would."

"At what?"

Now Shadow was the terrified one. He knew that once he uttered the word, there would be no taking it back. Saying it could drive her away and he didn't think he could bear that, but he had to know if there was even the slightest hope. "Love."

An odd look crossed her face. She crossed her arms and began pacing back and forth, shooting him the same odd look. He didn't know what to make of it.

"You don't want to love me, Shadow. I'm not worthy of such a thing," she said.

"Why not?"

"I'm dirty. Spoiled goods."

He smiled at her. "You're perfect for me then," he teased her.

"What do you mean?"

"You're spoiled goods and I'm a monster."

She stopped pacing. "A monster?"

"Well, by some people's standards, anyway."

Coming to stand in front of him again, she asked, "Why do you think you're a monster?"

"I don't think—I know I am. The man I killed the night we met wasn't the first person I've killed and he won't be the last, I'm sure."

Bree held his gaze. She sensed that this was the time to ask all of the questions she'd wanted to for so long. "Do you like it? Killing, I mean?"

"Yes."

"Do they deserve it?"

"Yes."

"Do you hurt people?"

"Yes."

"Do you like it?"

"Yes. Well, sometimes not, but it's necessary. Or sometimes I just enjoy toying with people because it's fun. It depends on my mood, I suppose."

"But you would never hurt me."

"No."

"Not even if I told people about you?"

"Not even then. I should to shut you up or punish you, but I won't. I don't think I could bring myself to do it. I'd sooner kill myself."

"Is the reason you like killing because of your father? Because of what he did to you?"

"Yes, and also because insanity seems to run in our family."

"So you think you're insane?"

His smile was self-deprecating. "I know I am. You don't live the way I live and enjoy the things I do without being at least a little insane. So, you see that you have been living with a monster."

Bree saw where many people would think that of him and she'd heard the things that they said about Marvin, too. However, she saw the brothers differently. Shadow could have killed her that first night and he'd had ample opportunity to harm her, rape her, or kill her ever since then, yet he'd only been kind and gentle with her. Rarely had he raised his voice to her and he'd never made a threatening move towards her after that first night when he'd pulled her hair. In her eyes, those were not the actions of a monster.

"You're not a monster, Shadow. You were twisted into the kind of person you are by the way you've been treated, but you're not a monster. Monsters don't take in stray women and treat them as well as you've treated me."

"Bree, don't fool yourself into thinking I'll change or that there's some hidden goodness inside me, because there's not."

She smiled at his warning. "I don't think you'll change, but there is goodness in you. You haven't hidden that from me."

There was a kernel of truth in her statement. "I guess you're right about that. I've always been good to Marvin, too."

"See?"

"Don't be too hopeful. While I'm being honest, I need you to understand that we're using you."

"Using me? How?" She became anxious again.

"These assignments you'll be given have a purpose and not one that I'm sure you'll like very much."

She saw his gaze sharpen. "Tell me."

"Come. Sit," he said, motioning toward the sofa. Once they were comfortably seated, he went on. "Both Marvin and I are rather touched in the head, I guess you'd say. Yes, we've had to be, but we also enjoy what we do. There are reasons for that, but I won't go into that right now. You need to understand exactly what you're dealing with and decide if you're going to stay or not."

Bree nodded. "Ok."

"What we want you to do is become a spy for us. We want you to become friendly with the women in Echo and report back to us the things they say that you feel are important. That's it. There's no reason to put your life in danger or anything like that."

She frowned. "How would I know what things are important?"

"Anything that's of a very personal nature. We don't care what recipes they've tried or other boring domestic topics. We'd like to know things about what their husbands are doing or anything that seems like a secret," Shadow said.

"And are you going to use these things against them?"

"Yes, if necessary, or maybe even if we're just bored," Shadow said.

"What if I don't want to do that, but I don't want to leave? Will you throw me out?"

He'd also thought about that and he knew that he wasn't going to be able to toss her out any more than he could kill her. "No. This is your home for as long as you want to be here."

"Ok. Do you ever hurt children?"

"No! Never! I promise you that. I've never been around them, but Marvin adores children. We would never harm an innocent child. Could you imagine Marvin doing anything to Pauline?"

Marvin loved Pauline, like everyone else in Echo, and he'd struck up a deal with Travis the year before. If the foreman brought her to see him once a week, he would continue paying him an increased wage. Therefore, she accompanied Travis every Friday and Marvin spent the day with her.

Bree smiled. "She's adorable. We have fun with her."

As time had gone on, Bree had slowly come out of her shell. She liked having lunch with the little girl and sometimes, she went for a walk with her and Marvin. Bree had been with them enough to know if there was any inappropriate behavior towards Pauline and she'd never seen any.

"I've seen them having lunch a couple of times and she's very cute," Shadow said.

"She's never seen you?"

"No, and she never will."

"Why do you still keep yourself in a cage?" Bree asked.

Shadow said, "I don't. I'm free this way. Can you really see me working on the ranch, doing business and such?"

"But there's so much you're missing out on," Bree said. "Friends, fun, family."

"Is that what you want? If it is, you should leave, because if you continue to stay here, that won't truly happen. If you want to settle down and have children, you'll need to find someone else to do it with."

"You don't want children?"

"I do, but that will never happen. How would they live like this, with a father they can't ever talk to their friends about? Not only that, they'd be outcasts. If you choose me, Bree, you're going to have to decide if you can forgo all of that," he said.

Her face showed her distress and indecision. "I don't know what to do."

"You don't have to decide right now. Take some time. It's a big decision. I'm going to get some sleep," he said. "I have things to do tonight."

"Spying?"

A wicked grin settled on his face. "Among other things."

She watched him exit the room, leaving her to ruminate on all he'd told her.

Chapter Eighteen

The warm, starry night was perfect for sleeping out in the open. Lucky lay on his back, watching the heavenly bodies move around the sky. It reminded him of all the times he'd done that with his Cheyenne friends and his wife. He tried to keep those thoughts at bay, but when he was alone at night like this, they wouldn't stay out of his mind.

He chuckled to himself as he remembered how he'd blundered when trying to engage in a conversation with Avasa for the first time. He hadn't known that the braves and maidens weren't supposed to talk to each other unless it was necessary. Of course, at that point, he didn't consider himself a brave.

She had been hauling water from the stream and Lucky had come along and tried to take the heavy water skins for her. She'd frowned at him and had shaken her head. He'd flashed her a grin and nodded. They'd gone back and forth about it until they'd heard laughter coming from the direction of the camp.

Avasa had become angry and embarrassed, yanking the water skins from his grasp and stomping off. Lucky had stood there trying to figure out what he'd done wrong.

Wild Wind had come to his rescue as he had so many times. "It is not your fault. You do not know our customs. It is an insult to help the women. They do not like it when we interfere in their work, just as we do not like it if they try to fix our weapons."

As a man who'd been raised to help women, Lucky couldn't believe what he was hearing. "So even if those bags were so heavy she had to crawl to haul them, I shouldn't help her?"

Wild Wind had grinned. "That is right, but other women would help her if she needed it."

"But us men aren't s'posed to?"

"No. You are not to talk to the maidens. It is considered unchaste for her to talk to a brave like that."

"Why? We were out in the open and I only offered to help with the water. That makes no sense."

Wild Wind had said, "To you, perhaps, but it is the way we do things. If you are going to stay here, you will have to get used to our customs."

Lucky had fixed his friend with a questioning look. "So if ya can't talk to the maidens, how do ya court 'em?"

Wild Wind had laughed. "You really do like her. Come, I will explain it to you."

Thinking back on it, Lucky laughed when he realized how hilarious his faux pas had been to his friends. He crossed his ankles and looked over at the lamb that lay close to him. Its dam hadn't made it through the birth and he'd been hand feeding it. It now regarded him as its mother and even slept in the tipi with him. He now knew how Win felt with Sugar.

"I s'pose you're hungry. Come, then, I'll feed ya for the last time tonight."

As he rose, one of the dogs barked. He froze in place and waited to see what had alerted it. He saw a deer bound across the pasture. While some would have smiled at the pretty sight, he didn't. If the deer was on the run, whatever was chasing it might come after the sheep. Quickly, he readied the bow that he'd kept near him in case it was needed.

Although the dog had barked, the sheep weren't spooked at all, which was a comforting sign. He waited for several minutes, but when nothing further happened, he put the bow back down and led the lamb into the tipi so he could feed it.

About halfway through the feeding, Lucky heard both of the dogs bark this time. He hurried from the tipi and collided with Billy. Since Lucky was heavier and already on the move, Billy was thrown onto his rear end.

"What the hell is wrong with you?" Billy asked.

Lucky didn't answer him. Instead, he scanned the pasture and tried to see beyond it, but the darkness hampered his vision. The dogs still barked, indicating that something was still around. The most they ever did when Billy or one of their other friends came was let out a few friendly woofs. These were not those types of barks.

Without speaking, he reached a hand down and helped Billy up. "Sorry," he whispered.

"What's wrong?"

"Somethin's around. A deer ran by and now the dogs are actin' up."

Billy started looking around, too, but he didn't see anything. He noticed that Bucky and Sheila were paying more attention to the lower part of the pasture. Using Indian sign, he told Lucky where he thought the predator might be.

"We should split up and meet in the middle. Get your bow," Lucky signed back.

After retrieving it, Billy took off in the opposite direction as Lucky. Circling the herd, Lucky silently commanded Bucky to stay with the herd while he took Sheila with him. Both men kept a watchful eye as they trotted silently along, but they hadn't encountered anything suspicious on the way. Sheila sniffed around, acting excited, but she didn't growl or seem overly concerned.

As they stood looking into the shadows close to the trees, the sheep on the opposite side of the herd set up alarmed bleating. Lucky sent

Sheila on her way and she sped across the field. By the time her and Bucky reached the place, the sheep had started to calm down again.

Billy and Lucky stopped running.

"Just stand still," Lucky signed. "There is more than one."

"Why are the dogs not growling more? If it were wolves or coyote, they should go after them," Billy signed.

"I know. It might be someone trying to steal a sheep or two. It would not surprise me," Lucky sent back. They continued signing.

"But they are still trained to go after them."

"Whoever this is, he is very smart. Did you see the way Sheila's tail wagged?"

"Yes. So?"

Lucky rolled his eyes and said, "They know the person or persons. He or she may have been getting the dogs used to them for a while, even bringing them treats."

Suddenly, Billy felt something hit the back of his legs and he cried out in surprise. He spun around, but didn't see anything. "What the hell?" Looking down, he saw a decent sized rock on the ground.

Lucky's expression turned fierce. "They're havin' fun with us now."

"Do you think it's some kids?"

"No. Kids wouldn't think to recondition the dogs. This is someone who knows what they're doing."

"Why would they give themselves away?"

"Because they enjoy doin' stuff like this. Who do we know like that?"

"Earnest."

"Right. Go get Win and then go get Homer. We'll have him track down whoever this is and my guess is it'll lead right to Earnest," Lucky said.

Billy knew when to protest something Lucky told him to do and when not to. He ran off to Win's cabin without another word.

Behind Lucky's tipi, Shadow grinned. *Going to go get that mutt, huh? Your dogs aren't the only ones I'm friendly with, Irish.* Keeping the tipi between himself and Lucky, he took off into the trees. Reaching their cover, he went over to a tree and crouched down to untie Barkley. The bulldog licked his face and whined.

Shadow ruffled his ears and then said, "Go play," while pointing in the direction of the sheep farm.

Barkley panted happily and raced away. Laughing softly, Shadow headed deeper into the forest.

Win helped guard the herd while Billy went for Homer. He concurred with Lucky that someone was messing with them, but he didn't think it was Earnest himself. The man knew nothing about animal behavior so he wouldn't have known how to recondition the dogs. As he was just coming back to meeting up with Lucky, a dog came running up to them.

"Barkley?" Win said upon seeing the bulldog.

Barkley panted and ran circles around the two men before jumping against Win's legs in greeting. This wasn't the first time the bulldog had come to the sheep farm. Since he'd treated the dog a couple months ago, Barkley had become fond of Win. Their dogs knew Barkley now, so Lucky thought that might explain their lack of aggression, but Barkley couldn't throw rocks.

Win knelt and pet Barkley. "What are you doing out? Did you escape? Earnest doesn't normally let him out at night."

"Hmm," Lucky said. "Maybe it was kids and it Barkley was around, maybe the kids ran off after they threw that rock at Billy."

Win said, "I can tell you don't really believe that."

"I don't."

"I agree. Barkley would have come to play with the dogs before that. No, he just happened to come along right after that. There was more than one person, you say?"

"I do. Unless it's someone that can run awful fast," Lucky said.

Win laughed. "That definitely leaves out Earnest. I've never seen the man run in all the time I've known him. Even as kids, I don't remember him running much."

"He could train in private and what about when he was away at boarding school?"

"I guess that's possible, but that was a long time ago. I'll ask Erin if he's in good running shape. He's been to see her a couple of times, so she'd know," Win said.

"Right."

Barkley let out a hoarse bark, which was echoed by the sheep dogs' voices. Homer pulled Billy along behind him, the big red coonhound eager to see all of his friends. Evan followed them. Homer stopped upon seeing Barkley. He'd never met the other dog. His hackles rose and he bared his teeth as a growl rumbled in his chest. Barkley was the peaceable type, however, and just bowed down, ready to play.

Homer snarled and growled louder before lunging at the bulldog. Billy yanked him back.

"Homer! Stop that!"

Homer's ears drooped and he sat down, but he still growled at Barkley.

"Barkley, go home," Win said. "Go home." He didn't want to see anything happen to Barkley.

Barkley gave Win a wounded look before trotting off into the night. It wasn't too long until he met up with Shadow again, who praised him. "Let's go home, boy."

Shadow ran, making sure to avoid any damp places where his deer-hide-encased feet would leave prints behind. These crude moccasins gave him the ability to travel both silently and rapidly. Because the deer hide was fresh, the scent would mask his own. It wouldn't matter if Homer led them to his ranch because it would simply seem as though they were following Barkly. He grinned as he ran home through the trees with his trusty friend at his side, thinking that Irish wasn't the only one who knew some Indian tricks.

Marvin jerked awake when someone pounded on his front door. He got up and threw on a robe before going downstairs. He opened the door and looked into Evan's angry face.

"What's wrong?" Marvin asked.

"Where were you tonight?" Evan asked, pushing his way inside.

Marvin said, "Come right on in, Sheriff. Oh, I see you brought company, too."

Lucky glowered as he passed Marvin. Both he and Evan looked at the staircase as Barkley came trotting down them. He greeted the two men as though he hadn't seen them in days instead of just that night.

"I've been right here, sleeping, or did you think this was the new way I'm styling my hair now?" Marvin said and closed the door.

"Your dog came to visit the farm tonight," Lucky said. "Not long ago, we sent him home."

"Oh, thank you. You didn't have to check on him, but I appreciate it," Marvin said. He was enjoying himself very much. "That's where you ran off to, hmm? He does this every so often. I let him out at bedtime and he wouldn't come back. He sometimes chases a stray cat or a rabbit. He woke me up not long ago."

Evan pushed Marvin up against the front door. "How did the dog get in the house if you were sleeping when he came back?"

Marvin didn't like being touched very much. He narrowed his eyes. "If you will allow me, I'll show you how."

"Fine."

Marvin moved out around the two men and led them out to the kitchen. Going over to the door, he showed them a much smaller door. "This is his dog door. Sir Isaac Newton is the said to be the inventor of such a thing, but I don't know if that's true or not. I had this made for Barkley. During the day, he comes and goes, but after bedtime, I lock it so he can't get out. As I said, he ran off tonight, so I left it open so he could get back in. What's this all about?"

Evan said, "Thanks for the useless information. There was a disturbance at the farm tonight."

"And you think Barkley did something?" Marvin asked, sliding the bolt on the dog door home.

"I don't," Lucky said. "But I think you did."

Marvin stepped right up to him, looking him in the eye. "And just what are you accusing me of? Are any of the sheep hurt?"

"No. Not this time. Mark my words, Earnest, if I find ya anywhere near our herd, I'll make sure ya never walk again. And if ya got someone workin' for ya, ya can make sure they know, too."

Marvin laughed right in Lucky's face before backing away slightly. "Why would I want to hurt your herd?"

"You don't want it to take off because it'll hurt your business. An alternate meat supply to compete with your beef."

Marvin's eyes narrowed. "I think you should look at the Terranovas instead of me. I'm doing quite well, you see. In fact, so well that I'm thinking getting out of the cattle business altogether. Or scaling back anyway."

"Does Travis know this?" Evan asked.

"If I've answered all of your questions, I'd appreciated it if you would leave so I can go back to bed," Marvin said.

His cold tone always meant that the conversation was over. "Yeah, we're done—for now. Watch your step, Earnest," Evan said.

"Goodnight, Sheriff. Mr. Quinn. Have a nice night. Give my best to your wife and Edna," Marvin said.

"Go to hell," Evan said as they left.

Marvin chuckled to himself as he mounted the stairs to go back to bed.

When Evan got home that night, he climbed into bed softly, trying not to wake his wife. He needn't have worried. She hadn't gone to sleep yet.

"What happened?" she asked.

Evan sighed and gathered her close. "Nothing. That's the problem. Homer led me back to Earnest's, but he was only following Barkley's trail. He doesn't like Barkley very much. I think he was hoping for another chance to take a bite out of him." He told her the rest of what had happened.

Josie said, "He's so evil. I think he's behind it somehow, too, but why?"

Evan said, "Earnest never does anything without a reason. It sometimes doesn't reveal itself until later on, but he always has some sort of motive."

"I think he's lying about his finances. If he was doing so well, why not make any repairs to The Shrine?"

This was what the locals called Marvin's house. The story around Echo was that Wesley Earnest's death had devastated Marvin and he'd turned the house into a shrine to his departed father.

"I don't know. Although, he did give Travis a raise last year. Maybe things have been improving steadily," Evan said. "Damn it! I know he's behind what happened on our wedding day and I know he's got something to do with this, too. There's got to be someone else working for him, but who?"

Josie put his hand on her belly so he could feel the baby kick. Instantly he began to calm down as he felt their child move. He kissed her and she said, "Evan, you're the smartest man I know and you're also patient. Just like you helped catch the men who killed your parents and sisters, you'll catch him, too. It's only a matter of time. It took six years to bring those killers to justice, but you helped do it. You'll get him, too."

The baby kicked as if agreeing with her, making Evan smile. "You're right. I will. I'm smart, but the smartest thing I ever did was marrying you."

"That's right and don't you forget it," she said.

Her confidence in him bolstered his resolve and as he lay there feeling his child move under his hand, that resolve turned titanium in strength.

Chapter Nineteen

Thad had lit a cigarette and put his feet up on the other chair in the sheriff's office. "So you want me to play spy, huh?"

"Yeah. You're not on a job right now and I could really use your help. I'll pay you," Evan said.

"Since when have I ever charged you for helping out with a personal matter? I don't want your money. Besides, I'd like to see him strung up as much as you would," Thad said.

"Well, this is still law enforcement business," Evan said.

"It's more personal and you know it. I'm not takin' any money from you. I got paid well on the last job I did. I'll start tonight."

"Ok. The boys and Homer are gonna be keeping a watch on things out at the farm."

Thad nodded. "Good. I can't do all their work for them."

Evan laughed. "I'll tell them you said that."

"So when's my nephew or niece gonna get here? Should be any day now, right?"

"Yep. You gonna stick around to see the baby born?"

Thad had just returned to town again after having been away for most of May. "I'm gonna stick around. I just need a different place to stay."

"Why? Are the Hanovers that full?"

Thad grimaced. "No. Phoebe and I are over. She was seeing someone else while I was out of town and I just can't get past it."

Evan slumped back against his chair a little. "Hell, Thad. I didn't know. When did this happen? Just now?"

"No. Back in March."

"March?" Evan asked. "You're just tellin' me now?"

Thad shrugged. "I didn't want to talk about it. Still don't."

Evan knew that Thad was hurting over the situation if he didn't want to talk about it. The bounty hunter talked about anything if it didn't matter to him. He could tell that this mattered very much to his friend.

"I'm sorry, Thad."

"It's ok. It's not like I was gonna marry her or anything. Maybe this other guy offered to. I don't know. So do you know anyone else who might have a room? I'm gonna miss that tub."

Evan's lips twitched. "Win has a nice tub."

Thad laughed. "I don't think him and Erin want me using it."

"Probably not. Don't let on to Aunt Edna that you need a place to stay. She'll tell you to stay with her."

Thad laughed even harder at that idea. "You're right. She would."

"You can always sleep on the sofa," Evan said. "I'll make her behave."

"I'll do that if I have to, but nobody makes Edna do anything," Thad said and got up. "I'll report back to you in the morning, boss."

"Ok. See ya then," Evan said, grinning as he thought how true Thad's statement about his aunt was.

Thad had made sure that Barkley was in for the night before making his first circuit around the property. He discovered nothing out of the ordinary before arriving back at the tree he was using for cover. He would have liked to have lit a cigarette, but the lighter flame and the glow from one would have given away his position. Hoof beats sounded on the driveway and he saw a lone rider come up to the house.

As he watched the rider dismount and tie the horse to the hitching post, he felt a jolt of recognition.

Phoebe? What the hell are you doing here?

He watched her walk into the house without knocking or using a key. Disbelief turned to fury and it was only giving away his presence that kept him from charging into the house. She'd been seeing Earnest? The thought of that he'd possibly been sharing Phoebe with Earnest made him nauseas.

Anyone but him, Phoebe. Please tell me it's not true.

He leaned against the tree as a single tear escaped the corner of his eye and trailed slowly down his face.

"Please, Marvin," Phoebe pleaded. "Please let me stay."

"Phoebe, you have to go. We're through. I've told you that several times," Marvin said.

"I know, but I love you," she said. "I need you."

"No, you don't. You're just lonely. I don't want to be with you when you're pining for someone else," Marvin said as he pulled Phoebe from his room.

"Is this a test? I've told you that I'm not seeing anyone but you now," she said.

Marvin would have welcomed this sort of declaration if he knew it had been a decision she'd wanted to make. He'd learned that Thad had broken things off with her, not the other way around.

"No, it's not a test. I'm just bored with you now and I've moved on. So should you," Marvin said.

"You don't understand. I'm pregnant."

Marvin halted on the stairs with her, staring into her eyes. He broke into laughter, startling her. "Oh, how splendid. You're with child and you think it's mine."

"Well, it's not Thad's."

"That means that you've been seeing a third man because it's not mine, Phoebe. I'm physically incapable of having children."

She grew angry. "You're a lying bastard."

Marvin pressed her against the wall and held her lightly by the throat. "I might lie about all kinds of things, Phoebe, but not that. If I thought there was any chance that you might have conceived my child, I would marry you tomorrow just so that I could raise it. I'd give almost anything to be able to father a child. No, this child belongs to the bounty hunter."

Then Marvin ushered her down the stairs and opened the front door. Moving her out onto the porch, he said, "Leave, Phoebe, and don't come back again. I don't ever want to see you here again."

He slammed the door shut and locked it, something he never did. Going into the kitchen, he locked that door, too.

Out on the front porch, Phoebe stood still for a moment before banging on the door.

"Marvin! Please! Don't shut me out! Please! I need you! Please!"

Marvin sat on the stairs, tears dripping from his eyes as he listened to her cries. The woman he loved was pregnant with another man's child. Pain unlike any he'd ever known gripped him as his masculinity took another blow. He'd never father a child and a child was what he most wanted in this world.

Phoebe leaned against the door, sobbing her heartache to the empty veranda. Finally realizing that Marvin wasn't going to answer the door again, she ran to her horse and mounted. Wheeling the horse around, she galloped down the driveway, unaware that the other man who loved her watched her speed away.

As Thad took up his usual position at the Earnest residence, he had to work hard to fight the urge to kick in Marvin's door and work him over.

He'd watched the place the past two nights, but never saw Marvin leaving the house nor anyone coming to the ranch. It was hard to block out the memory of Phoebe pleading with Marvin not to reject her.

That night, he had the feeling that his efforts were futile. It also reinforced his and Evan's belief that Marvin had someone working for him. Still, he took his job seriously and settled in for the night.

Shadow returned to the sheep farm after leaving it alone for a few nights. He circled the perimeter, assessing the situation. His highly developed night vision enabled him to see everything clearly even though there was no moon that night. Years spent in darkness had given him that advantage.

Scanning the field, he made out Lucky sitting right in the middle of the flock. Billy sat near the tipi and Win sat in a chair on the cabin porch. Shadow always admired his enemies' cunning and the way the three farmers had positioned themselves was very smart. Someone without his special vision wouldn't have been able to see Lucky and Billy.

Win was plainly visible, but that was by design. It gave any intruders the idea that he was the only one guarding the herd, thus giving them a false sense of security. His elevated position also gave Win a better position from which to see out over the field. Shadow also saw that Billy had Homer with him. It was a good thing that he'd made friends with most of the dogs around Echo so that they didn't make a racket whenever he came around various houses. Homer would have attacked him otherwise.

His objective that night was to kill one of their two rams. Breeding season would soon begin and losing a ram would hamper them. Slowly, he crept towards the pen. A movement to his left stopped him. It was Sugar. Shadow smiled until the burro flattened her ears and squealed. It was an angry sound.

The burro quieted when he stood still for a few moments, but as soon as he took a couple of steps forward, she let out another squeal. Shadow growled under his breath. He couldn't afford to have her make a commotion. He would have to come back another night.

Although he started backing up, Sugar grunted and advanced on him. Keeping a watch on the three men, Shadow moved towards the woods. Sugar squealed louder and rushed him. Shadow couldn't take the time to kill her, so he ran for the tree line. He almost made it when something pierced his shoulder.

The pain was excruciating and the force of the missle knocked him off balance. Shadow slammed into a tree with bone-jarring intensity. Calling on a deep well of determination, he steadied himself and reached behind him for what he knew had to be an arrow. He hadn't heard a gunshot, so an arrow was the only other weapon that could have hit him so swiftly. Fortunately, he was able to reach it. He couldn't run through the forest with it sticking out of his back. Bracing himself, he grabbed onto the arrow and yanked it out. He gritted his teeth until he was sure they would crack, but he never uttered a sound of pain. Letting it drop to the ground, he fled.

It was imperative that he stay ahead of them so he could reach the safety of the tunnel leading to his lair. His strength and excellent conditioning allowed him to run at almost full speed despite his injury. Warm blood ran down his back. He hoped his shirt would soak it up enough to prevent leaving a blood trail. Looking over his shoulder, he saw movement behind him. Homer was closing on him. Shadow stopped long enough to give him the command to stay and then ran away again.

Homer was still sitting there when Lucky caught up to him.

"Homer, sic 'em, please!"

Homer never did anything unless asked politely. He whined, but didn't budge.

"Sic 'em, please!" Lucky said louder.

The dog set out after Shadow again, but he wasn't sure who he was supposed to listen to, so he didn't run at full speed. Lucky cursed their unknown enemy. He must have gotten to Homer, too. Whoever it was had planned carefully, but he hadn't counted on Sugar. Lucky grinned as he followed Homer again.

Shadow was beginning to weaken, so he wasn't quite as alert as usual and he hadn't noticed Billy heading for him from his right flank. Billy jumped him and they rolled together. Shadow was thankful that it was almost pitch-black in the forest so that Billy couldn't see his face. Instinct kicked in and he swiftly dealt with the younger man.

Lucky and Win had taught Billy various fighting techniques and he was strong, but he was still no match for Shadow, who was a master at several fighting disciplines.

Billy got in a few good punches as they faced off, but he didn't expect Shadow to roll right at his legs. Pushing through his intense pain, Shadow took him down, grabbing his left arm at the same time. They came to rest with Billy on his stomach and Shadow on top of him. He shoved Billy's arm up behind his back so hard that it dislocated his shoulder

A debilitating, searing pain followed the pop Billy heard in his shoulder. He screamed and then passed out. Shadow sprang to his feet and ran again. He knew the woods around Echo better than anyone and he now took the most direct route to the secret entrance. Lucky would stop to help Billy so he was home free since he was sure that Win had stayed back to guard the farm in case someone else was working with him.

By the time he reached the entrance, Shadow labored heavily, his steps much slower and unsteady. He managed to pick up the tree branch he always used to erase his tracks and scrub the ground with it. Then he opened the door, slipping inside the tunnel, and secured the door behind him.

He leaned against the wall, gathering his strength so he could make it the rest of the way home.

Chapter Twenty

When Billy woke up, he felt disoriented until he realized he was being carried.

"Lucky?" he croaked hopefully.

"Aye, lad. We'll be home in just a minute."

"Let me down. I'm gonna be sick."

His intense pain combined with the rapid movements caused his stomach to roil. Lucky stopped and eased Billy down from his shoulder. He held Billy upright when his knees buckled. Lucky wanted to cry when he saw Billy's left arm hanging uselessly at his side. He'd thought Billy had just been knocked out, not injured.

Billy held on to Lucky for support while he heaved. The action increased his pain and he almost passed out again. When his stomach settled down, he said, "He did something to my arm. I think it's dislocated."

"'Tis. I've seen dislocations before. Can you walk?"

"I think so."

Lucky kept the pace slow to avoid jarring Billy's shoulder.

"When we find this son of a bitch, I'm gonna kill him, but I'm gonna make him suffer first," Lucky said. "And I'm gonna enjoy every second of it. I know how to do things to a man that'll make him pray for death."

"Can we not talk about that right now?" The images Lucky's statement evoked made him feel queasy again.

"Sorry, lad."

When they came around the front of Win's cabin, Lucky called out to him. "Help me get him inside."

Win jumped down from the porch and ran to them. "What happened?"

"I jumped that guy and the next thing I knew, he did something to my arm and it hurt so bad I passed out," Billy said.

They got him inside and sat him on the sofa. Erin came out of the bedroom.

"What happened?" she asked as soon as she saw Billy.

Lucky said, "Billy tangled with the guy who was here and he dislocated his shoulder. I got him, though. I found the bloody arrow. Good for him. I hope he dies, God help me."

Erin sat down next to Billy and began examining him. Billy winced a couple of times, but didn't flinch away from her gentle touch.

"This has to be reduced," Erin said. "I won't lie to you, Billy; it's going to be very painful. I'm going to give you some laudanum and some cocaine injections at the site to help, but it won't keep the pain away completely."

"Great," Billy said. "Why am I always the one who gets hurt? Last year it was the earthquake and now it's this."

Win had also looked Billy's shoulder over. "Whoever did this knew what he was doing and is very strong. This is something that has to be done in close contact. Did you recognize him?"

"No. It was too dark. He's bigger than me—not taller, but heavier. And he had long hair. I think it was brown. I'm not sure," Billy said.

Seeing he was becoming distressed, Erin said, "Don't worry about that right now. Let's get this taken care of for you."

"Ok."

Erin administered the shots and gave Billy a dose of laudanum.

"Lucky, sit on the other side of Billy," Win said.

"Why?"

"I want you to catch him," Win said walking over to Billy.

Lucky sat next to Billy, who watched Win intently.

"Billy, I'm going to make you sleep. That way, you'll be spared a lot of pain," Win said.

"You're gonna hit me?" Billy asked.

"No. I'll just use a pressure point. Just relax," Win said, putting his thumb against the sensitive area in back of Billy's ear. "Goodnight."

He gave the area a hard jab with his thumb and Billy's eyes fluttered shut. Lucky caught his slack body, giving Win a look of amazement.

"How'd ya do that?"

Win smiled. "That's a secret and not something to try if you don't know what you're doing."

Erin was also impressed. "I know those pressure points exist, but I've never seen anyone use them before. Let's take him into our room where we'll have more space."

Lucky hefted Billy and bore him into the bedroom, depositing him on the bed. As he looked at the Indian boy who'd become a little brother to him, the Irishman vowed to find the culprit and make him pay.

Shadow was indeed paying. Bree had gotten Marvin, who had raced to Shadow's bedroom, where she'd already lit several lamps. He was shocked at all of the blood on the sheets and carpet. His brother lay face-down on the bed, blood still oozing from the deep arrow wound.

"Shadow! What happened?" Marvin asked as he began looking at the wound.

Shadow's brain was foggy from the loss of blood. "Damn burro."

"What? Bree, go start boiling water and bring me some cloths from the cabinet in the bathroom," Marvin said. He might not be able to do ranch work, but he had acquired quite a bit of medical knowledge over the years so he would know what to do in case something like this occurred. It was imperative to stop the bleeding, especially since Shadow had already lost so much.

Bree hurried to do his bidding, her heart pounding with terror over Shadow's plight. She raced into the kitchen and put the water on to boil. Collecting the linens Marvin wanted, she ran back to the bedroom and gave them to Marvin.

"Thank you," Marvin said. "Go outside and dig up some dirt, preferably from the backyard. It's looser out there. You'll need to separate it from the grass. Can you do that?"

"Of course." She ran off again.

Out in the yard, she used a large spoon to dig up the dirt, making sure to leave the grass behind. She cried as she dug, terrified that she was going to lose Shadow. Other people didn't know him the way she did. If they knew about him, they wouldn't understand what made him do the things he did, why his heart was so black. They wouldn't see the kindness he'd shown her; they wouldn't see his sense of humor or intelligence. All they would see was the monster Shadow thought himself.

Once the bowl she'd brought with her was full, she rushed back to Shadow's bedroom, where Marvin was washing Shadow's wound and the blood from his back. He looked up as she came in. "Mix some water with the dirt until it turns to mud."

Bree left the room again. Marvin still hadn't been able to get Shadow to tell him what had happened. "Shadow, how did you get hurt?"

"Damn burro."

Marvin ground his teeth in frustration. "Shadow!" He slapped the back of his head.

The light blow roused Shadow. "What?"

"What happened?"

Shadow told Marvin his tale, but Marvin occasionally had to slap him again to get him to continue whenever he lapsed back into semiconsciousness. Bree returned with the mud and Marvin packed the wound with it to stem the blood flow and help it coagulate. He gave Shadow a dose of laudanum.

Once his brother slumbered, Marvin sat down in a chair and closed his eyes.

"Marvin."

Bree touched his shoulder lightly and he opened them. "Yes?"

"What should I do now? How can I help him?"

"There's not much else to be done at the moment. In the morning, I'll go to Dr. Avery and buy the appropriate supplies from her."

Bree's terror grew. "But then she'll know about him."

"No, she won't. I'm not going to tell her. Don't worry. I'll do everything in my power to keep him alive. I won't let him die. I can't. He's the only person who loves me and he's my other half. I don't expect you to understand. We need each other. If he dies, so will I."

Bree gazed at Shadow's still form and tears ran from her eyes. "I do understand."

Wonder stole over Marvin. "You love him, too, don't you?"

"Yes, I do."

Marvin took her hand and said, "I guess we have that in common."

"We have much more in common than you think, Marvin, but I don't want to talk about it right now." She squeezed his hand.

"You're right, Bree. There will be time for that later on. Go lie down with him and get some rest. You'll need it."

As they finished tending to Shadow the next morning, Marvin said, "You'll have to bear with Shadow. He's going to be very bad tempered. He always is when he's sick or hurt."

"That's ok. I can handle him," Bree said. "You might not think so, but I can."

Marvin smiled. "Actually, I do believe you. Something about you gets through to him. I don't know what it is, but I'm thankful for it."

"Thank you," Bree said as she ran a hand over Shadow's arm.

Marvin watched the loving gesture and he was both happy for his brother and a little jealous. Thoughts of Phoebe crowded his mind, but he buried them again. There was no point in dwelling on that hopeless situation.

"I'll be back. I'll go get those medical supplies from Dr. Avery," Marvin said.

Bree asked, "What will you tell her?"

"Don't worry. I already have a story prepared for her," Marvin said. "That's one of the things I'm best at. Strategy and conniving." He looked at his sleeping brother. "I've had to be in order to keep him safe."

"You're completely devoted to him, aren't you?" she asked.

Marvin nodded. "Yes. We are all each other has truly had for so long and I'll do anything for him. Everything I've done over the years has been for him, to try to make up for all of the horrendous things he had to endure until I found him. I should be going. I'll be back just as soon as I can."

As he passed by Bree, he put a hand on her shoulder. "Thank you for your help. I can't tell you how much I appreciate it."

"I'm just repaying all of the kindness you've both shown me," she said.

He smiled, patted her shoulder, and went on his way.

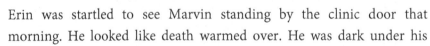

Erin was startled to see Marvin standing by the clinic door that morning. He looked like death warmed over. He was dark under his eyes and he looked older.

"Marvin, what's wrong?"

He gave her a sad smile and said, "May we talk inside?"

"Certainly."

Once they stepped into the waiting room, Marvin locked the door behind them. Erin became uneasy.

"Dr. Avery, I have a rather unusual request. I need medical supplies for a friend of mine. I can't tell you who she is because she's a very private person. She had an accident on her farm and is in need of bandages and other supplies."

"What kind of injury is it?" she asked.

Marvin lied very convincingly and now was no exception. "She tripped on a pitchfork. She has a couple of severe punctures to her calf. It was lucky for her that I had gone to see her and I arrived about a half an hour after this happened. She had stopped the bleeding for the most part, but she doesn't have the proper supplies needed. I washed it for her and applied a mud pack, but that will only last for so long."

Mud-packing wounds was a fast remedy that peoples from all over the world had used for thousands of years. Erin was surprised that Marvin knew about such things.

"Where did you learn that?"

"One of my friends from boarding school was the son of a doctor, and at one time I wanted to be a physician. He put me in touch with his father and I exchanged letters with him about all sorts of medical conditions. I read medical books and took notes, which I still have."

"Why didn't you pursue a career as a doctor?"

"My family lost quite a bit of money when the mines around here went dry. We needed our money to hang onto the ranch and money for medical school was out of the question. Then my parents passed away and building our business again became my main focus in life. I'm happy to report that things are looking up there."

"I see," Erin said. "I'm sorry to hear that."

"Thank you. Now, about those supplies." He handed her a small satchel.

"Yes, of course. I really would prefer to come see your friend," Erin said.

Marvin replied, "I would prefer it, too, but she won't budge. I'm afraid she doesn't want it known that we're seeing each other, so I would appreciate it if you didn't say anything about this."

"Of course. I'll get what you'll need," she said, going to the supply closet and putting iodine-treated gauze bandages, salve, and carbolic acid into the satchel.

Then she went back to waiting room, but stopped just before entering. Marvin sat on one of the chairs with his head in his hands. She surmised that whoever this lady was, he cared about her very much to be so upset.

"Here you are, Marvin," she said.

He raised his head and stood up. "Thank you so much," he said, taking the satchel from her. Marvin handed her a hundred dollar bill. "I think that should cover everything. If not, let me know. I'll be glad to give you more."

Erin took the money even though it was too much. He would have been offended if she'd refused it. "Thank you. That's very generous of you."

"It's well worth it."

Erin put a hand on his arm. "If things worsen, please convince your friend to let me come see her?"

Her kindness touched Marvin. "I will, and thank you again."

She nodded and he left.

Chapter Twenty-One

Josie sat up against the headboard as another mild contraction squeezed her. When it eased, she ran her fingertips over Evan's temple, smoothing his dark hair away from his face. He needed a haircut again, but he hadn't gotten it done yet. Looking down at her husband, she couldn't believe that she'd known him for a year now. And now they were about to become parents.

"Evan. Wake up." She tugged a little on his ear and giggled.

"What is it, honey?" he mumbled.

"I have something to ask you."

"Are you hungry again?"

She laughed. "No. I was wondering if you wanted to have a baby today."

Her words registered and Evan sat up, completely alert now. "It's time?"

Josie nodded. "It's time."

He grinned and put a hand on her stomach. "Our little deputy is ready to be born, huh?"

"Yes."

Leaning over, he gave Josie a soft kiss. "Well, Mrs. Sheriff, I guess I'll go get Dr. Avery."

"Not just yet," Josie said. "There's time. I'm so excited."

Evan sat against the headboard and put an arm about her shoulders. "Me, too. I can't wait to hold our baby."

"I know."

A stronger contraction hit her and Josie groaned a little. "I guess you should go get Erin."

"Right. I'll alert the old woman that the time is nigh, as she keeps saying."

Josie laughed. "I love hearing her say that."

"That makes one of us," Evan said as he dressed. "I'm glad she won't be able to say it anymore."

"Be nice, Evan."

He said, "That was nice."

She chuckled. She liked hearing Evan and Edna's banter. "Go get the doctor, Sheriff."

"Yes, ma'am."

"This really isn't fair," Billy said. "I almost missed your wedding last year and now I'm gonna miss your baby being born."

It had been a week since his run-in with Shadow and Billy was still in a lot of pain. "I'm bored as hell, I can't sleep, and I can't even get dressed by myself."

Evan felt bad for Billy, but he said, "Quit whining and put on some pants. You didn't think you were gonna get out of it, did you?"

"What? I just told you I didn't want to and I just told you I can't dress myself," Billy said. The laudanum made him very fuzzy.

Erin readied her bag. "Ok. I'm all set."

Win came back in the cabin. "Horse is saddled, doctor."

"Thank you, doctor."

Lucky had followed Win. "I'll help Billy get dressed and we'll be along."

"What's this 'we' stuff?" he asked. "I can't go anywhere. Look at me."

The Irishman smiled. "Well, we're all used to you bein' in your underwear now since you've been here all week, so you might as well get Edna used to it."

Evan laughed. "She won't mind, that's for sure."

Billy held his shoulder while he laughed. "I hate you guys. Ok. Let's go."

"We're only jokin', lad. You have to put pants on," Lucky said.

Billy frowned. "Make up your mind."

Evan said, "We'll see you at the house."

Evan paced and paced and paced. He didn't pace alone, though. He and Lucky passed each other in the parlor as Josie labored upstairs. Billy was sound asleep on the sofa, Win sat calmly in a wingback chair, and Thad watched Evan and Lucky pace from another chair.

After a particularly loud cry from Josie, Evan bounded up the stairs, certain that catastrophe had struck. Men weren't supposed to be in the room when their wives were giving birth, he knew. Therefore, he was hesitant to knock on their bedroom door and disturb those inside the bedroom.

He tried to call on his sheriff's composure, but right then he wasn't a sheriff. He was a scared husband and father who needed reassurance. None of the men downstairs were much help. He'd been over at Billy's parents' house with Arlene and Remus, but then he'd come over home again when things had progressed further along.

Josie let out a long groan and Evan's worry increased. He decided to knock, figuring the worst that could happen was that they would yell at him to leave.

He rapped lightly on the door. "Hello in there. I'm just, uh, I was wondering how things are going."

Erin said, "Everything is fine, Evan."

Relief made him grin. "Ok. Thanks. I love you, honey."

"I love you, too," Josie said through gritted teeth.

Now that he was up there, Evan didn't want to go back downstairs. He sat in the hallway instead.

"Evan?" Josie shouted.

"I'm right here."

"Where?"

"In the hallway."

"Why?"

"I got tired and had to sit down," he said.

He heard Josie giggle. "I'm a little tired myself."

Evan picked up the bantering rhythm that went on in their household at bedtime. "I don't know why. I'm the one doing all the work. Pacing is exhausting."

"I know," Josie said. "Husbands have it very hard during childbirth."

"We really do. I mean, you get to just lay back and relax. But me? Oh no. I gotta spend the time looking at a bunch of ugly guys downstairs. That's the real reason I came up here. I got tired of looking at them and Billy's snoring is enough to drive you crazy. He snores worse than you."

"I do not SNORE!" Josie protested and began pushing again.

Erin and Edna encouraged her while she groaned and screamed.

Evan couldn't stay away anymore and he opened the door, slipping inside. The three women looked at him in shock.

"What? You act like you've never seen a man want to be with his wife while she's giving birth to their baby," Evan said defensively.

Josie was thrilled to see her husband and reached out a hand to him. "If you stay, you can't tell me how to do this," she teased him.

He rolled his eyes. "Don't you know that sheriffs know everything about having babies?"

Edna snorted. "The only thing you know about it is making them."

"Shut up, old woman," Evan said. "I know more than you think I do."

Erin had never had a husband present for a birth before, but when Evan sat down on the bed with Josie, she knew he wasn't going to leave again. As long as Josie didn't mind, Erin wasn't going to object.

He turned to his wife. "Are you gonna take all day to have this kid or what?"

Josie grabbed his forearm and latched on as another contraction hit. Evan grunted in surprise over her painful grip, but said nothing about it. He watched her pant and he saw the pain in her beautiful face. But he saw fierce determination unlike anything he'd ever witnessed there, too. He stayed quiet, letting her concentrate, but he put his hand on her arm, offering her silent encouragement.

Erin said, "Keep pushing, Josie. The baby's crowning. Almost there."

Evan wished there was more he could do to help.

"Oh, God, I'm so tired," Josie said, slumping back.

Edna said, "Now, now. You better keep going. I'm waiting to hold that baby."

"I get it first," Evan said. "I'm the father after all."

"Well, I've been in here the whole time," Edna countered.

"I don't care," Evan said.

Erin said, "Ok, you can argue about this later. Josie, push."

Josie shook her head.

Evan kissed her and said, "If you don't get this baby born, I'm going to tell everyone that you snore."

She glared at him before gathering herself and pushing with the next contraction.

The number of people downstairs had grown as dawn had come. Tansy and Sonya were waiting there as well, ready to help. Not only did they hear Erin and Edna urging Josie onward, they heard her husband, too. None of them had ever known a man to be present in the birthing room, but Thad told them to calm down.

"This is Evan. He does all kinds of stuff no one expects him to. Why should this be any different? Besides, they didn't throw him out, so it must be ok," he said.

Watching their daughter come into the world together was the most beautiful experience of Josie and Evan's lives, and Evan held his wife while Erin tended to the baby. Once Erin had cleaned up the baby, she handed her to Josie, who cradled her, a look of wonder on her face as she looked at the little miracle they'd made.

Evan cried openly as he kissed Josie. "She's beautiful just like you, honey," he told her. "Thank you for our little girl. I love you so much."

"I love you, too," she said, crying right with him. Smiling tiredly, she said, "You can't tell anyone about my snoring now because here she is."

Evan chuckled. "Yep. Here she is."

"She has your dark hair, Evan," she said touching it.

He beamed. "Yeah, but she has your smile."

Josie laughed. "She hasn't smiled yet. How do you know that?"

"Call it a hunch. I am a sheriff, after all," he said.

The three women laughed at him and he joined them. Josie handed the baby to Edna, who also wept happy tears.

"Oh, my goodness. She's perfect! Look at that darling little nose and those sweet cheeks."

She didn't see Josie and Evan exchange a look.

Josie said, "That's right, Grandma. Now you have a pretty baby to play with."

Edna gave them a startled look. "Grandma?"

Evan became teary-eyed again as he said, "You became my mother all those years ago, and to Josie, too, so we thought it fitting that you be called Grandma."

Edna's throat constricted and she couldn't respond right away. "I can't tell you how honored I am. I'll be the best Grandma to her."

Josie said, "We know you will."

Erin said, "Sheriff, I'm kicking you out. Take your daughter to meet the rest of the family."

Josie watched Evan carefully take their daughter from Edna and smiled at the sight of the tiny baby in Evan's large hands. She fell in love with him all over again as she watched him with her. Then Erin shooed him from the room.

As they heard Evan descend the stairs, everyone in the parlor quieted. When he entered the room, he grinned and said, "Everyone, say hello to Julia Rose Taft."

Quiet exclamations and congratulations filled the parlor. Evan thanked them all.

"Uncle Thad, would you like to hold your niece?" he asked.

"You bet. It's been years since I've held a baby. The last one was you, as I recall," Thad said as he took Julia from Evan. Looking down into her pink little face, he said, "Well, Julia, welcome to the family. Boy, Evan, she looks like your pa an awful lot."

Evan swallowed hard and said, "I thought so, too, but I think she's gonna have Josie's smile. I hope she has blue eyes, too."

"She just might. You and Josie make beautiful babies."

"Thanks," Evan said.

Julia was passed around, seeming not to care about all of the fuss. Only Billy hadn't held her since he'd fallen asleep again. Lucky gave Billy's boot a hard nudge.

"Billy, wake up," he said.

Rousing, Billy looked around with bleary eyes. "What? Isn't that baby born yet?"

They all laughed at him and he spotted the little bundle in Lucky's arms. "Oh! My turn!" He held out his good arm.

Lucky chuckled and sat down by him. "I don't think ya takin' her with only one arm is a good idea."

He transferred the baby to Billy, who smiled at her. "Boy or girl?"

"Julia Rose," Evan responded.

"Congratulations, Evan," Billy said. "She's real pretty. Hi, Julia. I'm your Uncle Billy. We're gonna have a lot of fun together. I'll teach you how to paint and draw."

"That'll be nice, Billy," Evan said.

"Mmm hmm," Billy said, his eyes falling shut again.

Lucky put a supporting arm under the baby as Billy's head dropped onto Lucky's shoulder. Evan said, "I wish I had a picture of that, Lucky. Aunt Edna would get a real kick out of it."

Thad said, "I'll go get her."

When Edna saw the sweet sight the Irishman and the sleeping Indian made while they both held the baby, she laughed until her eyes swam with tears. "Thad, you go get Dan right now. I don't care if he's still in bed or not. I want a picture of that for Josie."

"Yes, ma'am," Thad said and left immediately.

When he returned a short time later with Dan, the photographer had them all crowd around the sofa so they could all be photographed with the baby. He took a couple of group pictures and then a few individual pictures with Evan and Edna and some other combinations before leaving. He promised to get them developed as quickly as possible.

Evan said to Julia, "I better get you back to your ma now."

Everyone said goodbye to the baby and Evan took her back upstairs.

Chapter Twenty-Two

As Erin and Win sat at dinner a week later, Win noticed how quiet she was.

"Penny for your thoughts," he said.

"Hmm?"

Win said, "I asked what you're thinking about."

"I was just thinking about a patient. Well, she's not a patient of mine exactly. A lady friend of Marvin's."

Win perked up at that. "She hasn't been to see you?"

"No. He keeps coming to buy supplies from me, which I don't mind, but I'm worried about her. He says she won't come see me and she won't let anyone come to her house, either."

"Why not?" Win asked. This sounded suspicious to him.

"He said that she doesn't trust anyone but him."

Win was quiet a moment, then, "When did he first come to you about this?"

"A couple of weeks ago. Why?"

"Right after the night that guy was here?" Win asked.

Erin nodded. "I guess so. You can't think he was involved."

"I can and I do," Win said. "The timing seems strange to me. What kind of problem is this woman having?"

"She tripped and fell on a pitchfork. He said she has two puncture wounds on her leg, so I've been giving him gauze and other things," she said. "It's for a woman, not a man."

"So he says. Erin, I wish you would listen to me about him. He's lying. I've known him since I was a kid and even then he was slippery and sneaky. He's insane," Win said.

Erin was irritated. "I haven't seen any evidence of that. What I've seen is a man who's concerned about a friend."

"Earnest doesn't have friends. He has employees and victims."

She pursed her lips and fell silent. The stubborn set of her jaw told Win that the discussion was over. He didn't want this to develop into a full-blown fight.

"Erin, I'm glad that he doesn't give you any trouble. I'm going to tell Evan about this, though. He's been working hard on this case and any lead is worth checking out," Win said.

"Fine," Erin said as she rose from the table. She took her plate to the counter and scraped the couple of bites into a can sitting there. Whatever scraps they had would be given to the dogs.

Win sighed. "Look, I don't want to fight about this. Can we agree to disagree?"

He joined her at the sink and scraped his plate, too. When Erin saw that he was genuinely sorry, she said, "Ok. I think that's probably a good idea."

"Good. I'm going to go talk to him and I'll check on Billy, too." He smiled. "When I get back, we can read our story."

"Actually, I have some charts to take care of," she said.

"Can't you work on them while I'm gone?" he asked.

She replied, "Yes, but I don't know how long it'll take me."

Putting his arms around her waist, he said, "Ok. I'll wait until you're finished."

"Ok," she said, but didn't sound thrilled.

His irritation showed. "Never mind. Have fun with your charts. Don't wait up. I'm not sure when I'll be back."

"Fine."

He strode from the cabin, his back rigid with anger. Pride prevented her from going after him. She couldn't help her opinion about Marvin. She knew that he and Evan had a history, but people made mistakes and she'd seen how kind Marvin was towards this woman. There'd been no hint of anything suspicious. It seemed to her that Win was overreacting about this.

It was irritating how he pushed aside her opinion, making her feel that she was being silly and naïve about Marvin. Until he gave her a reason to distrust him, she would continue helping him with his friend. She knew that she and Win would have to talk about this, but she wasn't looking forward to it. It was the first time that they'd argued about something. She put it all aside as she did the dishes and got to work on her charts.

Marvin looked at Evan and Thad with anger in his eyes. "I don't have time for this."

His attitude surprised Evan. Usually Marvin displayed smug amusement, but he was irritable and he looked harried and a little unkempt.

As they stepped into the foyer, Evan asked, "Where is he?"

Running a hand through his hair, Marvin asked, "Who are you looking for now?" He knew full well whom they were talking about.

Thad said, "The guy you sent to sabotage the sheep farm."

Hatred flashed in Marvin's eyes as he looked at the man who'd gotten Phoebe pregnant. "Don't you have other more important things to do than harass me? Like tend to your baby?"

Evan said, "Don't you worry about my daughter. This has you stamped all over it."

A malicious grin curved Marvin's lips as he kept his attention on

Thad. "I wasn't talking about *your* baby, I was talking about *his.*"

Thad's brow furrowed. "Have you finally completely lost your marbles? I don't have a baby."

Marvin's chuckle was a sarcastic noise. "I know you don't—not yet. Congratulations, Mr. McIntyre."

Thad stepped close to Marvin. "What are you sayin'?"

"Oh, I didn't realize Phoebe hadn't spoken to you about it. I'm sorry. She informed me a couple of weeks ago that she's with child. You see, we've been seeing each other for a couple of years now, or didn't you know?"

A shockwave of astonishment shook Evan and Thad. Evan hadn't known anything about Phoebe seeing Marvin. Thad didn't know that Marvin was aware of his relationship with Phoebe.

Marvin laughed at their stunned expressions. "I see you didn't. Oh, but I knew about you, Thad."

"You rotten bastard," Thad said, his voice filled with quiet rage. "Prepare to meet your maker." He pulled his gun and aimed it at Marvin's forehead.

"Now, now, Thad. If you kill me in cold blood, the sheriff here will arrest you and you'll never see your child," Marvin said.

"How do I know you're telling the truth about her being pregnant?"

"Ask her. I stopped seeing her a couple of months ago because I was tired of her lack of commitment. I love her and I've asked her several times to marry me, but she won't. I couldn't take the rejection any longer. The last time she came to see me, I told her never to come back."

Thad glowered at him, his finger itching to pull the trigger and rid the world of Marvin. "How do you know the kid ain't yours?"

"Because I'm incapable of fathering a child."

Evan spoke up. "You tried to tell me that about Louise, too, but you got her pregnant."

Fury sparkled in Marvin's eyes. "No, I did not!" He further shocked them by undoing his pants and dropping them. He pointed to the scar on his groin area and said, "This is from a botched inguinal hernia repair when I was fifteen. I can perform quite adequately in bed, but I can't impregnate anyone, which I'm sure pleases you no end. Ask Dr. Avery if you don't believe me." He pulled his pants back up and fastened them again. "Now, if you'll excuse me, I have things to do."

Thad had lowered his gun, numb with the realization that he was going to become a father at fifty-eight years of age. In this instance, he believed Marvin, having seen the proof of his previous injury. He'd gotten Phoebe pregnant. They'd always been careful, but nothing was foolproof.

Evan said, "All of this has no bearing on why we came here. Erin says you've been treating a 'friend' who was injured right around the time of the disturbance at the farm. Lucky shot the guy with an arrow, so he's gonna be laid up for a while. Seems funny that you're suddenly treating someone with a similar wound."

"Pure coincidence, Sheriff."

"Who is she?"

"I won't tell you. We're not ready for our relationship to be known."

"That's awfully convenient."

Marvin said, "You're grasping at straws. There's no one here who's hurt and there's no reason to divulge my friend's identity and give this town even more to talk about. It's no one's business. She's a very private person. As I said, I'm busy. Goodnight."

"Not so fast," Evan said. "Where's your houseguest? Miss Josephson? Is she the one who's hurt?"

"No, she's not. She went out to see the horses, I believe. She's very fond of them," Marvin said.

"I think we'll go find her," Evan said.

"Fine," Marvin said. "Be my guest."

Thad and Evan walked out of the house and Marvin slammed the door after them.

As they walked to the barn, Evan asked, "Are you ok?"

"I don't know. I can't believe it. I can't be a father at my age, Evan.

I'll be dead by the time the kid's twenty," Thad said.

Evan put a hand on his shoulder. "Thad, look at it as a blessing. You don't know that you're gonna die in twenty years."

Thad just looked at him. "I'll be seventy-eight and I've lived fast and hard. Men like me don't live to be ninety, you know. I can't believe this."

Evan said, "Maybe it's time to slow down."

"And do what? Being a bounty hunter is all I've ever known. It's too late for me to change careers. Besides, I get restless in one place. You know that."

Evan smiled as he thought about Julia. "Having a baby is more exciting than any chase, Thad. Trust me."

Thad sighed as they reached the barn. "I have to marry her, Evan, and the sooner the better. I don't even know how far along she is."

"It seems like you have a lot to talk about," Evan said. "I'm sorry, Thad. I know this is a shock, but it'll turn out all right."

"I wish I had your faith."

Evan fell silent as they began their search.

Meanwhile, inside, Marvin had alerted Bree that he needed her by ringing the lair bell three times. This was the number they'd settle on to differentiate whom Marvin wanted. She came through the secret door a minute later.

"What is it?" she asked.

"I need you to go upstairs to your room. Evan and Thad are here. They're looking for the person who tried to attack the sheep farm and they want to talk to you," he said.

"Oh. All right," she said. "I know what to do."

"Thank you," Marvin said.

"I'll do anything to protect him," she said.

Marvin smiled. "I know. Me, too. Go."

Bree hurried to the room they'd set up for her so it looked like she stayed there. Sitting down in the chair there, she waited for Marvin to call her to come down.

Not finding Bree, the two lawmen came back to the house.

When they came inside, Evan said, "I don't know what kind of game you're playing, but she's not out there."

Marvin's eyebrows lifted in surprise. "Oh. Maybe she came in and I didn't realize it. I was busy in my office going over some finances. I'll call her." Going over to the stairs, Marvin shouted, "Miss Josephson! Will you please come down?"

In a few moments, Bree appeared at the top of the staircase and made her way down. "What is it?"

Evan said, "Good evening, miss. I'd like to ask you a few questions, if you don't mind."

"Certainly. What's this about?"

Thad watched her, noting her calm demeanor. She seemed curious, but not nervous.

Bree was surprised by how good she was becoming at lying.

"Do you know who trespassed at the sheep farm a couple of weeks ago?"

She was taken aback. "At the sheep farm? Why would I know anything about that? I heard about it and about Billy being hurt, of course, but that's all I know."

"Who's Marvin taking care of?" Thad asked.

Bree gave him a level look and said, "I have no idea. He hasn't even told me and, frankly, it's none of my business."

Thad said, "Maybe it should be. I mean, he's had you here for a while and now he's seeing another woman. Do you know the kind of man you've been sleeping with?"

Bree became enraged. She slapped Thad hard across the face. "How dare you insult me as though I'm some whore?" She was fed up with men thinking of her in those terms and she wasn't going to allow it any longer. "Marvin and I are nothing more than friends. He's been kind and generous since I've been here. I asked if I could stay because I don't want to live alone and I don't know any single women who are looking for a roommate. I don't have to stand for this." She whirled around and proudly mounted the stairs again.

Marvin said, "I've had all I'm going to take. Your harassment has reached a new high and you've insulted my houseguest—a woman who has lost her father recently and has had to endure financial hardship in the wake of his death. Have you no compassion? Get out!"

Evan could have kicked Thad. Normally Thad used a little more tact than that, but the shock he'd received that night had obviously impaired his ability to keep a cool head. After Thad's insulting behavior, Bree wasn't going to answer any more questions.

"Let's go, Thad," Evan said, pulling on his arm.

Glaring at Marvin, Thad said, "If it's the last thing I do, I'm gonna find proof that you're behind all sorts of things and then you'll hang."

Marvin smirked and said, "Congratulations on your baby."

Evan yanked Thad out the door before he took a swing at Marvin.

Marvin sat on the stairs again, but this time, instead of crying, he shook with fury.

"You've made me very angry gentlemen and horrible things tend to happen when I'm angry. Very bad things indeed."

Chapter Twenty-Three

It was late when Win arrived home. He'd spent an hour or so with Billy and then he'd gone to Spike's where he'd sat and drank at the bar. He and Spike had chatted about this and that and then he'd played cards with Jerry. After that, he'd started home.

He tried to overlook Erin's continued defense of Marvin, telling himself she hadn't known him long enough to see what an evil man he was. It was hard because he felt as though she didn't believe him. He was her husband and she should trust him above all others.

Entering the dark cabin, he went into their bedroom, undressed, and got in bed.

"Win?"

He hadn't realized she was awake. "Yeah."

"I'm sorry about earlier."

Rolling over to face her, he said, "Me, too. I know you don't believe what I'm telling you, but it's the truth. Look what he did to Evan a few years ago. He's always tormenting Travis, and who knows what else he's done? We still think he was behind Evan's kidnapping last year."

"I know, but there's no proof."

"That's because he's smart and great liar. I don't know how he does the things he does, but we'll figure it out eventually," Win said.

"Seeing is believing. That's your motto, after all. Or it should be."

He frowned. "What's that supposed to mean?"

"It means that you don't believe in anything unless you have concrete proof of it. Well, I'm the same way. I just hate to see so much focus on Marvin when someone else could be responsible."

"Evan's the best lawman around, so if he thinks Marvin did it, then somehow, someway, Marvin *did* do it."

Win couldn't believe that once again, Marvin had somehow insinuated himself into another relationship and yet he had.

"If that's brought to light, then I'll apologize, but if it's not, I'm not going to ostracize the man for no reason."

"You have blinders on, Erin. You need to take them off. Why do you think so many people say things like that about him? Because it's true."

"Was it true when they said you couldn't be a good vet because you're Chinese? Or that you were strange because you kept to yourself so much? Or how about that you were nothing more than a bum, sleeping here and there? Everyone said those things, but they weren't true," Erin said.

He couldn't refute that and it made him even angrier. He rolled over the other way, got out of bed, and left the room. Erin heard the front door open and shut. She closed her eyes against the tears that filled them, but they snuck out from under her eyelids and trailed a slow path along her cheeks.

"When were you gonna tell me?" Thad asked, entering the kitchen at the Hanover House.

Phoebe jerked and almost dropped the pot of water she was putting on the stove to boil. He'd snuck up on her. She moved to face him. "Tell you what?"

His handsome face settled into a granite-hard expression. "That you're pregnant with my kid."

Phoebe looked around in panic, rushing to the hallway to make sure no one was there or in the other rooms downstairs. Returning to the kitchen, she said, "Don't talk so loud! Who told you?"

"Earnest. Who else? How could you do it to me? I thought I meant something to you," he said.

"You did. You do," Phoebe said, going over to him.

Staring down at her, Thad asked, "So you show it by sleeping with Earnest? It wouldn't be so bad if it was someone else, but why did it have to be *him*?"

"You'd never understand. I never meant to hurt you."

Thad snorted. "You're a liar. We'll have to get married so this baby has a decent home."

Phoebe shook her head. "I'm not marrying anyone and I don't even know that it's your baby."

"It is. Earnest can't father children because he had an injury when he was a kid. It's mine and I mean to raise it," Thad said.

Phoebe colored. "I don't want it."

His dark eyes narrowed. "You're not getting rid of it. If you don't want it, you'll have it and give it to me. Would marrying me be so bad?"

"Yes, because you'll always resent me for being with Marvin," Phoebe said. "We'll grow to hate each other and you know it."

Thad couldn't deny that. He'd never touch her again and he'd lost all respect for her. They'd end up fighting and that wasn't a good environment for a child.

"You'll have it and give it to me," Thad repeated.

"I can't have it. Everyone will know and I'll be shunned, an outcast. It'll be the same for you," Phoebe said. "Think about the baby. Everyone will always make fun of them."

"I'll protect them," Thad said. He looked at her abdomen and saw that it was thicker. "That's my baby and you're not gonna kill it."

Without another word, he left the kitchen, leaving Phoebe in a state of furious despair.

That evening around eight o'clock, Marvin had just come up from the lair after changing Shadow's dressing for the last time that day when he was startled by a knock on the kitchen door. He let out an exasperated groan when he saw through the door window that Phoebe stood on the other side.

Opening it, he asked, "What did I tell you?" He couldn't prevent the wave of desire that coursed through him even though she'd hurt him so much.

Her eyes were filled with hot rage. "How could you do it? How could you tell Thad?"

"I'm sorry about that. I didn't know you hadn't told him."

She pushed her way past him. "He wants me to keep it."

Marvin smiled. "So you're getting married then?"

"No! I'm never marrying anyone! I'm getting rid of it. I can't have it. I'll be subjected to all kinds of cruel treatment and you know it."

"What do you want me to do about it?" he asked. "It's not my child. I'm not the one that slept with him."

"I know that!" Her body shook with rage and despair and it was moment before she regained control of herself. "I'm leaving tonight for Dickensville, but I have something I need you to do first."

"Why couldn't I be enough for you?" Marvin asked as if he hadn't heard her. "I would have given you everything if you had married me."

Phoebe's face contorted with anger. "That's not important anymore! I don't want anything from you except for you to die!" she screamed.

Almost too late, Marvin saw the small gun she'd withdrawn from her cloak. He grabbed her wrist, but it went off. The bullet hit him in the thigh and he went down with a loud cry of pain. Phoebe fell with him because he'd kept hold of her wrist to prevent her from shooting him again. When she hit the floor, the gun became dislodged from her hand and it slid across the kitchen.

They scrambled for the gun. His injured leg hampered Marvin and Phoebe was a strong woman. She kicked his wounded leg and his hold on her loosened as agonizing pain ripped through it. Marvin found himself in a desperate struggle for his life because he knew if Phoebe got hold of that gun, she would kill him.

Boredom weighed on Shadow and he desperately wanted to go outside. He was starting to feel better since his wound was healing well thanks to the good care he'd been receiving. There was still a lot of internal damage, but the laudanum helped manage the pain. Now that darkness had fallen, Shadow was adamant that he was going to go sit on the porch. Bree and he argued about it.

Stubborn to a fault, Shadow rose from the chair where he sat and headed for the secret door to the cellar.

"Oh, no you don't," Bree said, trying to block his way.

He laughed and kept walking. "I'm just going to sit in a chair. That's all. I promise."

"I know you. You'll want to walk to the barn or something."

"I just promised you that I would just sit in a chair." He walked around her again, but she pulled on his good arm, stopping him.

"No! You shouldn't exert yourself by walking up the stairs."

"I'll be fine."

She could see he wasn't going to listen to her, but she had a way of keeping him in check at least a little. Crossing her arms over her chest, she said, "All right. I have a proposition for you."

"What is it?" he asked with a raised eyebrow.

"You may sit on the porch for twenty minutes, no more. And if you behave and go no further, I'll let you kiss me."

Desire flared inside him. "What sort of kiss?"

"A real kiss. But you don't get it until we come back down here."

"Done."

His quick acceptance amused her. "Ok. Let's go then."

"Yes, ma'am."

They were about halfway up the stairs leading to Marvin's office when they heard a gun go off. Shadow recognized Marvin's shout of pain and the sounds of a struggle ensued.

"Bree, I can't move faster than I am. Marvin has a gun in his bottom right desk drawer. You're going to have to help him. Go!"

"I've never shot a gun!"

"GO!" he roared.

Bree sprinted up the stairs, opened the door and went through it, shutting the closet door behind her to hide the still open secret panel. She retrieved the gun and followed the sounds of the fight into the kitchen. She was shocked to find Marvin struggling with Phoebe. They were both reaching for something. Bree saw that it was a small gun. Phoebe aimed a vicious kick at Marvin's wounded leg again and he lost his hold on her completely as he fought to remain conscious.

Phoebe crawled to the gun and picked it up. Bree saw that she meant to shoot Marvin and raised her own weapon, aimed as best she could, and pulled the trigger. The bullet hit Phoebe in the chest and she was flung onto her back. Bree shot again. Phoebe's body jerked and then was still.

Shadow had arrived, but he'd made sure not to step in any blood. It was second nature to him not to leave any trace of himself behind. "Put the gun down, Bree. She's dead. Go down and get the medical supplies."

Bree wasn't listening; she trembled and stared at the woman she'd just killed.

Marvin panted and pulled himself up into a sitting position, leaning on the sideboard for support. "Thank you, Bree. I'll never be able to repay you. I owe you my life."

"She's going into shock," Shadow said. He grabbed her arm and shook her a little. "Bree!"

She looked at him as though she'd just woken. "What?"

"Go get the medical supplies so you can bandage Marvin's leg so that he doesn't bleed to death before you can get Dr. Avery here. Now!"

Bree put the gun on the kitchen table and rushed to do as he'd said.

—————

The Tafts sat in their parlor while Josie held Julia and Evan worked on some embroidery. Edna dozed in her chair. Every so often, Evan looked at his women, as he called them. He was a happy man and he knew how blessed he was. A soft knock sounded on the front door.

Putting aside his project, he rose to answer it. Lucky stood on the other side and Evan smiled at him.

"Well, if it isn't Irish? Come on in."

Lucky stepped inside, his expression grave. "I need ya to come with me. There was a shootin' at Earnest's."

Josie and Edna started and Evan asked, "What?"

"I'm not sure exactly what happened. Miss Josephson came to get Erin. Win went with her and I came to get ya," Lucky said. "Marvin's hurt, but, uh, Phoebe, well, she's dead."

Evan's eyes closed and he pinched the bridge of his nose as he gathered his composure. He kissed his women, told them not to wait up, and followed Lucky out into the night.

Chapter Twenty-Four

When Evan and Lucky arrived on the scene, Erin and Win were there working on Marvin. Erin had confirmed that Phoebe was dead, but she hadn't moved the body. She'd begun treating the patient she could still help. Bree sat in the parlor. She'd refused a sedative, saying she wanted to be able to give an accurate account of her part in the whole situation.

Evan looked at Marvin. "Is he gonna make it, Erin?"

"Yes. He'll be fine."

"Damn," Evan said and walked further into the kitchen.

Marvin laughed, which surprised Erin. She expected him to be angry, not amused.

"It's all right, Erin. Outside of you and Bree, everyone else here wishes I were dead. I'm used to it," he said when he saw her expression.

"What happened?" Evan asked, kneeling next to Phoebe. Her death saddened him. He was also sorry for Thad, both for the loss of Phoebe and his unborn child.

He rubbed his forehead and rose to stand by Lucky, who glowered down at Marvin.

Marvin said, "Phoebe came and we started arguing. She was angry because I told Thad about the baby. I didn't know she hadn't told him, remember, Evan? You were here when I made that blunder."

They all looked at Evan. His expression showed his discomfort. No one but him knew Thad had been seeing Phoebe or that she was pregnant with his baby. "Yes, I remember."

The others exchanged stunned looks.

"She was going to have an abortion. I asked her why she didn't just marry him. I wish the child had been mine. Oh God! The baby," Marvin said and put a hand over his mouth. The tears that flooded his eyes weren't an act. "I begged her in the past to marry me, but she wouldn't. She didn't want to marry him, either." A snarl curled his lip. "Does that sound familiar, Evan? Louise's baby wasn't mine, either. I'd give anything to be a father, but that will never happen! Do you believe me now?"

"I'm not discussing that right now," Evan said, holding his temper in check. "What happened after you argued?"

"She wanted me to do something before she left. Die. I hadn't seen the gun before that. I grabbed her wrist, but she still managed to shoot me. We fought for the gun and fell down. It wound up over by the sink. We struggled for it and she got to it first. I thought that was it. I didn't know Bree was there until her gun went off. Phoebe fell and Bree shot her again. I think it was just a reflex at that point. The poor girl. First her father and now this."

"Where'd Bree get the gun?"

"My office," he said, feeling lightheaded. He shook his head to clear it. "I told her about it when she came here. If she was alone in the house and there was any trouble, I told her to use it. I owe her my life," Marvin said.

"So both you and Thad were seeing Phoebe?" Win asked.

"Yes. I knew about Thad, but only for the last year. I didn't know that she'd been seeing him even before that."

"Why did you stay with her?" Win asked, but he looked pointedly at Erin.

"Because I loved her so much. I was willing to share her, hoping that she would eventually choose me, but she wanted us both. I broke it off a few months ago, though. I didn't know that she'd stopped seeing him, until she came to tell me she was pregnant. She tried to tell me it was mine, but we know that's impossible. Isn't that right, Dr. Avery?"

Erin said, "Yes."

Evan asked, "You knew that, Erin?"

"Of course. I'm his doctor. I always do a detailed past history on my patients. He told me about the injury and I always do a physical exam. The type of hernia he had sometimes results in infertility, especially when the surgery isn't performed well. Based on the scarring, I could tell that the surgeon wasn't very skilled and it's possible that he'll have to have another surgery at some point," she said.

"And you didn't think to tell me?" Win asked.

"Why would I?" she replied. "He's my patient and I don't disclose patient information unless it's an emergency. The only reason I am now is because he gave me permission."

"Do you see what I've been trying to tell you?" Win demanded. "How twisted he is? Only a maniac would keep seeing a woman he knew was cheating on him. He hates Thad and I'm sure he enjoyed knowing that Thad was being cheated on, too."

Erin looked stricken and Lucky put a hand on Win's shoulder. "Win, come outside with me. Ya need to calm down."

Win smacked Lucky's hand away. "She's been defending him ever since she got here. She couldn't see what a sadistic rat he is. I hope you see it now. Because of him, Phoebe's dead—so is Thad's baby. Maybe next time I try to tell you something, you'll listen to me."

"Win!" Evan shouted. "Shut up and get out! Don't talk to her like that. Go on."

Win gave her a scathing look and left.

"I'm sorry, Dr. Avery," Marvin said.

Lucky grabbed his face roughly and squeezed it hard. "Shut your trap or I'll shut it permanently and gladly go to jail for it."

Erin finished with Marvin and put her equipment back into her bag. "I'll be back tomorrow to change the dressing."

Giving Lucky a wary glance, Marvin said, "Thank you."

Erin nodded and went to the sink to wash her hands, refusing to give into the tears that pricked the back of her eyes. Once her hands were clean, she dried them and prepared to leave.

"Erin, it'll be all right," Lucky said.

"I know you mean well, but I'd just like to leave now," she said, stepping around him.

Evan and Lucky watched her go, sympathy filling them for several different people.

Erin couldn't go home. She couldn't face Win and she didn't want to go to the Tafts' house. Instead, she went to Billy's. She was glad to see light in his loft windows.

He was surprised to see her when he opened the door. "Hey, doc. C'mon in. Where's the other doc? You're out kinda late."

Erin made it to a chair before she broke down.

"Oh, boy," Billy said. He didn't have a hanky on him, so he gave her a clean rag to dry her tears with. He sat down next to her. "What happened?"

Getting control of herself, Erin told him the whole sordid tale. "I know now that I've been a fool about Marvin, but he didn't have to rub my nose in it right in front of everyone. I deserve more respect than that. I'm his wife."

Billy had to agree with her. Yes, Erin should have listened to Win about Marvin, but Win also should have discussed it in private.

"Can I stay here, tonight?" she asked. "I don't want to see Win right now."

"Sure. Uh, I'm sorry that I only have a sofa up here," he said.

"That's fine. I'm not going to be fussy after I barged in here."

"You didn't barge in. I'm glad I can help. I can't believe it. So Thad and Marvin were both seeing Phoebe, but Thad didn't know it, but Marvin did, and Marvin can't make babies, so the baby was Thad's. And Bree shot Phoebe because she shot Marvin and was going to kill him. Do I have all that right?"

Erin nodded. "That's right."

Billy shook his head, got up to retrieve a bottle of scotch that sat on a table, and gave it to her. "You need this. Artist's orders."

She smiled a little at his joke and took a healthy swig of the liquor. It had been a while since she'd drank anything that strong, but she enjoyed the burn it created. Handing it back to Billy she sat back in her chair, suddenly very weary. "How's your shoulder?"

"Hurts, but not like it did. I cut back on the fuzzy juice." This was what he'd started calling laudanum. "I'm trying to get some more work done here since I can't do anything on the farm at the moment."

"I can understand that."

"Well, anyway. I'll let you get some sleep," Billy said. "If you need anything, just stomp on the floor right over by the sofa and I'll hear you."

She offered him a wan smile. "Thanks."

He gave her a one-armed hug and went downstairs. Erin blew out the lamps and lay on the sofa in one corner of the large studio. She wasn't used to sleeping by herself and she missed her husband lying next to her, holding her. Calling on the skill she'd developed over the years that had helped her sleep during stressful situations, Erin blocked everything from her mind and dropped off to sleep.

The next morning, she went home long enough to wash up and change before going to check on Marvin. Win wasn't around, but she saw Lucky.

"How're ya holdin' up?" he asked, giving her a hug.

Erin said, "I've been better, but I'll survive."

"Of course ya will. Things will settle down and ye'll work things out with Win. He's a reasonable man and he'll come to see that he shouldn't have acted like that."

"No, he shouldn't have. I can't talk about this right now, though. I have to get to work. I have to change Marvin's dressing and then I have patients to see," she said.

Lucky nodded. "All right. If ya need anything, let me know."

"I will, thanks."

<hr />

"How's your pain?" she asked Marvin as she readied her bandages and instruments.

He met her eyes. "My heart hurts worse than any bullet wound ever could."

"I'm sorry for your loss, Marvin."

A resigned smile flitted across his face. "Me, too. Bree is devastated, of course. I owe her my life, but I'd sooner that it was me who was dead."

"Do you mean that?"

"Yes. I only wanted to get the gun away from Phoebe. Despite what everyone thinks, I was deeply in love with her. She was the only person who ever loved me despite my many failings. I'm going to her funeral. Travis says it's tomorrow and he'll take me."

"You shouldn't do that."

Marvin said, "I know, but I have to say goodbye to her."

Bree knocked on his bedroom door. "Hello, Dr. Avery. Do you need help with Marvin?"

Erin smiled at her. "No, I'm fine. Thanks. How are you doing?"

Bree shrugged. "I don't really know. It hasn't sunk in yet, I guess."

"Are you sure you don't want a sedative?"

"I'm sure. It'll get better with some time," Bree said. "I'll be in the parlor if you need me."

"Thanks."

No one saw Win for two days. Evan had gone out to the Devil's Knob, a place no one but Win liked to go. The small valley's name came from the high moaning sounds the wind made as it moved across the caves in the rock walls and the huge rock formation that looked like a rope knot; it was one of Win's old haunts before he'd gone into business with Lucky and Billy and had built his cabin. Back then, he'd had no permanent residence and had used one of the caves in the summer because it stayed cool inside.

Win heard Evan calling for him, but he didn't respond. He lay in one of the caves near the top of a rock wall where he knew no one would try to climb. He needed time to cool off before he talked to his wife. He didn't become angry often, but once he was, his anger lingered a while.

"Ok, Win. I have the feeling you're here. If you are, just know that everyone's worried about you, including your wife. You can't hide forever. Don't stay mad too long. Nothing will get solved that way." Evan waited for about five minutes before leaving.

Up in his cave, Win closed his eyes again and went back to meditating.

The next night as she lay in bed, Erin heard someone knock on the door.

"Who is it?" she asked before opening it.

"Win."

She unlocked it, went back to their bedroom, and got back in bed. Her heart thudded inside her chest as anger and relief battled within.

"It's nice to know you're still alive," she said.

Win said, "I left you a note."

"Oh, yes. How silly of me. Of course that makes up for you not coming home for three days."

He sat down on the bed. "I'm sorry. I had to calm down. It would do no good for me to talk while I'm angry. I'm not very reasonable."

"Most people aren't when they're mad."

"I shouldn't have lost my temper—"

Erin sat up, glaring at him. "That's right. There was no need to humiliate me like that!"

"It wouldn't have happened if you'd just believed me in the first place," Win said.

"Are you happy that you were right and I was wrong? Don't you think I already feel stupid enough without your condescension?"

Win gritted his teeth against his rising temper. "Erin, I'm trying to be calm about this."

"Good for you! You berate me in front of our friends and Marvin and then disappear for three days and expect me to be calm about this? I don't think so," Erin said.

"You're right. I shouldn't have done that. I was wrong."

"Are you going to run off every time we have a fight? I don't call that very reasonable. What if I would have needed you? What if someone else would have needed you? Did you ever stop to think about that?" she yelled. "No, because you were too busy being smug and self-righteous. You haven't even been here to support Thad. He's heartbroken and all you thought about was your wounded pride."

Win stood up. "I'll go sleep in Lucky's tipi. We'll talk about this is in the morning when we're both calm."

"I have work in the morning."

"Tomorrow night then."

"I see. On your terms. Yes, Dr. Wu. We'll do it then," Erin said.

Win's heart was full of pain as he left the cabin. He scratched on the tipi flap.

"Come in, Win."

"How'd you know it was me?"

Lucky gave him a steady look as he sat down. "Well, seein' as your woman was yellin', I figured you must be the cause of it. Your windows are open."

"Oh."

"So himself has finally decided to show his face has he?" Lucky said this sort of thing when he thought someone was being conceited. "Nice of ya to come home with us humble folk again."

"I know I messed up all the way around," Win said. "I'm sorry."

"Well, it's not really me ya need to apologize to."

"I tried to talk to Erin about it, but she's still too mad."

"I'm not surprised. What if this had happened when she was almost ready to have a baby or somethin'? Would ya have slunk away then?"

Win put his head in his hands. "Not you, too."

Lucky laughed. "You're gonna hear it quite a few times, lad. There're a lot of people who are none too happy with ya."

"How's Thad?"

Lucky shook his head. "Drunk and in agony, as you'd expect to be if you'd lost the woman you loved and your baby. I know all about that. In my case, they're both still alive, God willin', so it's worse for him because death is permanent."

Guilt crashed down on Win. "I should have been here to help him."

"Aye. Ya should've been, but you're here now. You've got a lot to make up for, so ya better get started right away in the mornin' and go see Thad. We've been watchin' him so he doesn't kill Marvin. It's not Marvin's fault Phoebe and the baby are dead, but Thad's in too much pain to see it."

"I disagree with you on that."

"Oh? Why's that?"

"Because if Marvin hadn't kept up his twisted—"

"I'm gonna stop ya right there. Phoebe was a grown woman, Win. She knew right from wrong and no one forced her to sleep with two men. No one forced her to keep secrets the way she did and it was her decision to go over there to kill Marvin. Remember, Marvin had ended things with her, so she had no right to go after him like that. Phoebe's dead because of her own actions. Bree was only protecting her friend."

Win's hands fisted where they rested on his knees. "I can't believe you're defending him."

"I'm not. He's the most vile, evil, twisted bastard I've ever come across, but ya have to place blame where it goes, Win. See, I can see it a little clearer because I'm not as close with Evan as ye. A lot of what you're feelin' is because of his history with Marvin.

"And now we find out Marvin was tellin' the truth about him not being the father of Louise's baby, too. He admitted to the affair with her, but he didn't father the child. Remember he said he tried to convince her to go ahead and marry Evan? I'm inclined to believe him about that, too. He said he told Phoebe she should marry Thad.

"They say history repeats itself and 'tis true in this case, too. I know ya don't want to hear this, but sometimes you have to dig a little deeper for the truth. I told Evan the same thing. He didn't like it, but he admitted I was right. Maybe if Evan hadn't let his hate towards Marvin get the best of him, Marvin might have told Evan who'd sired Louise's baby. That man is as bad as Marvin, as far as I'm concerned."

"You're unbelievable."

"I'm just lookin' at it from all sides. You've all been goin' straight at Marvin, but he's like one of those sidewinder snakes, moving all different ways because that's how he gains the most traction without getting caught. Evan has to be just as sneaky and catch Marvin off guard. Marvin's the devil incarnate and has to be beaten at his own game. But that's not solving your marital problems. No, you're gonna have to eat some crow, I'm afraid, but the question is whether you're strong enough to stomach it so you can fix things. That's all I'm gonna say on the matter. Goodnight."

Chapter Twenty-Five

For the next week, Win and Erin argued over the situation and got nowhere. Each wanted to place blame, which resulted in an even greater divide. Neither of them would talk to their friends about it, each being very private people. They went about their work every day and came home at night.

Neither of them was very hungry and many of their dinners were only half-eaten. Erin worked on charts and Win went to see Lucky. Sometimes he stayed in the tipi and sometimes he slept on the sofa. Erin cried silent tears in their bed and there were times when the grief and anger got the best of Win and he cried tears of his own.

Evan and the rest were beyond concerned, but they didn't know what to do about it. Edna had some ideas, though. She'd been thinking about it almost nonstop that week and she'd come up with a plan.

One night she said, "Evan, you tell Erin and Win that I want to see them tomorrow night at seven and that it's an order. Then, once they're here, I want you to lock them in the house with me. They're not getting out until this gets settled."

"You want me to lock them in the house with you?" he asked.

"That's what I just said, sonny boy. Tomorrow night at seven. Get a padlock on that front door in the morning."

Evan smiled. If anyone was experienced enough to counsel the couple it was Edna. She'd been married for a long time and he was sure that she and his uncle had had their share of fights. Yet, they'd stayed married and had still been very in love when Rebel had passed.

"Ok. I'll tell them," Evan said.

Win arrived at the Tafts' shortly after Erin. He entered the parlor, his manner hesitant. Outside of his wife, Edna, the unofficial matriarch of their patchwork family, was the one he hated disappointing the most.

"Welcome, Win," Edna said.

Win looked at Erin, but she was concentrating on Edna.

"Thanks," Win said, sitting on one of the wingback chairs.

There came the sounds of two locks of some sort clicking shut on the outside of the front door. Evan had already secured the kitchen door.

"What was that?" Erin asked.

Edna smiled. "You're not going anywhere until we get this settled."

Win's disbelief was comical. "You locked us in here?"

"That's right. You're both acting like a couple of jackasses. Erin, do you still love your husband?"

Erin glanced at Win. Her heart cried out for him. "Yes."

"Win, do you still love your wife?"

"Yeah," Win said.

Edna harrumphed. "Well, you need to start acting like it. I'm going to tell you something about Marvin that people around here just can't seem to get through their thick skulls, including you two. By keeping up this arguing, you're letting him win. Since we came here five years ago, I came to see Marvin for what he is. He's evil, yes, but in a few ways, it's not his fault."

"What do you mean? I'm getting tired of hearing people defend him," Win said.

"Shut up!" Edna said, her sharp tone surprising them. "You'll hear me out."

Win looked properly chastised. "Yes, ma'am."

"Spike filled me in on some things about Marvin. I guess his parents weren't the nicest people either. Marvin learned a lot of his behavior from them, but something happened after his father died. It was an odd thing. His mother died first, but that didn't seem to faze Marvin much. They weren't close, I guess. But when his father died, he got worse; I don't know why. No one does."

"I'm not excusing his behavior, mind you. I'm just trying to give you some insight into the man. He thrives on creating suffering, which you know, and I'm sure he knows that things have been strained between you."

Erin said, "I haven't said anything to him. I treat him as quickly as I can and get out of there."

Edna chuckled. "You don't have to tell him. Marvin always seems to know things, but no one knows how. He has someone doing his dirty work and he has for years, but whoever this person is has never been caught. He's slick. I'm sure it's the same man who came to your farm, but he still got away. He's no dummy, that one. Neither of them is. Anyway, I want Erin to calmly explain why she's so hurt and angry."

Erin looked at Win and said, "You embarrassed me in front of everyone. It was very disrespectful and I felt like a moron. I still do. I based my opinions about Marvin on what I saw. People can have a perception about someone that may be false. I always try to give people the benefit of the doubt. Marvin never did anything to me.

"Through all of this, the only way he affected me at all was by making you angry and condescending towards me. He never caused me any personal harm and he never gave me any reason to distrust him. I'm not sticking up for him. I'm saying the real reason I'm angry is because you made me feel incredibly stupid for my beliefs and you enjoyed pointing out to me how wrong I was. I deserve better than that."

Win nodded. "I know how poorly I acted and I'm sorry. I've been doing a lot of thinking this week; I let my hatred of Marvin cloud my judgment and that was stupid of me. I got angry because I felt that as your husband, you should have believed me. I felt like you thought I was being stupid in believing what I do about Marvin. You're right; the issue really isn't Marvin. He just happened to be the catalyst in all this.

"I want you to value my opinion and I felt that since you didn't know Marvin and haven't been around to see some of the things he's done, you should have listened to me more. So when Marvin showed his true colors to you, I felt righteous and vindicated. But I lost my temper and went about things all wrong. I'm sorry."

Edna said, "See what can happen when two people sit down and talk about things rationally? You should have done that long ago. The two most reasonable people I know have been so unreasonable and caused each other unnecessary pain. Now, what are you going to do about it?"

Erin said, "I'm going to listen to your opinions more and not let pride get in the way of doing that, even if I don't agree with you."

Win met her gaze and smiled. "And I'm not going to be so smug when I'm right. I'll also listen better to your side of things and I promise to never embarrass you like that again."

She smiled back at him. "Thank you."

"Do you forgive me?" Hope beat inside his chest.

Erin's eyes filled with tears as she said, "Yes, I forgive you. Do you forgive me?"

"Yes."

He went to sit by her on the sofa and, not caring that Edna was in the room, he took Erin in his arms and kissed her.

Edna chuckled and got up from her chair. "I have to go do something in my room." She shuffled her way there and closed the door.

Erin thrilled to Win's touch and kissed him back with fervor. She'd missed him more than she thought it was possible to miss anyone. Being without him had been a torture she never wanted to endure again and she meant to work hard to make sure they were never apart in the future.

Holding the woman he loved, Win vowed to be more open-minded and not think that his opinions were the law. Erin was an intelligent woman, which was one of the reasons he'd fallen in love with her. It was an insult to her to not acknowledge her feelings and discuss them rather than trying to be superior to her. That wasn't the way to treat someone you loved.

As they parted, Win said, "I love you and I'm so sorry."

She put a hand on his cheek. "I'm sorry, too, and I love you, too, Dr. Wu."

He grinned. "Dr. Avery, I think we should go home and discuss this some more."

"I think that's a fine idea."

Win went to Edna's bedroom door and knocked. When she opened it, he said, "Thanks, Edna. We appreciate your help. You're a wise woman."

She came out into the parlor. "I'm glad you worked things out. Now, I don't want to hear about anything like this happening again. If I do, there'll be hell to pay."

"Yes, ma'am," Win said.

Erin hugged Edna. "It won't. Thank you."

"You're welcome. Now go on home and make up properly," Edna said.

Erin blushed and Win laughed. He knocked on the front door, assuming that someone was outside to let them out.

"Aunt Edna! All clear?" Evan hollered.

"All clear!" she shouted back.

Evan chuckled, unlocked the door, and opened it. "I'm glad that you two came to your senses."

As the couple stepped out onto the porch, Win said, "Your aunt knows what she's doing. She should charge for it."

"That's not a bad idea," Evan said.

They bid him goodnight and mounted their horses. As they rode down the lane, Win moved closer so he could hold Erin's hand. "You know, we still have that book to finish."

"That's right, we do," Erin said. "I think we need to do that. We were right at a love scene, too."

He nodded. "That's where we left off. I think that maybe we should have a love scene of our own. How do you feel about that?"

"Dr. Wu, it's like you read my mind sometimes. Now, about our book; when we start reading it again, I want to do the man's part."

"I don't know. That might be weird since it's a love scene."

"I think it would be funny."

Win let her hand go. "I'll race you for it. Whoever gets home first does the man's part. Is it a deal?"

Erin's answer was to put her heels to her horse and race away. Win lost no time in chasing her. He caught up to her and they grinned at each other as their horses galloped along through the night.

Epilogue

Summer in Echo began winding down and the sheep farmers were kept busy laying in supplies and food for the winter. Lucky and Win had planted a garden that year again and their friends helped them can the vegetables. They were given some of the food in return for their assistance.

Baby Julia had no shortage of doting aunts and uncles around Echo. It looked as though her eyes would stay blue, which tickled Evan no end. Josie was glad that Julia's dark hair wasn't lightening. Evan and Josie both loved that she was such a nice combination of them. Edna took the baby every chance she got, taking her grandmotherly duties very seriously.

Evan was minus his fill-in deputy. Thad had taken off on another job, but he really needed the time away from Echo to heal; every time he saw the Hanover House, his heart and mind were filled with thoughts of Phoebe and their unborn child. The double loss had inflicted great pain upon him. So he had escaped to parts unknown to do what he did best—catch bad guys.

Billy's shoulder healed and he began training with a vengeance, determined to be able to hold his own in any future clashes. His encounter with the unknown man had given him the impetus to become more of a fighter even though he was still a lover. He also decided that he was ready to find a bride of his own.

Edna's eyes almost popped out of her head one night when he showed up at the Tafts' wearing nothing more than the breech cloth Lucky had made for him. Billy had begged him to make one for him so that he could look like an Indian. He'd found some feathers and put them in his hair. When Evan let him in the house, if they hadn't known Billy, they would have thought an Indian brave had come to pay them a visit.

When Josie said this, Billy responded, "One did. Me. I *am* an Indian, after all, and I think I'm pretty brave, so yeah; I'm an Indian brave."

Edna was delighted. "Well, young man, you certainly have grown up well. I think you're a little taller, and look at all that muscle."

He grinned and said, "I'm glad you approve. This is your payment."

"For what?" Edna asked.

He crouched by her chair. "I'd like you to write a bride ad for me. I'm ready."

Edna gave him a doubtful look. "Are you sure? You're not quite twenty yet."

Billy nodded. "I know what I want. I see how happy Evan, Josie, Win, and Erin are and I want that, too. I'm ready. Will you please write it?"

She smiled and put a hand under his chin. "How can I resist that face? Of course I will. Let's start right now. Sheriff, we need some paper here."

Evan jumped up. "Yes, ma'am." As he went out to their kitchen, he grinned as he thought about Billy looking for a bride. He was sure that was going to be an adventure. He brought back a tablet and a pencil, which he handed to Edna.

She said, "All right. Now tell me what you're looking for."

Billy smiled and said, "Ok. Well, she should be …"

LT NDA BRIDEY

Marvin and Shadow's injuries also healed. It was a good thing that Shadow had such a strong constitution or he might have succumbed to the damage inflicted on him by Lucky's arrow. As his shoulder and back healed, he exercised it and did stretches to bring it back to normal strength and to prevent the muscles from becoming stiff.

While Marvin's leg knitted together, his heart was another matter. Bree and Shadow often found him just standing in the kitchen, staring at the spot where Phoebe had died. Bree had become very defensive of Marvin, much like a brother, and she tried to comfort him. Although she'd felt guilty for killing Phoebe, she wasn't sorry that she'd come to his aid.

At any time, Marvin could have hurt her or killed her because she knew about Shadow and many of their other secrets. However, he was generous and kind to her. There was more to the brothers that anyone knew and perhaps never would. She wasn't blind to their faults and dark sides, but she also knew that there were reasons why those sides existed.

While her relationship with Marvin was that of a sibling, her feelings for Shadow were in no way not sisterly. She'd fallen in love with him. Yes, he was violent, sadistic, and harsh when it came to other people, but he was gentle, indulgent, and protective of her. His patience seemed boundless and he never pushed about the physical side of their relationship.

Society would have been shocked that they slept in the same bed together, but it felt as natural to them as flying did to birds. Her nightmares had greatly subsided and it was because of Shadow. He held her when she was scared, soothing her and chasing away the darkness. How ironic that the man who lived in darkness should bring her such light.

Shadow was amazed every day that there was more room in his heart for someone other than Marvin. He hadn't thought it possible, and yet what he felt for Bree was true love. Heaven help anyone who ever tried to hurt her again. He had killed for her once and he would do it again if necessary.

Evan had taken Josie's encouragement to heart, and even though the clues weren't adding up at the moment, his instincts told him that they would. No matter how long it took, he would bring the murderer of the stranger to justice, along with the man who had caused so much trouble at the sheep farm. The sheriff was also still intent on finding his unknown kidnapper.

Evan wasn't so conceited that he wouldn't listen to advice from others. He thought long and hard about the things Lucky had said to him and he began to formulate a plan to find enough evidence on Marvin to lock him up for good and rid Echo of his evil presence. His Uncle Rebel had taught him to back off and be creative when coming up with another approach to an investigation. That's exactly what Evan planned to do. Yes, Marvin's days of tormenting people were numbered.

On a humid evening in August, Lucky showed Billy a picture of him and his wife.

"A photographer from some newspaper wanted to take some pictures of the tribe and the chief, Red Elk, let him. I paid him to make this for me," he said.

Billy looked at the beautiful dark-eyed woman with the long, black hair and his Irish friend next to her and he could see how in love they were.

"You had long hair?" Billy asked when he saw the golden locks flowing down over Lucky's shoulders and partway down his chest.

"Aye. The Cheyenne don't have barbers, ya know. Plus, it helped me fit in a little more," he said. "Billy, I'm going after them soon. This whole thing with Thad has gotten me thinkin' and I can't wait much longer. I need to know. I need to see Avasa and my child."

Billy saw the determined gleam in his eyes and knew that Lucky wouldn't give up on his mission. "I don't blame you. I'll help in any way I can."

Lucky clapped his shoulder and said, "Thanks. Now, how about we go to Spike's and have a pint or two? My treat. We might even strike up a card game. What say you?"

Billy got up and said, "Let's go."

And so Irish and the Indian set off for a night of fun.

Win and Erin spent a lot of time talking about their future, making plans for the clinic and for Win to officially open his own practice.

As they sat on the sofa together one night, Erin said, "You know, you should just build a practice off the back of the clinic. One side for animals and the other for humans."

She was kidding, but Win liked the idea. "That would actually work," he said. "There's room back there and we'd even be able to help each other sometimes."

Erin saw the advantages to that. "I'm a genius!" she joked.

Win hugged and kissed her. "Yes, you are. I'm very lucky to be married to such a smart, beautiful, talented woman."

She put her arms around his neck. "And I am lucky to be married to such a handsome and intelligent man. I'll never take you for granted."

"And I'll always show you how much I appreciate you," he said.

She gave him a coy look. "Dr. Wu, I think our bargain worked out very well, don't you?"

"I concur with your conclusion, Dr. Avery. It worked out just fine. I have a surprise for you."

She smiled at him. "What?"

"Our new book came today."

She gasped and playfully smacked his chest. "Why didn't you say so before now?"

He grabbed her wrist and kissed her palm, making her shiver. "Because we were talking about some serious stuff. But now it's time for fun."

"Go get it," Erin said.

Win hurried into their room and brought back two copies of their book and then went outside to put the cross sticks out. Coming back in, he and Erin settled on the sofa together. They each leaned against the opposite arm of the sofa so that their legs were entwined in the center of it.

"You start," Win said.

She squealed a little. "Ok. *The frigid wind swept down the mountainside, the snow-laden clouds above ready to release their frozen precipitation onto the world below ...*"

They read long into the night, swept up in the story and later, they were swept up in a whirlwind of passion. They were better for having gone through such a turbulent time because it had brought them closer. Since then, they'd made a bargain to be more understanding of one another, and to respond to each other with love instead of anger.

Both doctors knew that there would be times when they fought, but by keeping their bargain mind, they would keep their loving marriage alive and that was much more romantic than any romance book they would ever read.

The End

Thank you for reading and supporting my book and I hope you enjoyed it.

Please will you do me a favor and review "Montana Bargain" so I'll know whether you liked it or not, it would be very much appreciated, thank you.

Linda's Other Books

Echo Canyon Brides Series

Montana Rescue
(Echo Canyon brides Book 1)

Montana Bargain
(Echo Canyon brides Book 2)

Montana Mail Order Brides Series

Westward Winds
(Montana Mail Order brides Book 1)

Westward Dance
(Montana Mail Order brides Book 2)

Westward Bound
(Montana Mail Order brides Book 3)

Westward Destiny
(Montana Mail Order brides Book 4)

Westward Fortune
(Montana Mail Order brides Book 5)

Westward Justice
(Montana Mail Order brides Book 6)

Westward Dreams
(Montana Mail Order brides Book 7)

Westward Holiday
(Montana Mail Order brides Book 8)

Westward Sunrise
(Montana Mail Order brides Book 9)

Westward Moon
(Montana Mail Order brides Book 10)

Westward Christmas
(Montana Mail Order brides Book 11)

Connect With Linda

Visit my website at **www.lindabridey.com** to view my other books and to sign up to my mailing list so that you are notified about my new releases.

About Linda Bridey

LINDA BRIDEY lives in New Mexico with her three dogs; a German shepherd, chocolate Labrador retriever, and a black Pug. She became fascinated with Montana and decided to combine that fascination with her fictional romance writing. Linda chose to write about mail-order-brides because of the bravery of these women who left everything and everyone to take a trek into the unknown. The Westward series books are her first publications.

Made in the USA
Monee, IL
22 August 2020